SHATTERED Secrets

A HUDSON ISLAND NOVEL

CHRISTINA SOL

Shattered Secrets

By: Christina Sol

Published by: Sol Media LLC

Cover Design: LJ Anderson, Mayhem Cover Creations

Proofreader: Judy's Proofreading

Paperback ISBN: 979-8-9898861-2-8

✿ Created with Vellum

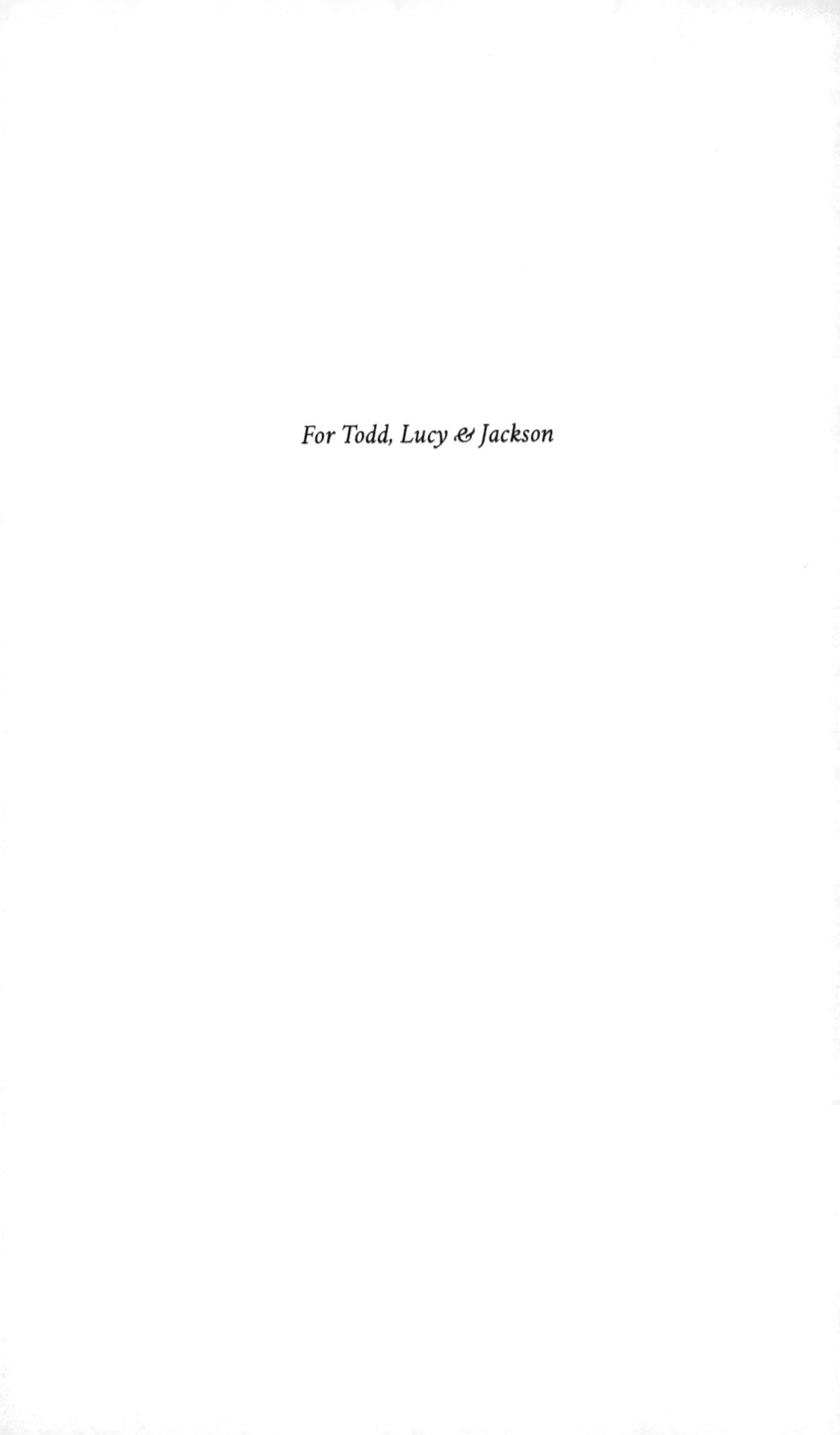

For Todd, Lucy & Jackson

CHAPTER ONE

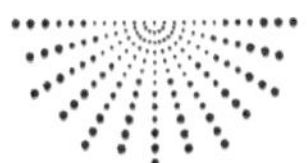

Matt Alvarez leaned back in the oversized Adirondack chair. He paid no attention to the unobstructed view of Puget Sound. Ignored the blue skies and the crisp breeze that whipped around him. He focused solely on his phone. Or rather, the email that he'd fired off moments earlier.

Holy fuck. What had he just done?

His fingers itched to call his captain, to tell the man who'd become a mentor and friend to disregard the email. Say he wasn't going to retire, after all. That he'd changed his mind and was still a detective with the Seattle Police Department.

Instead, Matt took a steadying breath. Then exhaled. He repeated the movements a few times until he recognized the tingling in his belly. Beneath that initial panic was something he didn't want to acknowledge, didn't want to admit.

Relief.

Knowing he no longer had to go back to Seattle, back to his old life, was a fucking relief. But one that shamed and embarrassed him. Getting shot had changed him in more ways than one.

Physically? Well, fuck. He'd worked damn hard to get back into shape. Some would say he was in better condition now than when he'd been on the force. And they wouldn't be wrong. He'd added twenty pounds of muscle, and his cardio fitness was ridiculous. However, he had lingering nerve damage in his right hand. It wasn't enough to sideline him from work, but it was enough to bother him.

Mentally? To put it simply, the shooting and the aftermath of it all had fucked with his head. Big-time. And unlike his body, his mind was still a work in progress. It didn't help that, while he'd still been in the hospital recovering from his gunshot wound, his personal life had imploded in a horribly spectacular manner.

Bitterness burned in Matt's chest, and he shook his head. To say that he'd been working through some serious anger issues over the last year was a gross understatement.

The forced downtime had made him take a step back and reevaluate. He loved what he did. Truly. Investigative work got his blood pumping. There was nothing quite like the rush of the chase, of catching those who thought they were above the law, of bringing justice to the victims who'd been wronged. But the longer he'd been away, the less sure he'd become about wanting to go back down that bureaucratic, red-taped path.

His finger hovered over the phone icon. With another shake of his head, he sighed and flipped his phone so it was face-down on the chair's arm.

At last, Matt took in the view. Mid-June in the Pacific Northwest was picturesque. The sun was shining and the dark waters of Puget Sound glimmered. Soft white caps dotted the horizon, and as he watched the churning of the sea, the tension in his chest released. God, he loved this place.

After getting shot, he'd undergone two surgeries and had been hospitalized for two weeks. After his release, his twin brother, Jake, and Jake's then-girlfriend, Carmen, had insisted he stay with them. So he had. It was safe to say Matt hadn't been the best roommate, but his brother had stuck by him.

Nearly a month later, when Jake had offered up his vacation home on Hudson Island, Matt had jumped at the offer. The minute he'd arrived, a weight had lifted from his chest. He'd still been in a world of hurt—both physically and mentally—but for once, he'd actually been able to breathe.

A little over a year had passed since that day. Aside from taking the ferry to Seattle to see his doctors, he rarely left Hudson Island. He barely kept in touch with his parents and knew his brother was acting as the go-between. Jake, the persistent bastard, visited him every month or so. It wasn't like he could refuse the guy since he'd been freeloading off him for the past year.

Basically, Matt was a miserable fuck. An angry, miserable fuck. But in all his wallowing, he'd carved out a small space for himself here. He'd made some acquaintances—fine, they'd become actual friends, friends who were recruiting him hard to join their organization, and—

His phone rang. Flipping it back over, he glanced at the display. Cade. Aside from his twin, Cade was his closest friend. He silenced the call. Seconds later, his phone dinged a text notification.

CADE

Call me back, you motherfucker.

Matt's lips twitched, then turned into a frown. A surge of anxiety warred with his earlier relief as reality set in. For the first time since high school, Matt was unemployed. Holy shit.

His phone started ringing again, and Cade's face popped back up on the display. Answering the call and putting it on speaker, Matt welcomed the distraction from his spiraling thoughts. "What's up, man?"

"What are you doing?" Cade replied.

Matt slumped into the chair and rested his head against the back, closing his eyes. "You're the one who called. You tell me."

"Dude. Seriously, what are you doing?"

Aside from wallowing in self-pity, Matt was doing jack-shit. "Nothing. What's going on?"

"Can you meet me in town?"

His knee-jerk response was to say no, but he knew Cade, like his twin, was a persistent fucker. "Sure. Where?"

"Ray's Diner."

Matt frowned, and he was thankful they weren't on a video call. He had no issues with Ray's Diner. In fact, it was one of his favorite places to eat in town—their fried chicken platter was fucking divine. His issue came in the form of a pint-sized waitress with rainbow-streaked hair. Scarlet Miller.

Well, the issue wasn't actually her. It was all him.

Scarlet was a young single mom who was chipper, sweet, and ridiculously pretty. For some inexplicable reason, Matt couldn't form words around the little sprite. *Literally* could not form words. After the first couple of weeks of stuttering and fumbling, Matt had stopped trying. Now he basically grunted and mumbled his way through every meal. It made him feel like an ass. An old, inadequate ass. He had no clue what the hell was wrong with him.

"You still there?" Cade asked, yanking him from his maudlin thoughts.

Matt cleared his throat. "Sure. Ray's works. What time?" His eyes narrowed at the chuckle he heard from the other end.

"Now. Can you meet me in fifteen?"

He paused. "Everything okay, man?"

"Yeah," Cade murmured. "We'll chat over food. See you soon."

Standing, Matt slipped his phone into his pocket, then bit back a grimace when it dinged another incoming text.

Christ, Cade was being needy. Pulling his phone back out, he prepared to send some sort of text making fun of his friend. Instead, he stilled.

The text wasn't from Cade. Rather, it was from Gavin Frazier, the owner of Hudson Security.

GAVIN

> You free to assist? We have a case that could use your expertise. You'd be working with Bean.

Instead of texting back, he hit Gavin's name and brought the phone to his ear.

"I take it this means I've caught your attention?" Gavin asked by way of greeting.

"More than," Matt replied. He'd helped out a few times with Hudson Security, and those experiences were part of the reason he'd officially put in his resignation. Gavin's company—and his employees—were solid, and they didn't have to wade through the bureaucratic bullshit.

"Good to hear. Can you come in later this afternoon? Say three—wait, hang on." Gavin's voice was muffled as he spoke with someone. "Make that four. Bean's got a program that needs to run for . . . hell, I don't know, but she says four works better."

Bean was Hudson Security's IT specialist. Though Matt was pretty sure her job description fell more in line with *hacker* than *IT specialist*. Regardless, Bean was a damn genius when it came to all things tech, so when she said she needed more time to do her thing, more often than not, she got her way.

"Sure, four works for me," Matt said, locking his front door and hitting the key fob for his truck. "Hey, Gavin?" He hesitated as he slid into the driver's seat, heart thumping nervously in his chest.

"Yeah?"

"That job offer still open?" The man on the other end went quiet, and Matt tensed.

Then, after what felt like forever, Gavin chuckled. "Fuck yeah, brother."

The tension in his shoulders eased, and he exhaled. "Great. I put in my resignation this morning."

Gavin's chuckle turned into a full laugh. "About damn time, man. You can bet your ass I'll have all the fucking employment paperwork ready for you to sign when you get here. No take-backs, dude."

Gavin was stoic. Serious. Many called him intense. So hearing his enthusiasm—something not many people were privy to—had the corners of Matt's lips lifting. "I'm looking forward to it. Later, Gav."

And he was looking forward to it. The few times he'd assisted Gavin's crew had been thrilling. They'd filled that gaping hole in him that had been steadily growing the longer he'd been on leave. Matt loved being a detective with the SPD. Putting the puzzle pieces together was a rush he couldn't fully describe. Not being able to do that in the last year had nearly driven him mad.

Right up there with that adrenaline rush? He'd sorely missed the camaraderie. Being part of a team. But that's one of the things that burned the most when he thought about the SPD. One of the reasons he'd decided to not return. To know a brother in blue had betrayed—

Nope. Do not *fucking go there.*

Matt focused on the short drive to Hudson Island's quaint downtown. The three-block hub was a far cry from Seattle, where he and his twin had been born and raised. There was zero hustle and bustle on Hudson. The little town was a throwback; all the locals were in each other's business, and gossip was a sport. But also, when push came to shove, those gossipy neighbors had each other's backs. And that's what mattered. That's why this little town was growing on him.

After pulling into a parking spot in front of Ray's Diner, he nodded to a couple of familiar faces and made his way into the busy restaurant. Brunch was in full swing, and the scents of bacon, pancakes, and other savory delights had his stomach growling. He hadn't eaten since his post-workout smoothie at the ass crack of dawn.

Martha, the spry octogenarian who owned the diner with her husband, Ray, called out a greeting from behind the counter. Matt waved at the sweet woman, then quickly scanned the restaurant. He spotted Cade at a booth along the far window.

Sliding onto the opposite seat, he lifted his chin at his friend. "Hey, man. What's going on?"

Cade returned the chin lift and pushed the menu toward him. "Order first, then we'll talk."

Matt's brow arched in question. It wasn't like his friend to hedge. Cade didn't beat around the bush. He was straightforward and to the point. It was one of the things Matt appreciated about the guy.

He pushed the menu back. "You know I always get the same thing. Now talk."

Cade picked up the menu, then set it back down, shifting in his seat like his damn pants were on fire.

Matt leaned back in the booth and draped his arm along the back. "Dude. Everything okay?"

Cade nodded, crossing his arms over his chest. "Yeah, sorry."

Matt took a sip of his ice water and waited. When Cade remained silent, he let out a sigh. "Are you going to tell me what's up or not?"

"Right. So you know how Poppy officially moved in a couple weeks ago?"

Matt nodded and eyed his squirmy friend.

"Well, as you know," Cade continued, "when Poppy moved in, we adopted two cats. And as you also know, I'm heading over to London at the end of this week for a fight."

Matt nodded again. Cade was a former MMA champion —basically an MMA legend—and now one of the most sought-after and successful coaches in the world. Two of his fighters were headlining a huge UFC fight card in England the following weekend.

Matt made a circular motion with his hand. "Aaand?"

"And I'm bringing Poppy and the twins with me."

"I thought the twins were interning this summer at Hudson Security?" Poppy's sons were great young men who'd just finished their freshman year at the University of Washington.

"They are—and Gavin knows—but I wanted to surprise them with a European vacation. After the fight, we're gonna take about three weeks to travel around."

Staring, Matt prodded, "Sooo . . . you need me to watch your cats while you guys are gone?"

"Yeah. I'd usually ask Dante, but he took Rebecca and the kids to Seattle to visit our folks for a few weeks. Our parents haven't had a chance to spend much time with their new baby and—"

"Dude, stop." Matt held up a hand, halting his friend's verbal diarrhea. If Cade was babbling, something was seriously wrong. "I have no problem watching the cats. You know that. Why are you acting so weird?"

"What?"

Matt arched an eyebrow.

Cade took a deep breath, then his words left him in a whispered rush. "I'm gonna propose to Poppy when we're in Europe. I was thinking the Eiffel Tower, but is that too cliché?" His friend shook his head. "No, that's too cliché. I shouldn't do anything too touristy, right? Yeah, I definitely need to stick with something original. But what about—"

"Take a fucking breath, brother." Matt laughed and kicked Cade under the table. "Look at me." When panicked eyes stared back at him, he did his best to rein in a chuckle. "Poppy's not going to care where you propose to her. She's not pretentious like that. So if you want to propose to her? Just do it. If you want to sweep her off her damn feet with roses and champagne and the Eiffel freaking Tower? Do it. And, dude, if you have the twins with you, then all the better. It'll be perfect, Cade. Stop overthinking it."

Cade let out another breath. "You think?"

"Yeah," Matt said, happy to see some of the earlier panic subsiding. "You're making it way too complicated. Keep the ring on you and just ask her."

"Simple as that?" Disbelief colored Cade's features.

Matt shrugged. "You obviously know her better than I do, but even I know she doesn't care about fancy. You and the boys are what matter most to her. However, my one piece of advice is to do it early on in your trip. That way, *this*"—he waved his hand at his friend's anxious expression—"is curbed. I mean, as entertaining as this freak-out is, I suspect you guys want to actually enjoy your time in Europe—"

"Hi, Matt," a sweet, melodic voice interrupted. "Can I get you anything to drink besides water?"

Everything inside him locked up like a hundred-pound

weight had suddenly dropped onto his chest. He glanced at the young woman in the old-fashioned bubblegum-pink waitress uniform. Scarlet's kind smile, her vibrant brown eyes, and her rainbow-streaked hair had his tongue twisting and the words sticking to his throat.

"I'm good," he mumbled. *Fuck.*

For a split second, her smile seemed to slip, but then it was back in full force. "Well," she said, topping off Cade's coffee, "I'll give you guys a minute to look over the menu, and I'll be right back."

"Holy shit," Cade said once Scarlet was out of earshot. "And I thought I had problems."

Matt glared at his friend. "What's that supposed to mean?"

Cade looked at him like he was a dumbass. Which he probably was. "We've known each other a long time, man, and it's honestly getting painful to watch."

"I don't know what the hell you're talking about." He was pretty sure he knew exactly what Cade was talking about, but he wasn't going to admit shit.

"Right." Cade took a sip of his coffee as his eyes rolled. "Just ask her out already."

Matt stilled. "I still don't know what you're talking about."

"Don't bullshit me, dude. You just talked me down from the proverbial ledge, and now I'm going to return the favor."

"No, thanks," he grumbled.

Cade continued as if Matt hadn't spoken, "Yes, you've been a growly-ass beast since you moved here, but you *can* speak. In fact, you speak perfectly fine with everyone whose name isn't Scarlet Miller. Then you're *that.*" Cade waved his hand in Matt's face. The fucker.

Matt shook his head and took a drink of water. He couldn't deny anything Cade was saying. It was all true. He'd been a grumpy asshole—and he was certain many would say he still was—but he *could* have normal, friendly, polite conversations with people.

Unless they were Scarlet.

He could count on one hand the number of times he'd spoken to her without tumbling over his words.

"You like her," Cade said. It wasn't a question. He opened his mouth to add more, but Matt kicked him again.

"Hey, guys," Scarlet said, approaching their table. "What'll it be today?"

Matt managed to speak like the mature fucking adult he was supposed to be as they placed their orders—making it the fourth time he hadn't stumbled over his words around her—and Scarlet left with a chipper, "Your food will be right out."

When her back turned, Matt dropped his chin to his chest. He glanced up at Cade's chuckle, then let out a resigned sigh. "Remember when you were in middle school and the super pretty, super popular girl that didn't know you existed asked to borrow a pencil?"

The smile on Cade's face grew. "Oddly specific, but yeah?"

"I gave her my pencil and acted all cool, like it was no big deal . . ."

Humor twinkled in his friend's eyes. "But inside, you wanted to puke?"

"Exactly." Matt nodded to where Scarlet was helping a table across the diner. "It's a bit like that."

Cade laughed and shook his head. "You're stupid. You know that, right?"

He shrugged.

"It's not like you don't know her. Scar's one of Poppy's closest friends. Just ask the woman out already."

"I can't."

Cade tilted his head. "Why?"

His friend had to be fucking kidding him. "Come on, De la Rosa, you know why."

Cade's eyes narrowed as he leaned across the table and dropped his voice. "You won't ask her out because she's a single mom?"

Matt reared back, and his jaw dropped. "Fuck you, man," he hissed. "That's not the reason I can't ask her out."

Cade pulled away, crossing his arms over his chest. "Then what is?"

Jesus Christ, did he have to spell it out for the fucker? "Duuude. She's *way* too young for me."

Cade looked at him like he was a moron. "What are you talking about? She's in her twenties."

"She's twenty-*three*."

"And?"

He glared at his friend. "You're fucking kidding me, right? I'm forty."

Cade shrugged. "Yeah, but you're immature as fuck."

Matt rolled his eyes. Cade was nuts. His best damn friend, but fucking nuts.

Pursuing Scarlet was out of the question. He was too old, too grumpy, too . . . everything. *It's out of the question, Alvarez.*

Her laughter carried across the diner, and he frowned. Yeah . . .

He just needed to keep reminding himself of that.

CHAPTER TWO

Sporting a giant smile that was mostly genuine—because the tourists at table four were nice, but so stinking extra—Scarlet moved between the diner's center tables and topped off coffees. The lunch break to-do list she'd been compiling in her head had gone out the window the moment Matt Alvarez had shown up. She knew she needed to swing by the grocery store to pick something up, but for the life of her, she couldn't remember what. That's what the guy did to her brain. Fried it. Completely.

It took everything in her to not cringe. So what if Matt was the epitome of tall, dark, and handsome with some growly hotness thrown in? Because seriously, could she be a little more obvious? She'd been practically drooling over the poor guy.

She stilled mid-pour, and the cringe won out. After flashing a smile at her customers and ensuring they didn't need anything else, she hustled to the beverage station for a fresh coffee pot.

So what if she and Matt had shared a moment a few months back, leaving her crushing hard ever since? Okay, maybe it hadn't exactly been a *moment* per se, but rather an interaction. Of sorts.

She frowned. Okay, fine. Maybe it hadn't even been that.

All Scarlet knew for certain was that the interaction had been the first time she'd gotten the hint that Matt Alvarez even knew she existed. Yes, he'd come into the diner countless times over the last year and she'd waited on him. However, he usually limited his replies to one-word answers. No small talk, no pleasantries. Just right to the point. Which was fine. After all, that growly-hotness thing totally worked in his favor.

But on that particular Saturday a few months back, she'd taken Daisy to the playground and met up with her good friend, Poppy. Unfortunately, Eli—Poppy's dickweed of an ex—had shown up and started spewing vile shit at them. In the middle of the playground! But within moments of the asshole's appearance, Matt had swooped in.

All six-plus feet of the man's muscular goodness had stepped in front of her and put a stop to Eli and his crap. For sure, she'd always been fascinated by Matt. But after that? Scarlet had become the president of the Matt Alvarez fan club.

Was it a little sad? A bit pathetic? Yeah, she could admit that it was. But no one had ever stood up for her before. Besides, her little case of hero worship was harmless. After all, if the curt answers, grunts, and growls of the past few months were any indication, she'd gone back to being a nobody to him.

Which was fine. Truly. The man was way, way, *waaay* out of her league. But that didn't stop her from crushing on him. Because he'd stepped in when he hadn't needed to. That meant something to her. So regardless of whether she was on his radar or not, she'd happily and proudly continue being a card-carrying member of his fan club.

A bell dinged, and she made her way to the pickup window. After double-checking the orders against the ticket, she loaded her tray and strode toward the table with two of her favorite regulars. "Hi, ladies—"

The loud rumble of engines had her flinching. Her stomach dropped as her attention swung to the diner's main window. Three gleaming black-and-chrome motorcycles were pulling into parking spaces along the street. Catching sight of the riders, Scarlet let out a breath, and the sudden tension that had held her body captive eased.

All the riders were tricked out in jeans and expensive-looking Harley Davidson gear. Two bikes held couples who looked to be in their sixties. On the third was a similarly aged solo rider with a giant teddy bear riding bitch. She was sure there was a technical term for riding bitch, but that's all she'd ever heard it called. God knew she'd been that bitch countless times.

"Scarlet, honey?"

She startled but thankfully kept her serving tray level. Heat rushed over her face as she swung her gaze back to the table. "Ohmygod, I'm so sorry, ladies! Here you go, Mrs. Abbot," she said, donning a wide smile and placing a short stack of blueberry pancakes in front of the woman. "And for you . . ." She set a bowl of salmon chowder gently down in front of Mrs. Abbot's partner in crime, Mrs. Yoshida. She nodded to the window. "I'm sorry, ladies. I got distracted by the teddy bear."

Mrs. Yoshida picked up her spoon and gestured toward the window. "I imagine you'll be seeing a lot of those fancy motorcycles over the next few weeks."

Scarlet's blood chilled, but she managed to keep the smile on her face. "Oh yeah?"

"There's a well-known motorcycle group that does

charity work . . ." Mrs. Abbot's nose scrunched. "They're not like that television show."

Mrs. Yoshida scoffed. "Please. Like you and I didn't watch *Sons of Anarchy* together every week and wish we were thirty years younger." She winked at Scarlet. "But it's true. That group is mostly retirees from the Seattle and Tacoma areas."

"They raise money for local children's hospitals, veterans homes, wounded service members . . . that kind of thing," Mrs. Abbot added.

Relief settled Scarlet's twisting stomach. "Oh, well, that's really nice." And the complete polar opposite of her experience with motorcycle clubs.

Mrs. Abbot nodded. "June at Comfort Food heard from Bonnie, who obviously must have heard from her husband—"

"The *mayor*," Mrs. Yoshida interjected with a playful eye roll. Because yes, Mrs. Bonnie Green often referred to her husband by his title.

"—that the group is having a monthlong retreat at the Pacific View Resort. Each week has a different theme, so there'll be members in and out all month."

Scarlet grinned. There was something sweet about seeing the island's gossip train in action. "I'm not gonna lie, ladies, retirement sounds like a fun gig. Thank you for the heads-up about the retreat." She appreciated it more than these two would ever know.

The pickup window bell dinged again, and she gave the women a nod. "That's my cue. Enjoy your meals and let me know if there's anything at all that I can get you, okay?"

The next few minutes were a blur of running food, refilling drinks, and taking orders. With her tray loaded with more amazing food that had her stomach grumbling, she made her way back to Cade and Matt's table. Nerves had her heart beating double time.

Be cool, Scarlet. Do not *fawn over the man. Just. Act. Normal.*

"Here you guys are. Bacon double cheeseburger with cheddar, and a side salad with balsamic." She set Cade's plate in front of him, then grabbed Matt's. "And the fried chicken platter with fries and extra slaw." She placed a few additional napkins on their table. "Can I get you guys refills on your drinks?"

Matt gave a single shake of his head.

"I'm good, Scar. Thanks," Cade said. "Oh, hey, how's Daisy doing? I know for a fact that Rocco is missing her like crazy."

Scarlet's heart warmed and all her nerves evaporated at the mention of her daughter. Her sweet four-year-old attended a home-based day care run by Cade's sister-in-law, Rebecca de la Rosa. Rocco, Cade's three-year-old nephew, obviously also attended and he and Daisy were BFFs. Which was probably the cutest thing ever since Daisy was so stinking shy. However, Rebecca and her family were living over in Seattle this month, visiting with their extended family.

"Well," Scarlet began, "I can safely say the feeling is one thousand percent mutual. I mean, don't get me wrong, Daisy likes Miss Katie and Miss Flora—"

"They're two teachers from the elementary school who're filling in while Rebecca, Dante, and the kids are out of town," Cade clarified for Matt.

"Yeah, they're great. But . . ." Scarlet winced. "They're not Rebecca. And they're *definitely* not Rocco, so my sweet girl has been a bit blue. But she and Rocco had a video call yesterday, which was absolutely hilarious." The way the kids' faces had lit up upon seeing each other had been too precious for words.

Cade chuckled. "I'll bet. It would've been fun to be a fly on the wall for that."

"Oh, it was pretty comical." She grinned, then patted the

table. "I'll let you guys eat. If there's anything else I can get you two, just let me . . ." She trailed off as she noticed Martha hustling her way. Her heartbeat tripped at the worry etched on the older woman's face.

"Scarlet, honey," Martha said, her usually loud, boisterous voice hushed. "You need to get over to Rebecca's. Flora just called and said that little Daisy got into an accident."

Scarlet gasped, and her breath locked in her throat. Her chest clenched painfully tight.

"Flora said Doc Buchanan was on his way over, but they called for an ambulance as well—"

Martha could have said more, but Scarlet didn't stick around to find out. Her baby was hurt. That's what screamed in her brain. She needed to see Daisy, be with her, hold her . . .

Heart thudding loud in her ears, she dashed to the diner's back office and grabbed her purse from her locker. She flew out the back door and sprinted the two blocks to her apartment. They lived above Hudson Island Antiques, and her ancient white Corolla was parked in the alley behind the building.

Digging into her purse, Scarlet ran through the alley's opening, straight to her car. Her hands trembled as she yanked out her keys. Panic threatened to consume her, and a sob stuck in her throat when the key chain dropped with a clatter to the ground. Bending to retrieve them, she yelped when a hand touched her back. She shot up and spun on wobbly legs.

"Scarlet," Cade said, taking a step back, hands raised in the classic I'm-not-going-to-hurt-you gesture. "Everything's gonna be okay. Let us drive you to Rebecca's."

Her chest heaved with ragged breaths as her gaze shot to the hulking man standing behind Cade. He'd spoken, but she hadn't heard a word. "I'm sorry, what?"

"We've got you, Scarlet," Matt said. His deep, raspy voice was calm and soothing, and it chipped away at the fear crawling up her spine. "You're upset, and you shouldn't be driving. We've got you."

Before she could make heads or tails of what was going on, Matt steered her toward the Corolla's passenger door and opened it for her. Taking the keys from her hand, he helped her get seated and secured her seat belt. She could only stare mutely as he gently closed her door and rounded the hood.

At the driver's door, he adjusted the seat all the way back before climbing in. "Deep breaths," Matt said, starting the car and pulling out of the alley. "We'll be there before you know it."

"Hang in there, Scar," Cade said from behind her, squeezing her shoulder.

She flinched. She hadn't realized Cade was in the car with them. Tears prickled the backs of her eyes, and she pressed her clasped hands to her lips. "Please, Matt," she whispered. "Please hurry."

Images of her sweet girl flooded her mind.

Daisy this morning, strapping on her shoes. Her bright-blue eyes sparkling with joy. She'd been so stinking proud of herself for doing it all on her own. Like a big girl. Never mind her pink light-up sneakers were on the wrong feet.

Daisy last night, requesting another bedtime story, but not for her. No, the extra story had been for her beloved Mr. Slothy because "he likes your voice, Mama."

"Scarlet, we're here."

Matt's deep timbre had her eyes flying open. Rebecca's house stood ahead of them, and for a moment, she couldn't breathe. She recognized the two EMTs coming out the front door; Colton and Nora were regulars at the diner.

They didn't look panicked. They didn't look harried.

Instead, they were casually walking down the front steps. That had to be positive, right?

Her door opened, and she startled. Glancing up, she found Matt holding his hand out to her, a calm expression on his face. Good god, how long had she been sitting there? She grabbed his hand and scrambled out of the car.

"Nora! Colton!" she called out, meeting the duo at the base of the steps, Matt and Cade at her back.

"Hey, Scarlet." Nora's reassuring smile did nothing to soothe her galloping heart. "Daisy will be fine."

Colton nodded. "Doc's with her now. There's a chance she fractured her forearm."

Scarlet gasped, and her stomach lurched.

"But we don't know for sure," Colton continued, reaching out to squeeze her shoulder. "You'll want to go to Doc's for an X-ray."

"I know this sucks, hon," Nora said, "but Daisy was in good spirits when we left. Doc and Flora were able to calm her down. They're in the kitchen with her."

Despite the tears threatening to choke her, she managed to thank them for their help. With sympathetic nods, Nora and Colton said their goodbyes.

Scarlet took a moment to gather her courage. Staring at the closed front door, she sucked in a couple of deep breaths. Her hands were still trembling, but there was nothing to be done about that. *You can do this. You have to be strong. For Daisy.*

Another loud exhale, and then she squared her shoulders, pasted a smile on her face, and went inside.

CHAPTER THREE

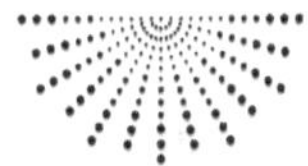

Scarlet's bravery just about slayed him. Her entire frame was trembling, but she forced her shoulders back and walked through Rebecca's front door with a carefully composed expression on her face.

Following close behind, Matt passed a gated front room with a number of kids sitting in a circle and singing a familiar nursery rhyme. The young woman leading the group sported a strained smile as she called out to Scarlet, "She's in the kitchen with Flora and Doc."

They neared the back of the house, and Scarlet came to an abrupt stop in front of Matt. His hands shot to her waist to keep from knocking her over. Letting go, he easily looked over the top of her head, since she didn't even come up to his chin, and into the kitchen.

Doc Buchanan—Hudson Island's favorite doctor and father to one of Matt's good friends—stood at the kitchen island with Daisy seated on the counter in front of him and Flora standing beside him.

The little girl was wearing a pink dress with purple and pink unicorns on it, dirt smearing her entire front. Her legs dangled over the edge, and he could see her skinned knees. Her black hair was pulled into a ponytail that was half undone, and her matching pink unicorn bow was askew.

The corners of his lips twitched. The kid looked like a hot mess. An adorable hot mess, but a hot mess for sure. Regardless, her giggles filled the room. Doc must have said something funny.

Matt glanced down at Scarlet. She'd gone completely still. Frowning, he placed his hands on her slim shoulders and squeezed. Then, bending so he was closer to her ear, he whispered, "Breathe, sweetheart. She'll be fine, but you need to breathe."

With a nod, Scarlet complied. Her hand came up and squeezed his, and it was his turn to go still.

"Thanks," she murmured. After another breath, she stepped away from him and into the kitchen. "Hey, baby girl."

Daisy's head whipped toward her mom, and in the span of a heartbeat, the little girl's expression went from smiling to devastated. Her giant blue eyes widened, then tears streamed down her face. As she cried, she reached for Scarlet and winced in pain. She'd obviously been holding it together until now, until she saw her mom.

Scarlet carefully gathered her daughter in her arms and rocked her, whispering comforting reassurances.

Matt rubbed the center of his aching chest. Plain and simple, his heart broke for the sweet kid. Daisy wasn't even his—hell, he'd only met her a handful of times—but her tears were like a two-by-four to the chin, and her hiccupping cries tore his guts out. He looked over at Cade. The despair and sympathy on his buddy's face mirrored his own emotions.

Running a hand over his closely cropped hair, he caught Doc's eye. "Hey, Doc. How can we help?"

Doc shook both his and Cade's hands in greeting, then said, "We'll need to head over to the clinic for X-rays."

"What happened?" Scarlet asked in that soothing voice, steadily swaying side to side.

"I falled down," Daisy wailed.

Her distress had Matt sucking in a breath and shooting a frantic glance at Doc.

The man chuckled, giving him and Cade a soft smile. "The little peanut's going to be fine, boys."

"Oh my sweet girl," Scarlet said. "You fell down? Is that how you hurt your arm?"

Daisy nodded, and her lower lip wobbled.

Flora held out a small stuffed unicorn to Daisy, who shook her head and burrowed deeper into her mom's arms. "We were all coming in from playing outside, and she tripped," Flora explained. "But when she fell, she landed on the edge of the bottom step."

"I falled down really hard," Daisy said with another loud hiccup.

"You sure did, honey," Flora said. "And you landed right on your forearm."

"It hurts, Mama."

Scarlet pressed a kiss to the top of Daisy's head. "I know, baby."

Matt's gaze flicked around the room. Holy shit, why the hell was everyone still standing around? They needed to move. Not chitchat about what had happened. He waited a moment, expecting the others to recognize the situation's urgency, but Flora and Scarlet continued to quietly discuss Daisy's fall.

Nope. He was done waiting.

"I'll drive," he said, pulling Scarlet's keys from his pocket. He nodded at Cade. "Call Poppy. Scarlet's going to want her friend." He turned to Scarlet. "You can sit with Daisy in the back and—"

"Oh, can I now?" Scarlet's eyebrow arched, and an

amused look flittered over her face.

Matt wasn't quite sure if she was being sarcastic or not, but it didn't matter. They were wasting time. Daisy needed to be attended to. Immediately. After all, what if her arm wasn't the only thing that had been injured?

His chest seized. Holy shit, what if she'd hurt her ribs in the fall? "Doc, you'll want to do a chest X-ray just to be sure. What if her fall—"

Doc laughed and slapped him on the shoulder. "Calm down, son."

"I'm perfectly calm," he replied, making sure to keep the annoyance out of his tone. "But her arm isn't going to X-ray itself, now is it? Let's get moving, people."

Placing his hand on Scarlet's lower back, he ushered her out of the kitchen.

Forty-five minutes later, Daisy's giggles filled the exam room, and Scarlet finally let out a relieved breath. The arm X-ray had revealed a fractured ulna, but luckily, it didn't require surgery. As for Daisy's ribs, Doc hadn't believed there was any damage during his initial exam—there was no apparent bruising and she didn't show any signs of pain when he'd poked and prodded her ribs. However, whether Matt had intended to or not, he'd planted that seed in Scarlet's brain. When she'd asked Doc if he could do a chest X-ray just to be sure, she was certain he'd balk. But to her surprise, he'd simply said, "I understand. I'm a father and would do the same thing. I'd hate to miss something."

In the back of her mind, she flinched at the added expense because she knew her crappy insurance wouldn't cover the cost of the additional scan. It didn't matter, though.

She'd happily take on extra shifts—hell, she'd get a second job—to make sure Daisy wasn't injured beyond her arm.

Thankfully, the chest X-ray had confirmed no damage to Daisy's ribs.

Doc had given Daisy some over-the-counter medication to dull the pain, and now his nurse was distracting her sweet little girl with an impromptu puppet show.

"We're doing a fiberglass short arm cast," Doc said as he fit a stocking-looking thing over Daisy's arm. "The fiberglass is lighter than plaster, and since this peanut is so petite, it'll be more comfortable for her."

Scarlet nodded, listening to him further explain that it would take between four and six weeks for her arm to heal, but with her being so young, it could be even sooner.

"I'll have you bring her back in three weeks," Doc continued. "We'll take the cast off and do another X-ray. From there, we'll see if we need to recast or move her to a splint for the final weeks of healing." He paused in applying the padding and nodded to the door. "Why don't you grab something to drink in the waiting room? After this padding, I'm going to apply the cast tape, and I think Daisy wants to surprise you with the color she's picked out." He looked down at her daughter and waggled his eyebrows. "Isn't that right, peanut?"

Daisy nodded, a giant grin growing on her cherub face. "The color's gonna be a surprise, Mama!"

Rising from the plastic chair, Scarlet leaned down and kissed the top of Daisy's head. "All right, baby. I can't wait to see what color you picked out." She caught Doc's eye and pushed back a wave of emotion. "Thanks, Doc."

"Of course, dear." He inclined his head toward the door again. "Now get out of here. We'll call you in about twenty for the big reveal."

Heading down the hallway, Scarlet let out an unsteady breath before she turned the corner to the waiting room.

"Hey, Scar. How are you holding up?"

Her head jerked up at the familiar voice. As her gaze locked on her friend, the emotion she'd been holding back surged forward, and a tear spilled free.

"Oh, sweetie," Poppy said, rising to envelop her in a hug.

Scarlet took a moment and leaned on her friend. From the day she had arrived on Hudson Island just over a year and a half ago with a toddler on her hip, Poppy had been like a big sister. The woman was, hands down, the closest friend she'd ever had.

Scarlet didn't trust many people—hell, she could count on one hand the number of people she trusted—but Poppy was one of them. She knew she never had to worry about Poppy stabbing her in the back or having some sort of ulterior motive, unlike her "friends" from before. Poppy was nothing but kindness, and while Scarlet was pretty sure she didn't deserve the other woman's friendship, she was hanging on to it with a death grip.

"Come sit," Poppy said, steering her to the waiting room sofa. "Cade filled me in on what happened. How's Daisy doing?"

Wiping away a couple of stray tears, Scarlet relayed the information Doc had given her. "When I left the room, she was in good spirits, so I don't know why I'm still so shaky." She held up her trembling hands and frowned.

"Give yourself a break, Scar. This is the first time Daisy's ever been hurt. You're allowed to be scared, Mama."

Scarlet never wanted to go through this ever again. Her heart couldn't take it. Yes, she knew it wasn't realistic to keep her daughter wrapped in a protective bubble for the rest of her life, but holy moly did she want to.

Glancing around the empty waiting room, she let out

another breath. Her forehead scrunched as she sank deeper into the couch. "Where are Cade and Matt?"

"Oh!" Poppy gave her a one-armed hug. "That's from Cade. He says he's sorry, but he had to take off. And . . ." She dug in her purse and pulled out a familiar set of keys. "These are for you. Matt also apologized, but he said he needed to get going, too. However, he did ask that I text him updates on how you and Daisy are doing."

Scarlet's eyes widened in surprise.

"Your face right now?" Poppy laughed. "You know, I can give you Matt's number so you can text the guy directly. I mean, after all this time, he's finally started speaking to you in full sentences. Who knew it would take Daisy breaking her arm for that to happen?"

Scarlet chuckled, and her face heated. Unfortunately, Poppy was aware of the teeny-tiny-sadly-one-sided crush she had on the man. "Yeah, that was an unexpected twist."

"Come on, girlfriend." Poppy leaned back so they were shoulder to shoulder. "What's going on there?"

"Nothing." And wasn't that the sad truth?

Poppy elbowed her in the side. "Riiight."

"I'm serious. He and Cade were at the diner this morning, and Matt was his usual mumble-one-word-answers-only self. But then Martha told me about Daisy, and I bolted out of there. One second I'm running to my car, and the next second Matt's in the driver's seat, Cade's in the back, and they're taking me to Daisy."

In hindsight, she was thankful Matt had driven her. She had zero recollection of the time between getting into her car and seeing Daisy in Rebecca's kitchen. It was all one giant, panic-induced blur.

"I don't know, Pop. I don't know why, but Matt was just there. Cade, too," she rushed on. "Cade was there for me, too."

Poppy shook her head. "Scar, my man will be the first one to admit that he was just along for the ride. That whole thing? That was all Matt."

It was Scarlet's turn to shake her head. "You're reading too much into it. Matt was just being nice." And she appreciated it. Truly. But she knew his assistance didn't mean anything. Just like her little crush on him.

"What's going on in that head of yours?" Poppy asked after a few moments of silence.

"I knew Matt was nice. I mean, he's friends with Cade, so he couldn't be a giant asshat, right?"

Poppy smiled. "True. But . . ."

She shrugged. "But nothing. It's just that he didn't have to go out of his way for me today. But he did, and it was really kind of him." It had been a long time since a man had been kind to her. At least, one who didn't want something in return. But that was most likely a reflection of her. Of the type of men she'd surrounded herself with.

She fought a cringe. Holy crap, all this stress was making her reflective. And *not* in a good way.

Scarlet met her friend's gaze. "You know when you have a crush on someone who you don't really know? And then when you actually get to know them, the person becomes more real?"

Poppy frowned. "Like real bad or real good?"

She shrugged. "Like real good, but it's in a way that makes you realize how ridiculous your crush is." And hers really, really was ridiculous.

Her friend's frown deepened. "I'm not following, Scar."

She let out a sigh that sounded pathetic to her own ears. Because that's what she was. Pathetic. With a side of delusional tossed in. "I've been crushing on Matt since the moment I laid eyes on him. He's crazy hot and does that sexy growly thing, you know? And did I mention he's smoking hot?"

Poppy chuckled. "Once or twice."

"But my crush on him was safe since I didn't know him. At all. Kinda like when you're crushing on a movie star. It's safe, right? Like, there's no way in hell you're ever meeting that movie star in person, so it's totally okay."

Poppy's lips pursed, and her eyes narrowed in confusion. "But you know Matt."

"Sort of." Scarlet released another sigh. This one defeated. "There's no way he'd go for someone like me."

Poppy pulled away, annoyance etched on her face. "What's *that* supposed to mean, Scarlet Miller? You're amazing."

She rolled her eyes. God, she loved her friend. Why couldn't Poppy have been her sister for real? Holy shit, if she'd had Poppy in her life from the get-go, then—

No. No matter all the shit in her past, Scarlet would never wish it away. Because without all the chaos and trauma, there wouldn't be Daisy. *She* was what mattered. Everything else paled in comparison.

"I'm serious, Scar," Poppy said, bringing her back to the present. "Do you think he's out of your league or something?"

She gave her friend her best don't-be-dumb-of-course-he's-out-of-my-league expression.

"Might I remind you, young lady," Poppy said in her most prissy mom voice, "that you lectured me not too long ago when I had doubts about Cade and thought that *he* was way out of *my* league."

"That's because you were being stupid." When Poppy's mouth dropped open, Scarlet held up a hand and kept talking. "You're a successful business owner who's raised two sons basically on your own. Two sons who are sweet and funny and who both got full-ride academic scholarships to one of the best schools. You're not out of *anyone's* freaking league."

"And you aren't either, Scarlet."

She met her friend's gaze, and for a moment, silence surrounded them. Poppy was one of the few people who knew about her sordid and checkered past. Not all of it—she made damn sure no one knew all of it—but her friend knew enough. "While I appreciate the sentiment, Pop, we both know that isn't true."

Poppy shook her head. "We're going to have to agree to disagree on this one, friend."

"Oh, come on. The man could have anyone." She let out a sigh. "Besides, everyone would just think I'm a gold-digger since he's so much older than me."

Poppy snorted. "You forget that you know each and every member of the gossip train. And they know you. They'd never think that."

She pursed her lips together. "Yeah, well, still. I'm not sure what he'd see in me. I mean, Matt's a Seattle PD *detective*. The man has a whole freaking career. I'm a waitress living paycheck to paycheck, hoping to keep her daughter in clothes that fit."

"Whatever. You're a great mom, and I know for a fact that you live frugally because you're trying to set aside money."

Scarlet opened her mouth to argue but snapped it shut when Poppy arched an eyebrow. Fine. She'd asked her friend about the different types of savings accounts she could set up for Daisy and herself, so denial was out of the picture. Still, she appreciated what Poppy was trying to do. She really did. Having someone be her cheerleader was a precious novelty.

"But, Pop, that doesn't take away the fact that I'm a ninth-grade dropout who doesn't even have a GED." Who'd been more than happy hanging around her local motorcycle club, doing whatever they'd told her to do. She hadn't been good enough—or old enough—to be anyone's old lady back then, but that's what she'd been aiming for. God knew they'd been the antithesis of the altruistic motorcycle club she'd learned about this morning, but she'd turned a blind eye to everything. Until it had become impossible.

That was another thing that needed to be kept under wraps for . . . well, forever.

She rubbed her suddenly throbbing temples. "Look, Poppy, I'm exhausted and don't know what I'm talking about. Please forget I said anything, okay?"

"But, Scar—"

"Mama!" The familiar patter of little running feet came to a sudden halt, and there was Daisy. Holding her right arm out in front of her, a giant grin stretched over her face. "Look, Mama! It's pink!"

Scarlet's heart squeezed, and she let her daughter's excitement wash over her. Let her sweet girl's joy temper the nerves and worry simmering in her gut.

They were going to be okay.

She'd just have to figure out the details later. The clinic did payment plans, right? *No, don't dwell on that.* As long as they had each other, they were good. However, knowing that she was all Daisy had was also utterly terrifying.

Stop! She needed to keep focus, needed to keep her wits about her.

"Scarlet, dear," Doc said, pulling her from her spiraling thoughts. He gestured to the exam room. "We can go over the care instructions for Daisy's arm."

Poppy patted her back. "Take your time. I'll wait for you."

Giving her friend a grateful nod, Scarlet rose. She smiled for her daughter, scooped her up, and settled her on her hip.

As they followed Doc into the exam room, Scarlet oohed and aahed over the tiny hot-pink cast. But the sour rock in her gut remained. Her baby had gotten hurt.

CHAPTER FOUR

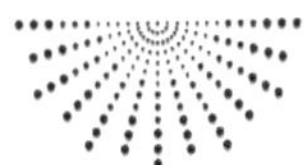

"Well, that was a crazy morning," Cade said, closing the door to Doc's clinic behind him. Poppy had shown up fifteen minutes earlier and was going to wait for Scarlet and Daisy so she could accompany them home.

"I'll say," Matt replied as they began the short, four-block trek from Doc's back to their cars, which were still parked at Ray's Diner. "Don't think either of us had any of that on our bingo cards for today."

Ever since coming to Hudson Island, most of Matt's days had been pretty mellow. Routine even. Hell, some would say his days were flat-out boring. But he would say they were therapeutic. A word that up until last year, he'd never given much headspace to.

Matt's time on Hudson had been focused on getting back into shape—both physically and mentally. He was easily stronger, faster, and more skilled than he'd been while on the force. After all, he spent most of his time working out. From his sunrise runs, then sparring or helping out with training at Cade's fight gym, to brushing up on his tactical skills with

Gavin's crew, he was in impeccable form. He'd never been stronger.

His mental recovery was another story. After the shooting, he'd started going to therapy twice a week—as mandated by the SPD. Eventually, those bi-weekly sessions had morphed into monthly, then into calls every six weeks. He could admit to himself that he'd come a long way. The anger, frustration, and bitterness he'd wrestled with when he'd attended his first appointment had eased considerably.

Hours on his therapist's couch and numerous sessions pounding the shit out of a heavy bag had helped him realize that while some of his issues stemmed from getting shot, the largest culprit was what had followed the attack. Namely, the implosion of his marriage.

The fact that he could even pinpoint where his issues came from was a win. Forget that his therapist kept reminding him that avoidance coping wasn't the healthiest. He'd fucking live.

"So, my friend, I know why *I* had to split," Cade said in a nonchalant way that Matt knew was anything but. "I have a meeting to get to. But why did *you* leave so fast?"

Matt suppressed a sigh. Because more than anything, he'd wanted to stick around. Wanted to know that Daisy was okay. That *Scarlet* was okay. But fuck, ever since they'd met, he'd barely strung together more than a handful of sentences in her presence. So it hadn't been his place to stay. At all. Even if he was always hyperaware of her, always trying to make sure she and her daughter were okay.

But there was no way in hell Matt was telling Cade any of that. Avoidance coping? Absolutely.

His phone dinged. Grateful for the interruption, he pulled it from his pocket and read the text from Gavin. He sent up a prayer of thanks to the universe, fired off a quick response, and turned to his friend. "I also have a meeting."

Cade's brow furrowed. "With who?"

"Gavin." As of thirty fucking seconds ago, his four o'clock meeting had moved to half an hour from now.

"Are you assisting on one of their cases again?"

Matt was tempted to give a vague answer, but Cade was his best friend. He paused mid-step and let out a breath. "Actually, no."

Cade stopped, and the concern on his face grew. "Everything okay, man?"

The corners of Matt's lips twitched. "Yeah," he said as he resumed walking with Cade in step beside him. "So . . . I put in my resignation this morning. Officially. And I'm going to work for Gavin." He looked at his friend in wonder. "I'm apparently signing paperwork and all that shit today."

Cade stared at him for a moment, slack-jawed. Then he let out a deafening whoop and pulled Matt into a bruising hug. "It's about fucking time, brother!"

Matt laughed and slapped his friend on the back. A weight lifted from his shoulders. Holy shit, saying it out loud —with this kind of reception—was such a damn relief.

"Thanks, man." He shook his head, still not quite believing it was all real. "Even with the medical leave I took, and then the additional extensions, I still had another five weeks of vacation and sick time racked up. But I figured enough was enough."

"Fuck yeah, man!" Cade said, clapping his hands together.

Matt laughed at his friend's exuberance.

"So you're here permanently, then?"

Matt nodded and the corners of his lips pulled up. "That's the plan."

"Good," Cade said. "You keeping your place in Seattle or selling?"

His house in Seattle had been sitting vacant for the last year. As much as he liked the old Craftsman, too much shit had gone down within those walls, within that city. Sure, he'd still return once in a while to visit his brother, sister-in-law, and folks since they all lived there, but otherwise, he was done with that chapter of his life.

A glance around Hudson's charming downtown had his insides settling, relaxing. There was no baggage here. No soul-crushing memories. Though it had taken a while, he finally accepted that this little slice of the Pacific Northwest was his new home.

"Selling." Matt shrugged. "Looks like you're stuck with me."

"I'm glad to hear it," Cade said with another backslap.

Matt smiled as they reached their vehicles. He was glad, too.

"Well, after you meet with Gavin, swing by the house around five. We'll throw some steaks on the grill, crack open a couple beers to celebrate your new job, and run over all the cat stuff."

With a chuckle, Matt opened the door to his truck. "Will do. But isn't the cat stuff just food and water?"

"Oh fuck no, man. Poppy has a whole routine with those damn cats." Cade heaved out an exasperated sigh, but his grin told a different story. The guy would do anything for his woman, crazy cat routines and all. He was that besotted. Not that anyone could blame him. Poppy was pretty cool.

Matt's mind flashed to Scarlet, and he wanted to kick himself. There were a million reasons why he needed to stay away from the young woman. And he would. He wasn't the kind of man she needed in her life. She deserved a partner who didn't have as much baggage as him, and someone who was a whole hell of a lot closer to her age.

Waving goodbye to Cade, Matt told himself that his concern for Scarlet was based solely on the events that had transpired this morning. It was *neighborly* concern. That was it. That was all it could be.

Twenty minutes later, Matt pulled into the Hudson Security parking lot. He crumpled the wrapper of the protein bar he'd just wolfed down and stuffed it into the small trash bin next to his seat. Taking a deep breath to quell the sudden nerves in his stomach, he made his way to the building's front door.

"Hi, Mel," he said once he was buzzed inside, greeting the receptionist he'd met on a handful of occasions.

"Good afternoon, Mr. Alvarez," she said, motioning to the small seating area. "Gavin's expecting you and will be right out."

"Thanks, and you can just call me Matt or Alvarez."

"Of course, sir."

Matt suppressed a cringe. He understood formalities. He did. But damn if *sir* didn't make him feel ancient. Taking a seat, he blew out another breath.

Holy shit, this is really happening.

Matt didn't have to wait long before Gavin opened the door separating the reception area from the secured offices.

"Mel," Gavin began, "I know you two have already met, but Alvarez is officially joining our team. Can you get him set up with access cards and all that good stuff? We'll be meeting in the main conference room for a couple hours."

"You got it, Gavin," she said, then turned and flashed Matt a smile. "Welcome to the team. I'll have everything you need ready by the time you leave today."

"Appreciate it," he replied, once again impressed by the efficiency of the operation. With the SPD, it had taken two full days to get a new key card when his had suddenly stopped working.

Following Gavin, he took in the open floor plan of the

office space. In the center was an array of workspaces and tables that reminded him of his former bullpen. However, unlike his former bullpen, the area didn't induce claustrophobia. The entire far wall was floor-to-ceiling windows—bulletproof, of course—that made the space feel enormous.

To the left were closed doors, which he knew led to management's private offices. To the right, where they were heading, waited numerous conference rooms.

Entering one behind Gavin, Matt waved at Bean, who was seated at the end of the large conference table, laptop open in front of her. She returned his wave with a smile, then refocused her attention on her screen.

"Alvarez, have you met Esmerelda Abara?" Gavin asked, drawing Matt's attention to the woman who walked into the conference room behind them.

Esmerelda looked to be in her early to mid-thirties, five-five, and athletically trim. Dressed in sky-high heels and a light-gray pantsuit, her white blouse popped against her bronze skin. Her long, wavy black hair was slicked back into a high ponytail. Simply put, the woman was stunning. But more than that, there was a sharp, no-nonsense air about her.

"Esmerelda keeps this place running and everyone in line," Gavin said. "She handles all the logistics for the teams and—thankfully—all the HR paperwork, too. She works remotely from Seattle and comes into the office for a day or two every few weeks, but she'll be relocating to Hudson soon."

"In your dreams, Frazier." She chuckled and held out her hand. "Welcome, Mr. Alvarez. I've heard a lot about you."

Accepting her firm handshake, he said, "Matt, please. Or just Alvarez is fine."

"Drop the formalities. Got it. And please, call me Esme." She opened the manila folder she was carrying and held out a small stack of papers. "Fill these out and bring them back to

me before you leave today. I'll get you set up in our system."
She glanced at Gavin. "Discuss compensation, please. Prefer-
ably *before* you get into the cases. Then text me immediately
with the final number."

"Yes, ma'am," Gavin said with a salute.

Esme turned on her heel, closing the door behind her.

Gavin gestured to the conference table and sat at the
opposite end from Bean, who was now speaking into her
headset. "As Esme mentioned," he began, "we never talked
compensation."

Matt would take the job regardless—he was pretty sure
they both knew that—but he was still curious to hear Gavin's
offer. Hudson Security was a world-renowned firm with
deep pockets. Plus, all the employees Matt had encountered
seemed to be doing fine money-wise. But what did he know?
At worst, he assumed he'd be paid about what he'd made as a
detective with the SPD, which had been a six-figure salary.
Nothing to sneeze at.

Luckily, he was in a position to be flexible. After all, he
lived rent-free at his brother's place, had a sizable savings
account, and was pretty damn frugal. It also helped that he'd
had a top-tier divorce attorney, courtesy of one of his brother's friends, so he'd come out of that clusterfuck relatively
unscathed. Financially, that is. Once he sold his house in
Seattle, he'd be more than comfortable.

"We're not much for titles around here," Gavin said, "but
the deal's full-time and salaried. Most likely some travel with
expenses covered by the company. We pulled how much you
were making at SPD—"

Matt's eyebrows shot up.

"What?" Gavin grinned, nodding toward Bean. "Blame
her. She came up with the info."

"There's nothing to blame me for," Bean said, ending her
call. "You were a government employee; it's all public infor-

mation. You just need to know where to look." She threw him an innocent smile and shrugged. "And I do."

Matt chuckled. "Even if it wasn't public information, I'm sure you'd find it."

"And you'd be correct." She gulped down some sort of fluorescent-green drink, and Matt tried not to cringe. "Truthfully, I didn't realize detectives made that much. But seeing as you've been with the SPD for over eighteen years and steadily worked your way up, it makes sense. Not a bad gig. I'm surprised they didn't try harder to keep you."

"They did." But there had been too many extenuating circumstances.

"Well, lucky us, then." Bean toasted him with her glass. "Besides, this gig is better. Trust me."

"Speaking of," Gavin said, giving Bean a pointed look. Which had her eyes rolling and Matt biting back a laugh. "How does double your old salary work?"

His jaw dropped. There was no way he'd heard that right. "Are you serious?"

"Very."

No way. "That's nearly three hundred grand."

"I can do math, Alvarez."

Bean smirked. "Told you the gig's better here. *And* there's no bureaucratic bullshit. Just Gavin's bullshit."

Gavin tilted his head toward Bean. "What she said. There's also full medical, dental, 401(k), and all that shit. You in?"

For a moment, Matt could only blink.

"Is that a yes?" Gavin waved his phone in the air. "I need to let Esme know before she comes back in here and stabs me or something."

Bean snorted. "Like she'd ever be so obvious." She caught Matt's gaze. "Don't let Esme's pantsuits, spreadsheets, and impeccable organizational skills fool you. That chick's a badass. Pretty sure she could kill you with her baby toe."

A grin spread over Matt's face, and he nodded. "Hell yeah. Let's do this."

He wasn't quite sure what he'd just gotten himself into, but he studied the two people in the room with him and felt no trepidation. Gavin Frazier was solid. Easily one of the smartest and best men he knew, not to mention the deadliest. And Bean. He had no clue what her last name was, or her first name, for that matter, but he was beginning to think that was intentional. Rumor had it the petite brunette dynamo was one of the top hackers—oh, sorry, *IT specialists* —in the world.

Then there was the woman handling his HR paperwork, who was apparently Black Widow in disguise. Everyone he'd met at Hudson Security was top-notch. Yeah . . . this was a team he wanted to be part of.

"Welcome aboard, Alvarez," Gavin said, sliding a pen across the table. "Now fill out that paperwork because Bean wasn't lying about Esme."

Once Matt's HR paperwork was completed, Esme came to collect it. She was heading out to catch the ferry back to Seattle, but she promised he'd have a copy of all his employment paperwork in his new, secure inbox within the next two hours. Of that, he had no doubt. The woman screamed competence.

Gavin placed a bottle of water next to Bean, then held one up to Matt, brows raised in question. At Matt's nod, Gavin tossed the bottle over and retook his seat. "As you know, we have a number of high-profile clients and usually ten to twenty cases going at any given time. Right now, one such client has a twenty-four-year-old son who's gone missing. The family believes he was abducted while on vacation down in Mexico. The son had round-the-clock security with him, but they were subdued. We've gathered some intel and would like you to take a look. We know what we think, but I'd like to get your opinion."

"You don't think he was abducted?" Matt asked, breaking the seal of his water and taking a drink.

Gavin shrugged. "I'd like you to take a look before sharing my thoughts."

"That's fair. I'll happily take a look at what you've got."

A ding from Bean's computer, and her subsequent curse, had their attention moving to the woman.

"What's up, B?" Gavin asked.

"Got a hit," she said, her nose scrunching as she typed. Then, turning her attention to Matt, she clarified, "I have a facial recognition program running constantly that monitors Hudson's comings and goings."

"Like the Hudson Security property?" Matt asked.

"Well, that too, but I meant Hudson Island."

His eyes widened in surprise. "How the hell do you monitor an entire island?"

A grin played at the edges of her lips. "Basically, the only way on our lovely island is the ferry"—she held up a hand, forestalling the comment on the tip of his tongue—"I *know* there are technically other ways, but ninety-nine point nine percent of people come through the ferry terminal. So, I have my program monitoring the cameras there. I get a notification when anyone on the local, state, or federal watch lists visits. Then depending on who they are and what they've done, I inform whoever needs to know."

Matt's brow furrowed. "Is that le—"

"Excuse me?" The glare she sent him made his balls shrivel and his mouth slam shut. Right. No asking her about the legalities of shit.

"You're a fast learner." Gavin chuckled. "So, the personal security side of our operation is pretty straightforward.

People need bodyguards; we assign them accordingly. The investigative side, like the Mexico case, is more complicated. That's where we could use your help. Oliver handles everything originating outside the US and has a couple cases he'd like extra eyes on."

Oliver MacKay was the second-in-command of Hudson Security. Though Matt had never met him personally—the man wasn't based out of Hudson Island—they'd been on a handful of video calls together.

Matt's phone dinged an incoming text.

"Sorry about that," he said, pulling his phone from his pocket with the intention of silencing it. When he glanced at the text from an unknown number, however, he frowned. "Do you mind if I check this real quick?"

"Everything okay?" Bean asked at the same time Gavin said, "Go right ahead."

Opening the text, a photo filled his screen. He smiled.

It was a picture of Daisy with a giant grin. Her lips and part of her cheek were stained bright blue from the Otter Pop she held in her good hand. She was wearing the same unicorn outfit as earlier, but now a tiny hot-pink cast covered her right forearm. Her beloved Mr. Slothy was clutched in the crook of her left arm. The text underneath read, *Thank you SO MUCH for everything!*

Letting out a breath, Matt put his phone on silent and placed it face-down on the table. "Sorry about that."

"Holy shit," Bean murmured, eyes wide as she stared at him.

Taking a drink of water, he looked at her in question.

"Damn, Alvarez." She fanned herself with a manila folder. "I don't think I've ever seen you smile like that. Warn a woman next time, will ya?"

Matt choked, and water sprayed from his mouth. Gavin laughed, so Matt flipped him off. Clearing his throat, face hot, he wiped up the spilled water with the napkin Gavin had tossed at him. "Uh, thanks, Bean. I think."

"No, thank *you*. And thank whoever it is that texted you."

"You know Scarlet from Ray's Diner?" When they both nodded, Matt continued, "Her daughter, Daisy, broke her arm at day care this morning. Cade and I were there when Scarlet got the news, so we drove her." He waved at his phone. "She just sent me a picture of Daisy in her cast."

Bean grimaced. "Yikes, poor kid. Is she okay?"

"Seems like it."

"Good. Kids are resilient." Gavin glanced at Bean. "Can we get back to work?"

"Ease up, boss," she said as an image popped up on the conference room's wall-sized Smartboard. "Unlike you jokers, I'm capable of multitasking. Now, back to my facial recognition program . . ."

CHAPTER FIVE

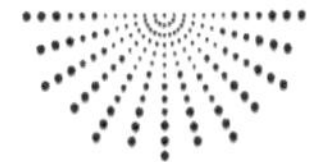

They spent four solid hours going over Hudson Security's current cases, with Matt giving his initial assessments of the information Gavin and Bean presented. He'd asked many questions and even questioned some of the intel that had been gathered. The time had flown by, and frankly, it had been amazing. Fucking exhilarating. His body was still buzzing with a level of excitement and energy that he'd forgotten existed.

God, he'd missed this—collaborating with a fierce team to put the various puzzle pieces together—and he was so damn grateful to have another opportunity.

Nodding along to the radio, Matt pulled into Cade and Poppy's driveway and parked. He was looking forward to decompressing with his friends over steaks and beers after an already fulfilling afternoon. As he shut his truck's door, he noticed a familiar car parked off to the side. An older-model white Corolla.

Scarlet was here.

Just like that, nerves sparked in his gut. What was it about this pixie that had him on edge? Shaking his head, he took the steps of the front porch two at a time and let himself in. The laughter and heckling of Poppy's twins reached his ears. No doubt they were giving Cade shit about something. Following the noise, he entered the kitchen.

"Hey, Matt!" Carter said. "You've known Cade for forever, right? Is it true that in college he tried to memorize all the dance moves in *Dirty Dancing* so he could pick up chicks?"

Matt grinned at his friend. These kids had his buddy's number. That was for damn sure. "Well, boys, I'm not at liberty to confirm or deny." But he nodded at the twins, who howled with laughter.

"Asshole," Cade muttered with a chuckle, knocking into Matt's shoulder. "Glad you could make it, man. Grab a beer."

Not needing a second invitation, he grabbed an IPA from the fridge, then scanned the full kitchen island. "Bottle opener?"

"Drawer behind you," Cade replied, gesturing with his beer bottle.

It took a few seconds of rummaging through the obvious junk drawer before he found a Seattle Seahawks bottle opener.

"Was that Scarlet's car out front?" he asked, turning back to Cade. He knew damn well it was, and by the look his friend was giving him, Cade wasn't buying the bullshit he was spewing.

Cade smirked and gestured toward the hallway. "They're in the TV room setting up Daisy with some movies. Do me a favor." He grabbed a tray of steaks. "Poppy wrote up a list of the cat stuff, but I think she left it in the front room. Grab that and meet us out by the grill?"

"Sure thing."

"Boys!" Cade called as he headed out the back door. "Grab the corn and start shucking. Your mom's got a table all set up for you guys."

Matt chuckled at the good-natured complaining the twins dished out. Beer in hand, he made his way to the front of the house—and then detoured to the TV room, which was basically a mini movie theater with kick-ass recliners and amazing surround sound. After all, it would be rude to not stop in and say hello to the ladies, right?

He grimaced. Yeah . . . that was too much bullshit, even for him.

Peeking inside, he frowned. A Disney cartoon was playing with the volume on low, but the room was empty. How had he missed them?

Turning toward the front room, he came to an abrupt halt. Daisy was kneeling on the sofa by the front window, with her back to him, playing quietly with Mr. Slothy and a stuffed unicorn. Mr. Slothy was in her good hand, and he appeared to be racing across the back of the couch. The bright-pink cast covered part of her right hand and ended just below her elbow, but that didn't prevent her from holding the unicorn firmly by the scruff. Or was it a mane? Regardless, the way the animals crashed into each other looked like some kind of stuffed animal demolition derby.

"Hey, Daisy," he said quietly, not wanting to startle her. "You didn't want to watch the movie?"

She peered over her shoulder and stared at him for a few moments, her doe eyes wide, before shaking her head. "Mr. Slothy's tired of *Frozen*."

"Oh yeah?" Walking deeper into the room, he lowered himself onto the love seat across from Daisy, careful to give her plenty of space. While he'd been around the little girl countless times, he'd only interacted with her on a handful of occasions. He knew she was shy. Besides, he was a big guy, and she was a teeny-tiny little thing. He didn't want to crowd her or make her uncomfortable. "What are Mr. Slothy and Mr. Unicorn up to?"

She held up the unicorn. "She isn't a boy, silly. She's a girl."

"Sorry," he said, holding up his hands. "My bad. I hope I didn't hurt her feelings."

Daisy giggled, and warmth bloomed in his chest. He wasn't the best with kids—not because he didn't like them, but because he didn't come across many in his daily life—so he was thankful Daisy wasn't scared of him.

"What's her name?" he asked.

"Baby Unicorn."

He grinned. Of course it was. "Are they pretending to be race cars?"

She shook her head. "Mr. Slothy and Baby Unicorn are running, but Mr. Slothy falled down, and now he's hurt."

"Oh no. Is Mr. Slothy okay?"

Daisy shook her head again, and her shoulders slumped. "His arm hurts, and he's crying. He's sad. He's scared, and he wants his mama."

As her lower lip jutted out and began to tremble, worry crept up his spine. "Can I see?"

She looked up at him and nodded. His breath caught in his throat. The sweet girl's eyes were glassy with unshed tears. Holy shit, this kid was breaking his heart.

Hurrying closer, he sat on the coffee table between them and held out his hand. "Can you show me where Mr. Slothy is hurt?"

She held out the stuffed animal's arm.

Matt didn't know what the hell he was doing, but he was going to make this kid smile if it killed him. "Just as I thought," he said, carefully turning the stuffed animal's arm left, then right. "It looks wonky. I think Mr. Slothy's going to need a cast just like yours."

Daisy gasped, and her blue eyes went wide with excitement. "He does?"

Matt nodded, thankful her sadness seemed to be forgotten. He jiggled the stuffy's arm. "I think so. We should put his arm in a cast just to be safe. You're his mama, so what do you think?"

She grinned. "To be safe."

"Do you know if Mr. Slothy likes the color blue?"

Her head bobbed up and down. "It's his favorite color."

"Nice. It's my favorite color, too." He pursed his lips in thought. "Can you make sure Mr. Slothy doesn't move? I have to get the cast supplies, but I promise I'll be right back."

"Okay," Daisy said, pulling Mr. Slothy into an embrace that reminded him of how Scarlet had held her daughter earlier this morning. When the little girl patted the stuffed animal's back and softly shushed, his chest squeezed tight.

Holy shit, this kid . . .

Matt rose and rushed to the kitchen. Yanking open Cade's junk drawer, he grabbed what he'd spied earlier. He was back beside Daisy in under thirty seconds.

"All right, Otter Pop, you hold—"

"Otter Pop?" Daisy giggled. "My name is Daisy."

"Huh." He pointed at her mouth. "Well, you have blue Otter Pop all over your face, so I think I'm gonna call you Otter Pop from now on."

"Mr. Matty, you're silly."

He winked at her. "Right back at ya, Otter Pop. Now, you hold Mr. Slothy still, and I'll put the cast on him. It'll be just a quick procedure. It won't hurt him at all." He bit the inside of his cheek to keep from chuckling as Daisy hung on his every word. He lifted Mr. Slothy's right arm. "Is this the arm Mr. Slothy hurt?" After she nodded with that darling smile on her face, he said in his most serious tone, "Be sure to hold him really still, Otter Pop."

Tearing a length of the blue painter's tape he'd stolen from Cade's junk drawer, Matt carefully wrapped the stuffed animal's arm, making sure to explain every little step to Daisy. He also made sure to add a little strip over the top of its paw, just like her cast.

Once finished, he lifted Mr. Slothy and inspected his work. "What do you think?" he asked, presenting Daisy with her blue-casted stuffy. "You guys match now."

She took the toy from his hands and gave it a hug. "Thank you, Mr. Matty!"

He chuckled. If Mr. Slothy had been real, all his bones would have broken from her squeeze.

"Mama, look!" Daisy held her stuffy in the air. "Me and Mr. Slothy match!"

Matt turned, and heat rushed over his face. Scarlet stood in the room's entryway, leaning against the wall. The soft smile on her face made his heart beat double time.

Holy shit, he was in trouble.

Scarlet's heart was in her throat, and she was teetering on the edge of melting into a puddle of mushy goo. She was also pretty sure the wall was the only thing holding her upright. Because the way Matt stared at her, with that blush washing over his cheeks, fell somewhere between adorable and smoking hot.

When she'd realized Daisy wasn't in the TV room, she'd gone looking for her. And come across this moment: big, tough Matt Alvarez making an arm cast for Mr. Slothy. To match her daughter's. *Holy wow, be still my freaking heart!*

She should have announced herself, but she'd stood transfixed, watching him carefully wrap the blue tape around Mr. Slothy's arm. He'd explained to Daisy how it wasn't going to hurt her beloved stuffy. How she was doing a great job holding him still. How she was an amazing mama to Mr.

Slothy. And just like Scarlet, Daisy had been mesmerized by each and every word.

Her chest squeezed tight. No one had ever done something like this for Daisy. Ever. And the way her little girl's face shone bright with joy had tears prickling the backs of her eyes.

"See, Mama!" Daisy said. "His is blue and mine is pink. It's our favorite colors!"

Blinking the tears away, she smiled at her daughter. "Wow! You and Mr. Slothy are basically twins now!"

Daisy scrambled off the couch with Mr. Slothy tucked under her arm. "Thank you, Mr. Matty," she said, rushing out of the room. "Mama, I gotta show Poppy!"

"Walk, please!" Scarlet called out, smiling when Daisy slowed.

Alone with Matt now, she took a deep breath in for courage. Holy crap, she totally felt like a loser middle schooler striking up a conversation with the most popular boy in high school. Looking anywhere but his face, her eyes caught on his enormous hands. His long, tan fingers were fiddling with . . . Baby Unicorn?

Her gaze swung to his, and that blush on his cheeks deepened. Though it must've been a trick of the light because, holy shit, there was no way *he* was embarrassed. Either way, there was something seriously swoony about this giant, muscular man holding a pink unicorn.

She cleared her throat. "Thank you for doing that for Daisy. Getting a pink cast made it fun for her and distracted her from what happened, but now that Mr. Slothy has a matching blue cast, she'll be even more excited."

"It's not a problem. I figured the way she was crashing her stuffies into each other, there was bound to be some damage to one of them." He shot her a grin that had her stomach doing somersaults.

Good lord, that's a lethal smile.

"Well, it was really kind of you. And I hope you don't mind that I texted you that picture of Daisy earlier." His head tilted to the side, so she rushed on, "I got your number from Poppy. I wanted to thank you for all your help this morning and show you that Daisy was doing good." Holy crap, if she didn't take a breath soon, she was going to pass out. But still, her mouth kept on blabbing. "I hope that's okay. Getting your number and texting you, I mean. I didn't want to over-step, but I really did appreciate all your help—"

Matt held up a hand, and her words came to an abrupt halt. "You're fine, Scarlet. Really. I appreciated your text, actually. The blue Otter Pop smile was great."

She finally took that breath, tucking her fists into the pockets of her denim shorts. She never knew what to do with her hands. "Yeah, she's pretty cute. I usually don't let her have more than one. She gets a little crazy with all the sugar, but today was . . ." She shrugged. "And to top it off, the twins were in charge of the popsicles."

"Are they really popsicles?" he asked, tone light and teasing. "They don't have sticks."

Scarlet stared at him for a moment, and the corners of her lips twitched. "They're stickless popsicles. But popsicles nonetheless."

He pursed his lips. "We may have to agree to disagree on that." He smiled, and again, her stomach flipped. "Judging by the amount of blue on her face, which may be permanent at this point, I assume she was able to con a few more Otter Pops out of the twins than they actually admitted to you." Leaving Baby Unicorn on the sofa, he stood and ran a hand through his closely cropped black hair. His tan, tattooed forearms were strong and corded, the veins popping just so.

She lost all train of thought. Her mouth might have even dropped open.

Gah! Focus, girl! Yanking her gaze away from the arm porn, she took in his wide shoulders and strong torso. There was no ignoring the way his T-shirt hugged his powerful chest. The guy was straight-up ripped and—*gah! Stop eye-molesting him!*

"Um," she squeaked before clearing her throat. "The steaks are almost ready. We're all outside if you want to join us." Ohmygod, she could feel the warmth washing over her face.

His lips split into a broad grin. "All right. I'm going to grab another beer. Can I get you anything?"

"I'm good, thanks," she said, back to squeaking. "I'll meet you outside."

More than anything in the world, she wished that the ground would magically open up and swallow her whole. No such luck. Apparently, her steady voice was a thing of the past. But holy crap, in her defense, she'd never seen Matt smile like that. And when he'd helped Daisy earlier, he'd been so soft and sweet—and so, so sexy.

Good god, she wanted to clobber herself in the head. This crush had been fine when she hadn't really known the guy. But now? When she'd gotten a glimpse of the man behind the somber expression and growly, one-word replies? Now, it was a bad, bad idea.

An hour later, they had finished the simple but amazing dinner of steaks, corn on the cob, and baked potatoes. Once the dishes were loaded in the dishwasher and the kitchen was clean, everyone gathered around the gas fire pit, relaxing while the twins entertained them with tales from their first year at college.

Scarlet laughed at their antics, though a small part of her was envious. The twins were only four years younger than her, yet it felt like a lifetime separated them. Their stories seemed so foreign. As did their easygoing attitudes and exuberance. It was like watching a movie about the charmed college experience. She knew their lives hadn't been silver spoons and luxury—Poppy was like her big sister, so she knew about their struggles—but their obvious confidence left her in awe.

Daisy squirmed in her lap, and she tightened her hold, inhaling her daughter's fruity scent. For the millionth time that evening, she wondered what she was doing here with these amazing people. How the hell had she gotten so lucky to land in their orbit?

She'd moved to Hudson Island nineteen months ago. And yes, she knew the exact day. Hell, she could probably narrow it down to the exact hour she'd stepped foot off the ferry. Coming here was the best thing she'd ever done. She'd immediately started working at Ray's Diner, and within a week, Poppy had befriended her. She'd cherished their relationship ever since.

Poppy had given birth to the twins at sixteen and spent the following years fighting and struggling but had come out on top. The twins, who were kind and kick-ass in their own right, were thriving in college, and Poppy owned and ran one of the most successful boutiques on Hudson. More recently, she'd found blissful happiness with a great guy who, as Scarlet's favorite gossip train ladies liked to say, wasn't at all hard on the eyes. The woman truly was her role model. If Scarlet could be half as awesome as Poppy, she'd die happy.

She smiled as the twins switched to teasing their mom about her new cats, Ripley and Bishop. While their crew was going to be away in London, Matt had agreed to watch the two felines. Apparently, her friend was a bit neurotic with the cat-care plan. Two bullet point pages of the cats' daily activities and feeding schedules. It was a bit extra, but also so very Poppy that Scarlet had to laugh.

"Poppy?" Daisy asked, her tiny voice quieting the group.

"Yeah, sweetie?"

"Can I play with the kitty cats when you're not here? I think they'll be sad."

"Of course, sweetie," Poppy replied.

Matt, who was seated next to Scarlet, reached over and squeezed Daisy's foot. "I think you're right, Otter Pop."

Scarlet furrowed her brow at the nickname, but when Daisy giggled, her stomach did that flipping thing again.

Holy shit. Matt Alvarez and her daughter had an inside joke.

"How about," Matt began, "when you want to play with the cats, you let your mama know, and then she can let me know? Then we can get you over here to make sure the cats aren't sad. Sound like a good plan?"

Daisy nodded, then yawned and leaned back into Scarlet's chest. "A good plan, Mr. Matty."

Scarlet had been acutely aware of the man sitting beside her for the last hour. It actually helped that he was so close. It meant she didn't have to make eye contact. It also helped that Daisy was sitting on her lap, growing more tired by the second. She knew she shouldn't use her daughter as a buffer, but she couldn't resist.

Truthfully, Matt made her nervous. He was just . . . a lot. Handsome, intelligent, and surprisingly kind. It was intimidating. She didn't know what to say to him and constantly worried she'd make a complete fool of herself.

It was easier to talk to him when she was at the diner, taking his order. She was well-practiced at that kind of small talk. But this kind? Where everyone was sitting around, shooting the shit? It was completely different. She didn't know how to do this. At all. So, like the coward she was, she hid behind her sweet little girl.

Daisy twisted and looked up at her. "Mama, we have to make sure Ripley and Bishop aren't sad. Poppy said I can visit them, and Mr. Matty will take me."

"I heard, baby." Giving Matt a smile, Scarlet ran a hand over her daughter's head. "I'm sure Ripley and Bishop would love to see you while everyone's gone."

"Maybe they can come live with us?"

Soft laughter filled the air as hopeful blue eyes gleamed up at Scarlet. "I think Ripley and Bishop would be happier here. This is their home, sweet girl, but we'll come visit."

"Promise?" Daisy asked, bottom lip sticking out.

She nodded, and Daisy let out another yawn. "On that note, I hate to break up the party, but we should be getting home."

Rising, Scarlet adjusted her hold on Daisy, who'd snuggled into her like a little monkey.

Everyone stood, and Poppy made her way over, enveloping both Scarlet and Daisy in a hug. "Even though our flight to London isn't until Friday, we're planning to head over to Seattle on Wednesday. Cade needs to check in at the Seattle gym, and we're going to see his folks before we take off. But I'll check in with you tomorrow, okay?"

"Please do." She returned her friend's hug. "I'd love to see you before you take off."

"Thanks again for coming out, Scar," Poppy said, shifting her attention to Daisy and gently bopping her on the nose. "And you, missy. You make sure to take care of that arm of yours, okay?"

Following the group into the kitchen, Scarlet helped Daisy wave goodbye to the guys. "Thanks for having us, Cade. The steaks were divine."

"I'm glad you liked them," he replied. "And you two are welcome any time."

"Oh, come on, Scar," Carter protested. "Forget the steaks. Have you ever had better shucked corn in your life?"

"Impeccably shucked corn," Dylan added. "Not a husk thread in sight."

She chuckled. These two never failed to make her laugh. "Pardon me. The steaks were okay, but the *corn* was amazing. Thank you, guys."

"That's right, girl," Carter said, holding out his fist.

With a shake of her head, she bumped her fist against his. "If I don't see you two before you leave, have fun in London."

In the living area, she spied her things on the floor by the fireplace. "Hang on, sweet girl," she murmured, bending to reach her purse and tote bag.

"Here, let me get that for you," Matt said, suddenly next to her. He picked up both items. "I'll walk you out."

And just like that, the nerves were back.

"Um, thank you," she said, trailing him to her car.

With Daisy's cast, maneuvering her into the car seat was a bit of a task. As Scarlet finally got the buckle to click, she nodded at the front seat. "Hey, Matt? If you could put my bags up front, I'd appreciate it."

"You got it." He rounded the hood and deposited her things on the passenger seat. After closing the door, he held up a hand. "Hang on a sec," he said, then rushed into the house.

By the time Scarlet had her driver's side door open, he returned wearing that grin that did something to her insides.

Opening the back door, he peered in and said, "Can't have you forgetting Baby Unicorn, now can we?" He tucked the stuffy next to Daisy in her car seat.

Scarlet bit her bottom lip to keep from sighing. *Who is this guy?*

"Thank you, Mr. Matty," Daisy said, giving him a tired smile.

"Any time, Otter Pop."

Scarlet had no clue where the Otter Pop thing had come from, but damn if it wasn't the cutest thing she'd ever heard. Clearing her throat, she got in her car and paused to meet his gaze. "Thanks again, Matt. For everything."

Grabbing the frame of her door, he said, "You're welcome, Scarlet. You in?" At her nod, he closed the door and tapped the roof twice. "Drive safe."

CHAPTER SIX

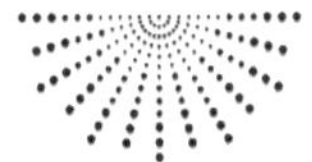

"Hey, Scarlet. How's it going?" Four Dumas gave her a friendly smile and placed a coaster down in front of her. He was the owner of Monty's Tavern and also its head bartender. She knew the man fairly well as he was Poppy's closest friend and honorary uncle to the twins.

Older, in fantastic shape, and ridiculously attractive—what was it with this town and all the hot older men?—Four was a bit of a grump. However, the man's jet-black rockstar hair, dark-indigo eyes, and killer smile forgave a lot of his overall grouchiness. Sure, that was one thousand percent superficial. But it was also one thousand percent accurate.

"I'm good, thanks." She wasn't. Between getting jabbed countless times by her daughter's feet and clobbered twice by her cast, Scarlet had barely gotten any sleep the night before. She was freaking exhausted.

She'd gotten up at six, dropped Daisy off at day care by seven, and worked the breakfast, lunch, and pre-dinner shifts. More than anything, she wanted to go home, take a hot shower, and crash. But that wasn't in the cards. It was only five, and she had about two hours to kill before she had to pick up Daisy. The last thing she wanted to do was make herself dinner, so here she was.

"What can I get you to drink?" Four asked.

"Oh, just a water for now." She wasn't much of a drinker, and with how tired she was, if she had a sip of alcohol, she'd probably be out for the count. Besides, she wasn't made of money, and dinner at this place was already a splurge.

"You got it. Menu?"

She nodded. "Please."

"How's Daisy?" He handed her a menu. "I heard she broke her arm."

The corners of her lips twitched. *Ahhh, you gotta love small towns.* "She's better, thanks. Honestly, if she didn't have a bright-pink cast on, you'd never know anything was wrong." She scanned the menu and found the least expensive appetizers. "Can I get a side of fries and cup of your *zuppa toscana?*"

"Coming right up, Scar. Hey, man. What can I get you?"

Following Four's gaze, her pulse quickened as she realized who had claimed the barstool beside her.

"The Wave Breaker Pale Ale, please," Matt replied. "Hey, Scarlet. How are you?"

"Here you go." Four placed a pint glass on the coaster in front of Matt. "Menu?"

"Thanks, and no on the menu. I'm waiting for the guys. I'm a little early." Matt took a sip of his beer, then asked her, "How's Daisy?"

Scarlet glanced between the two men, and she knew her eyes were wide. Outside the diner and Poppy, her social skills were a little rusty.

"Let me know if you need anything," Four said, shooting her a wink and heading to the other end of the bar.

Facing Matt, she gathered her wits. *Answer his question. There's no need to be nervous, dammit.* Right. "I was just telling

Four that Daisy's good. The cast hasn't slowed her down one bit."

He looked around, brow furrowing. "Is she here?"

"No. She apparently had plans tonight and wasn't going to let a cast stop her." Scarlet smiled, recalling her shy little girl's determination this morning. "I was going to keep her home from day care today, but she insisted on going. She didn't want to miss pool day."

"Pool day?"

She nodded. "Flora and Katie set up a bunch of kiddie pools in the backyard and had a pool party with ice cream and treats. They have this calendar in the playroom and all the kids have been counting down the days. Daisy's been looking forward to it for weeks."

"Not gonna lie, that sounds like a damn good time. Wait." He frowned, and a crinkle between his eyebrows popped. "Can Daisy get her cast wet?"

"No, but Flora somehow got her a special cast-covering baggie thing. It's even pink. So Daisy's all good. Then tonight, they arranged for a projector and screen to do a backyard movie thing for the kids with sleeping bags, endless chicken nuggets, and popcorn. Daisy really wanted to stay for that—and Daisy never wants to stay for those things—so here I am."

"Wow, that's quite the day. I'm glad she's bounced back." Matt stared at her for a moment, and it took everything she had to not squirm. "Are *you* doing okay? I imagine that yesterday was a roller coaster for you."

Surprise had her thoughts scrambling, and she moved her gaze to her glass of water. "Um, yeah. It was quite the nerve-racking day for sure." She peeked back at him with a bright smile. "But I'm fine."

A complete lie. Yesterday had been horrendous. She'd used every bit of acting skill she didn't know she possessed to hold it together. To not reveal her utter terror and heartbreak at seeing her daughter injured for the first time.

It had taken longer than usual to get Daisy settled last night, and after forty-five minutes of tossing and turning in bed, of crying that she couldn't get comfortable, Scarlet had tucked Daisy into her own bed beside her. Once her daughter had finally fallen asleep, she'd carefully snuck out of bed, hopped into the shower, and cried her eyes out.

Hours later, as she'd lain in bed with her daughter kicking and whacking the crap out of her, her mind had raced. What if Daisy had been injured worse? What would she have done? What if *she* got injured? What would happen to Daisy then? Who would look out for her?

The rabbit hole she'd gone down hadn't been pretty, but in the wee hours of the morning, she'd concluded that she needed to step it up and act like an adult. She'd avoided so many things for fear of getting her name in the system, but it wasn't just about her anymore. She had to think about Daisy, and it killed her that it had taken her baby getting hurt for her to realize it.

Scarlet didn't know anything about wills or stuff like that, but she needed to sort it all out. Because if anything happened to her, Daisy would be all alone. And that was unacceptable.

On top of her to-do list was talking to Poppy and Cade to see if, worst-case scenario, they'd be willing to take Daisy. If they declined, she wasn't sure what she'd do. No other backup person came to mind. Aside from Poppy, Ray and Martha were the only ones who knew anything remotely about Scarlet's past. They loved Daisy, but they weren't an option. They were in their eighties.

It was Poppy and Cade or foster care. And while she didn't know anything about Washington State's system, she imagined they were all the same. She'd grown up in and out of South Dakota's and wouldn't wish that on her baby.

She would figure something out. She had to.

"Scarlet?"

She jerked, and her eyes flew to meet Matt's. *Ohmygod, what were we talking about?* "I'm so sorry. I totally spaced out there."

"You okay?"

"I'm fine," she said, waving her hand like her brain lapse was no big deal. "But I suppose I'm a little more tired than I thought. I'm sorry, you were saying?"

"I asked what time you had to pick up Daisy tonight?"

"Oh." She glanced at her watch. Just under two hours to go. "Seven."

"Here you are, Scar," Four said, setting a bowl of soup and a plate of fries in front of her.

"Oh, Four, I ordered a cup." She gently pushed the bowl to him.

"Did you? Oh well, I'll just charge you for the cup." He shrugged. "You may as well eat that since it's here. What kind of sauce do you want for your fries?"

She suspected Four knew exactly what he was doing. Embarrassment sprouted in her belly, but she ignored it. She hated the charity, the pity. However, she was a realist and had put her pride aside countless times to survive. If the man wanted to give her extra food, she wasn't going to be an idiot and refuse it.

"Thanks, Four. And ketchup, please." She flashed him that chipper smile she'd perfected at the diner, then took a sip of soup and bit back a groan. This was way, way better than the canned tomato soup that was on rotation at home. She turned to Matt, determined to converse like a normal human being. "What are you up to tonight?"

"We all figured we'd get one last dinner in to catch up

before Cade heads out of town." His chin lifted when Four refilled his water. "And we figured we'd do it here so we can harass this guy at the same time."

"Dude, do you really want to harass the last person that touches your food?" Four winked at Scarlet as he set a small ramekin of ketchup next to her plate.

"The man makes a good point," she said, munching on a fry. "By 'we,' you mean . . . ?"

"Cade, Gavin, Joe, and Quinn."

"Ahhh. Team Testosterone. Nice."

"Team Testosterone?" Matt's lips tipped up in a grin, and for a second, she forgot how to breathe. "I wouldn't exactly say that."

She chuckled and dipped a french fry in ketchup. Chomping down on the crispy, salty goodness, she smiled at him around her bite. "I would."

His gaze shot to her mouth, and she stilled. "You, uh, got a little . . ." He pointed to the side of her mouth, his attention never leaving her lips.

Her tongue darted out and landed on a hint of ketchup. Matt's brown eyes heated, and butterflies took flight in her belly. The sound of her racing pulse filled her ears.

He jerked back, clearing his throat, gaze flying everywhere but at her. "All good."

Whoa. What the hell was that?

Unsure what to do with her hands, Scarlet grabbed her water and waved at her plate. "Feel free to have some fries while you wait."

Matt took a gulp of beer and shook his head. "I'm good, kid, but thanks."

Her spine straightened, and she narrowed her eyes at him. "I'm sorry, but by 'kid,' are you referring to me? Because we've established that Daisy's not here."

He winced. At least he had the decency to look contrite.

"Shit, Scarlet. I'm sorry. That was rude. I know you're not a kid." He ran a hand through his hair and grumbled, "It's just you're a lot younger than me, you know?"

She pasted her diner smile back on her face and nodded. She understood. No one would ever accuse her of not being able to read a room. Matt's silent message was loud and clear: Whatever that moment had been a second ago? He wasn't cool with it. She was a *kid*. Too young and immature for him. *Got it.*

See . . . this was exactly why it was so much easier crushing on someone she didn't actually know. It had all been harmless fun when he'd simply been the quiet, handsome friend of a friend who came into the diner. But now here she was, crushing on Matt Alvarez—who she now kinda sorta knew—and feeling like a goddamn idiot.

———

Before Matt could apologize again, Four was in front of him, nodding toward the entrance to the bar area. "The crew's here," he said, the three words curt.

Yeah . . . Matt could read the message on his friend's face. And he wholeheartedly agreed. He was a fucking dumbass. A dumbass who'd just hurt Scarlet's feelings. *Fuck.*

"I'm sorry again, Scarlet." Standing from the barstool, he hesitated. Shit. He had no fucking clue what to say. "I'll see you around, okay?"

"It was good to see you," she replied with a bright smile before returning her attention to her soup.

It was good to see you. He'd heard her say those exact words, countless times, to various customers at the diner. All with that sunny—fake—smile. Holy fuck, he really was an asshole.

Regret weighed on his shoulders as he made his way to

his friends, lifting his chin in greeting. He'd known Cade for forever and they were basically brothers, but over the last year, these other guys—Gavin Frazier, Joe Buchanan, and Quinn O'Conner—had become good friends, too.

Now that Matt was officially working for Hudson Security, he imagined he'd be getting to know the people working there as well. For the first time in a long, long while, he was looking forward to making new connections. That's what he'd missed the most while being away from the force. That brotherhood, that bond, that solidarity.

"Long time no see, man," Joe said with a grin.

Matt shook his head at his friend. He'd had a meeting with Joe and Gavin earlier that afternoon. Joe headed up Hudson Tactical, a joint venture between Gavin's Hudson Security and Cade's De La Rosa Gym, which provided hand-to-hand combat and tactical training for law enforcement.

Taking a seat next to Quinn, Matt said, "How's it going, Sheriff?"

Quinn shrugged. "Good. Work is work, Alex is still putting up with my dumb ass, and Annie's finally sleeping through the night. So I really can't complain at all."

Matt smiled. Quinn's wife, Alex, was a wonderful woman, and their daughter was pretty cute. "How old is Annie now?"

"Almost seven months."

"Wow, already?" When he pictured Annie, he saw a tiny little newborn bundled in pink blankets.

"I know, right?" Quinn rubbed his chin. "She hasn't quite figured out the crawling thing, so she just kind of rolls everywhere."

The proud grin on his friend's face had a pang of jealousy socking Matt in the gut. If only his ex-wife . . . *Nope. You're not fucking going there!* "That's great, man," he said, pushing those dark thoughts away.

"Thanks. I've been told by the gossip train ladies that we

need to enjoy it now because once she starts moving, it's apparently a whole other ball game."

Matt tapped his pint glass to Quinn's. Unwanted jealousy or not, he was truly happy for the guy.

After a waitress took their orders, the conversation shifted to Cade's upcoming trip. Excitement buzzed around the table as his friend talked about the upcoming fights in London. Two fighters from his gym were getting their first title shots, and Cade was confident both would take home a belt.

Matt listened with half an ear. From where he was seated, he had a clear view of the bar. And of Scarlet. Her back was to him, but that didn't matter. If anything, it allowed him to fully take her in. She wore jeans and a simple dark-gray T-shirt. Her long black hair, with its streaks of pinks, blues, and purples, was in some kind of intricate braid that fell to the middle of her back. She was petite—no more than an inch or two over five feet—so her Converse-clad feet barely touched the barstool rungs.

"Isn't that right, Matt?" Gavin asked, pulling his attention away from Scarlet.

A brief scan of the table showed all eyes were on him. *Shit.* "Sorry, what was that?"

Gavin nodded toward the bar. "Scarlet. Xander was asking about her. She's single, right?"

Matt's hand tightened around his beer. Xander Bonetti was a personal security officer with Hudson Security. Good guy, somewhere in his mid- to late-thirties, former Special Forces. He was often assigned to clients who had families since he was good with kids. *Fuck.*

"As far as I'm aware," Matt said through gritted teeth.

"Great. I'll let him know." Gavin smirked. The fucker. "That is, unless you have some kind of objection?"

"No objections here. It's a free country."

Xander and Scarlet would probably get along great. Which would be for the best. Even if the thought of seeing them together made Matt want to gouge his own eyes out.

He had no business being jealous. No business thinking of Scarlet in any non-platonic way. There were seventeen years between them. That was a ridiculous age gap. Hell, that was a larger age gap than Poppy had with her twin *sons*.

However, now that he had somehow found the ability to speak to Scarlet, he couldn't seem to stop. Like he was trying to make up for lost time. Which was why he'd called her kid earlier. It had been his way of reminding himself that he needed to back off. But he shouldn't have said that. It had been an asshole move. *Shit, what a clusterfuck.*

Since the day he'd laid eyes on Scarlet over a year ago, Matt hadn't been able to figure out what it was about her that captivated him. She was just so damn alluring. Her warm smile, her slight but curvy figure, her soulful brown eyes—

Holy. Fuck. Soulful brown eyes? What the hell was wrong with him? He needed to rein it the fuck in because nothing could come of this . . . thing . . . he had for Scarlet. Aside from friendship. Not that he was opposed to friendship. But he also wasn't a complete idiot. He knew it was a terrible idea to be so attracted to someone he needed to stay friends with. Still, there was no excuse for being a dick.

"Christ, Alvarez," Gavin grumbled. He glanced at Cade. "I thought he had a better poker face than this?"

Cade shrugged. "Usually, he does."

"I agree," Joe said, taking a sip of his beer. "I'd say this may be a case of extenuating circumstances."

Matt glared at his friends. "What the hell are you guys talking about?"

Quinn chuckled. "You look like you're about ready to devour the poor girl."

"*She's* the extenuating circumstance," Joe clarified with a grin.

"At least he's speaking full sentences to her now," Cade said. The traitor. "That's a plus."

Quinn elbowed him. "Well, you gotta start somewhere, I suppose."

"You guys are dumb," Matt grumbled, rolling his eyes.

Gavin barked out a laugh. "Nice comeback."

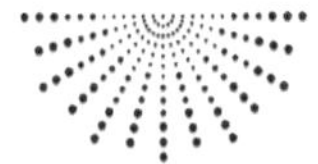

CHAPTER SEVEN

"Hey, lady!"

Ripped from her thoughts, Scarlet spun toward the voice with a hand on her chest. She grinned as Poppy gave her a side hug and settled onto the barstool Matt had vacated. "Twice in one day? What a treat for me!" They'd grabbed coffee earlier during her morning break.

"Cade said he was meeting the guys here for dinner, and the twins are hanging with some of their high school friends, so I figured I'd come over and harass Four."

"Why does everyone want to harass me?" the man grumbled as he set a coaster in front of her and topped it with a glass of ice water.

Poppy rolled her eyes. "Oh, please. You know you're gonna miss me when I'm away."

"You keep telling yourself that, cuz." Four chuckled at Poppy's glare. "The usual?"

"Please," Poppy said, giving up her mock irritation and gesturing to Scarlet's nearly empty bowl. "And I'll have what she's having, plus an order of the beef carpaccio with extra crostini."

"You got it," he said, placing Poppy's cocktail down on a second coaster. "Scarlet, do you like chocolate?"

About to take a sip of water, she raised an eyebrow. "Is that a real question?"

Four grinned. "I take it that's a yes?"

She tapped the tip of her nose. "Got it on the first try."

"Uh, what about me?" Poppy asked.

"You're a given, Pop. You'll do dessert before dinner every time."

Scarlet bit back a smile at the look Four gave Poppy. It could only be described as *duh*.

"Our head chef put together a new dessert, and I'd love to get your opinions on it. It's an espresso chili torte. Flourless chocolate cake, chili salted caramel, white chocolate espresso mousse, and spiced dark chocolate ganache with a raspberry puree and cacao nibs. You two in?"

Scarlet's eyes nearly bugged out of her head. "Again, Four, is that a real question?"

Laughing with his hands held up, he said, "Hey, you never know. I'd hate to presume anything."

"You can always presume me and chocolate are a go." She grinned. "Always."

"Noted. I'll be right back, ladies." He tapped the bar top, then disappeared into the kitchen.

"I take it Daisy's doing the big backyard-movie-night thing?"

Scarlet looked at Poppy in surprise. "How did you know?"

"How do I know anything, Scar?"

Her lips pursed, the corners lifting, and she nodded. "Small town."

"Yup," Poppy said, popping the *p*. "Flora and Katie ordered a bunch of these adorable plastic kiddie bento boxes that look like popcorn bags. The shipment was delayed, but thankfully, it arrived this morning. They wanted to make sure each kiddo had a souvenir from the first annual back-yard movie night."

"Of course they did." Both women had come in individually while Scarlet had been working at the diner this morning. They'd apologized profusely for what had happened with Daisy, and while she didn't blame either of them at all—it was a crazy unfortunate accident—she appreciated the sentiment.

Scarlet eyed her watch, then her friend. "I have another hour-plus before I need to leave to pick up Daisy. Want to fill me in on today's gossip?"

"Oh please," Poppy said, bumping her shoulder. "The diner is gossip train central. I'm sure you've got way more juicy tidbits than I do."

A burst of laughter had Scarlet glancing over her shoulder. It looked like the guys were having a good time. *Well, that's just stupid.*

"What's stupid?" Poppy asked.

Dammit. She hadn't meant to say that out loud. But in for a penny and all that . . . She tilted her head toward the table of men. "That much alpha male hotness in one place should be outlawed."

Cade and Matt, along with Gavin Frazier, Sheriff Quinn O'Conner, and Joe Buchanan, who was the son of Doc Buchanan—a silver fox in his own right. They were a formidable bunch.

Poppy chuckled. "You won't get any arguments here. They're a good-looking bunch, all right."

"I'm surprised all the single ladies on the island aren't here throwing their panties at them." She nodded to Four, who was making his way over, plates in hand. "I mean, I'm pretty sure they already do that with the hot bartender-slash-owner, so why not expand their scope?" Poppy mock-gagged—maybe even real-gagged—just as Scarlet had expected. With a laugh, she added, "Hey, just because Four's your pseudo-brother doesn't negate the fact that the man is smoking hot."

"Good god," Poppy said, making a time-out signal with her hands. "Please, no more talk about Four like that."

Scarlet sighed when Four placed a plate of decadent chocolate goodness in front of her. "Holy shit. This looks fantastic."

"Let me know what you think, ladies. Honest opinions."

Grabbing the small spoon, Scarlet took a bite and groaned. "Ohmygod, this is amazing." She glanced at Poppy, whose eyes were closed in bliss.

"Add this to the menu," Poppy said. "Please. And if you're planning on giving a piece to Cade, you should give it to me instead." She glanced at Scarlet. "I'll split it with you."

"I think that's a great plan." Scarlet took another bite and let the savory chocolate, tart raspberry, and slightly bitter cacao nibs melt in her mouth. She sighed again. Freaking heaven.

Four chuckled as he made his way down the bar. "I'm glad it meets your approval, ladies. I'll be back out with your dinner, Pop."

While relishing each bite, Scarlet surveyed the restaurant via the mirror behind the bar. The main tables appeared to be full, but the bar was nearly empty. Aside from her and Poppy at the counter and the high-top with the guys, only one other high-top was occupied. Surprising. Then again, she didn't tend to go out on Tuesday nights. Or any nights, really. She'd just heard that the place was usually packed every day of the week.

Poppy bumped Scarlet's shoulder with her own, and their gazes caught in the mirror. "Don't look now, but I'm pretty sure Matt hasn't taken his eyes off of you since I got here."

Scarlet couldn't hold back a snort. "Right."

"I'm serious, Scar."

She shook her head. "Oh, trust me. There's *zero* interest there."

"But—"

"For real, Pop. He called me *kid* earlier. Believe me, I'm nowhere on that man's radar." Scarlet kept it light, kept her tone joking and fun. That's what she knew Poppy—and everyone else—expected from her. Still, her eyes found Matt in the mirror. He was talking with Quinn, and she quickly looked away.

"Well," Poppy huffed, "I wouldn't rule him out."

"Ever the optimist, I see." She slung an arm around her friend and squeezed. "You're too sweet, Pop. So aside from the fights, what are you most looking forward to doing over in London? You guys are going to travel around, too, right?"

Scarlet knew it wasn't exactly the slickest subject change, but when Poppy replied with gusto, she was totally fine with it. She'd never traveled for fun, so she was thrilled to live vicariously through her friend. And after fifteen minutes of hearing about the plans for their trip, she was also okay admitting that she was the tiniest bit envious of her friend. Nearly three weeks in Europe? Uh, yeah. Freaking amazing.

"I'm so excited for you, Pop. But I can't lie, I'm going to miss you. I mean, who am I gonna go on my morning coffee breaks with?" Scarlet was friendly with lots of people on Hudson Island, but she really only hung out with Poppy. Out of habit, she mostly kept to herself.

"I can think of someone," Poppy said, pushing her empty bowl away and leaning back on her barstool. "He's tall, hand-some, a little bit rough around the edges . . ."

Scarlet groaned. "Just because Matt says full sentences to me now doesn't mean he likes me like *that*. Again"—she pointed at herself—"*kid*."

Poppy smirked. "Who said anything about Matt? Besides,

I'm sure there's no shortage of men who'd be more than happy to join you for coffee."

She could only shoot her friend a get-real look.

"What?" Poppy was the picture of innocence. "Besides, when was the last time you went out on a date?"

Scarlet managed to hold back an eye roll. Barely. She loved Poppy, she truly did. But now that the woman was all loved up with her hunk of a man, she was trying to get everyone else equally loved up.

Hard pass.

Scarlet shrugged. "It's been a while."

A thoughtful look crossed Poppy's face. "You know, Scar, I can't recall you going out with anyone since you moved here. You've been here what? A year and a half-ish?"

"Yup." She pinned her friend with a *look*. "Been kinda busy, you know?"

Poppy's mouth went slack, and her cheeks pinked. "Oh, I'm sorry, sweetie. I know . . . I didn't mean to imply . . ."

"I know." She playfully elbowed her friend. The last thing she wanted was to make Poppy feel bad. "Look, when I'm not working, I'm with Daisy." She shrugged. "That's how it should be. Dating is just not something I'm interested in right now." Or ever.

Even before he'd called her a kid, Scarlet had harbored no interest in going on an actual date with Matt Alvarez. Not that she had anything against the guy. It was a clear case of it's-not-you-it's-me.

Her mind flashed to the one and only date she'd ever been on. It had taken place a few months before she'd moved to Hudson Island. She'd been working at a diner in Arizona and one of her regulars, Aaron, had been persistent in asking her out. She had always declined. Until that last time, when her co-worker, who was friends with the guy, had overheard and volunteered to watch Daisy for free.

Being put on the spot, she'd relented. Not her finest moment.

As Scarlet had gotten ready, she'd been so damn nervous. She'd never gone on a date. There'd never been any need. In her old life—before Arizona and all the secrecy—she'd been a permanent fixture of the local motorcycle club. Because she'd been there so long, the guys hadn't wanted to waste their money on taking her out. And yeah, that was a direct quote.

Aaron had picked her up right on time. She'd thought they were going to a restaurant, so when he'd pulled up to a Burger King drive-through and told her they could just eat back at his place and hang out, unease had crawled up her spine. For good reason. The minute she'd walked through his apartment door, he'd pounced.

Scarlet shook her head in an attempt to clear the memory from her brain. It didn't work. Her stomach soured, and the chocolate torte in her belly threatened to come back up.

She had fought Aaron with everything she'd had and managed to get away. By the time she'd made it home, she'd sported a raging black eye and blisters on her feet. So yeah. She wasn't rushing to go on any dates. Like ever again.

Slinging an arm around Poppy's shoulders, she squeezed and said, "I'm happy you're happy, girl, but you don't need to play matchmaker. Let the gossip train ladies do that. After all, I'm well-versed at avoiding their meddling."

"Fine." Poppy heaved a dramatic sigh that had Scarlet's lips twitching. "But, Scar, you're so amazing, and Daisy is so fun. I just want you to be happy, too."

"I am. I promise." An image of Daisy from that morning flashed in her mind, and her heart squeezed. "My little girl is everything to me. I just want to focus on her. Give her a good life, you know? Like you did with the twins." More than anything, she wanted to provide her daughter with the kind of life that she'd wished for growing up. One that had nothing to do with possessions and everything to do with love and security.

"I do, sweetie. You know I do." Poppy reached out and held her hand. "As someone who's been in similar shoes, believe me when I say that you're doing an amazing job with Daisy. But don't forget . . . *you* deserve some happiness and fun, too."

Scarlet didn't, but she smiled at her friend, anyway. "Maybe when Daisy's a little older."

Poppy blew out another exasperated big-sister sigh. "That wasn't a flat-out no, so I guess it will do."

As Scarlet smiled at her friend, the alarm on her phone sounded. "That's my fifteen-minute warning," she said, snoozing the alarm. She placed enough cash down to cover her meal and a generous tip, then hopped off the barstool. "I have to go pick up Daisy."

Poppy stood as well and pulled her into a hug. "I'm so glad we ran into each other tonight, Scar."

"Me too," she said, returning the hug. "I'm gonna miss you, but have so much fun!"

Poppy held her at arm's length. "Now, I'm not playing matchmaker, but make sure you get Daisy out to visit the cats with"—she nodded to the guys' table—"you know who." Scarlet arched an eyebrow, and Poppy's eyes widened in mock innocence. "What? It's for Daisy's sake, not yours."

"Riiight." Rolling her eyes, she hip-checked her friend. "Text me when you get back."

Scarlet called goodbye to Four as she made her way out, then waved to Cade at the table of guys. Her breath caught when Matt shot to his feet and rushed her way.

"Hey," he said, shoving his hands into the pockets of his jeans. "I wanted to apologize again for making things awkward earlier."

"You're totally fine," she said, unable to meet his eyes.

"How about I give you a call this weekend?"

Her heart knocked hard in her chest, and her gaze swung to his. *Holy shit, what?*

"If you guys are free—um, you and Daisy, that is—we can bring her to visit the cats. I'm sure they'd enjoy her company more than mine."

Right. Daisy. Cats. Just like Poppy had said.

Her alarm sounded again, and she'd never been more thankful for an interruption. "I have to go get Daisy," she said, shutting off the alarm and shoving her phone into her back pocket. She looked up at him. "But I'm sure she'd love that. We're pretty open on the weekend, so feel free to text me some times that work for you."

She wanted to pat herself on the back. Her reply had been nice and nonchalant. *Like I've got my shit together.*

"Great. I'll talk to you later, then." Matt gave her a smile that had her stomach doing stupid things.

"Great, see ya!" She bit the inside of her cheek to keep from cringing. *A little bit too enthusiastic there . . .*

She waved at the rest of the table and Poppy, who'd joined their group and was wagging her eyebrows. Ignoring her friend, Scarlet hustled out of Monty's Tavern.

Oh. My. God. What the hell had she just agreed to?

CHAPTER EIGHT

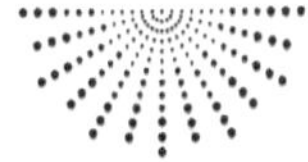

S carlet placed the clean pan on the drying rack next to the small pot and wiped her brow with the back of her hand. It was times like this when she wished her cute little apartment came with a dishwasher. But no. *She* was the dishwasher.

She grimaced. There was no real reason to complain. Even though it was older, the two-bedroom, one-bathroom apartment was larger than any place she'd ever lived, and it was conveniently located right above Hudson Island Antiques, which was only a couple of blocks from Ray's Diner. It also had come fully furnished, an absolute blessing since she'd arrived with only what she'd been able to fit in her car—two large suitcases and some random odds and ends.

The apartment even boasted two balconies. The bigger one was off the living room and had a gas grill that she had every intention of learning to use. One day. The smaller balcony was accessed through her bedroom and had a white oversized wicker chair with a matching little end table. It was one of her favorite places to unwind. After Daisy went to bed, Scarlet would often sit out there and relax, or she'd lie in bed with the sliding glass door cracked and listen to the sounds of her little town closing down for the day.

She'd really lucked out with this place. Mr. Wayland, who owned both the antique store and the building, was Martha's nephew, so he'd given her a screaming deal since she worked at Ray's. The building's second floor housed her apartment and another larger apartment that he used as a vacation rental. She was certain he could have charged her much, *much* more in rent, but she wasn't going to question it.

Still. It had been the longest week ever, so she had a right to gripe a little bit. She was exhausted and so thankful it was Friday. Mercifully, Ray and Martha allowed her to only work the weekday shifts so she could have the weekends with Daisy.

At the thought of her daughter, guilt pierced her chest.

She had messed up this week. Big-time.

Scarlet would be the first person to admit that she didn't know much about raising a kid. Growing up, her parental figure had been questionable at best. Gross negligence was what one judge had ruled. So, while she'd been pregnant, she'd practically lived at the library, reading as many books as she could on parenting. But nothing had prepared her for the reality of it all. Especially not as a single parent.

The newborn phase had been more than rough. But as soon as Scarlet had figured out that her daughter would sleep for long stretches on her chest, she had taken advantage of the information. She'd slept in a recliner, Daisy on top of her, for a solid year. Some books said co-sleeping was bad, others said it was good. All she knew was they'd both gotten rest in that position.

Once Daisy had started crawling, Scarlet had become strict, setting firm boundaries for her daughter. As Daisy got older, Scarlet refused to bend because, frankly, their situation didn't allow for it. It was a safety issue. If they were at a playground and she called Daisy over, she needed her child to comply immediately. Luckily, Daisy always did. And she never protested the rules.

Except for the evening she had broken her arm. She'd begged and pleaded to go to the day care's pool day and movie night even though Scarlet had wanted to keep her home to rest. Her daughter didn't ask for much—the kid was more than happy with her small collection of stuffies and coloring books—so she'd relented. She had stupidly thought it would be okay.

Then, on Wednesday morning, Daisy had been a mess. Constant tears, beyond cranky, and refusing to listen. Which was *not* like her daughter. At all. Yes, kids could be little assholes, but Daisy wasn't like that. Truly. People often liked to joke that Scarlet must have Daisy on a steady stream of Benadryl because the little girl was so easygoing.

So Scarlet had called in at work and kept Daisy home from day care. By mid-morning, her daughter's hand had puffed up like an exploding marshmallow. Not knowing what to do—aside from freaking out—she'd rushed over to Doc's clinic.

In a nutshell, Daisy had overdone it at the pool day and movie night.

Doc had removed Daisy's cast, put her arm in a sling, and given her some ibuprofen. The swelling had gone down later that night, so he'd been able to recast her arm on Thursday. But she had to keep her arm in a sling for the next twenty-four hours.

Scarlet pinched the bridge of her nose. It hadn't even occurred to her that the pool day and movie night would be too much for her daughter. After all, they were only kiddie pools with a few inches of water. She'd figured the kids were just hanging out and playing and splashing, not full-on swimming or anything . . . it would be fine.

She'd been so, so wrong.

She was officially the world's worst mother. She was the one who'd allowed her child to overdo it.

"Look, Mama," Daisy called out from the kitchen table. She held up a piece of paper with her left hand. "I can still draw! It's a rainbow!"

Scarlet made out the shaky rainbow and what she assumed were blue clouds and a giant yellow sun. Giving the counter a final wipe, she moved to where her daughter was seated and ran a hand over Daisy's head.

"That's beautiful, baby girl," she said, playing with the ends of her daughter's hair. "Why don't you start putting your crayons away now? It's almost time for your medicine, and then it's bedtime." Daisy's face scrunched, and Scarlet smiled. "Don't worry, it's the cherry-flavored medicine. Not the yucky pink one."

Daisy immediately brightened. "Okay. Can you put this on the figyator?"

"Sure thing. When you're done putting the crayons away, grab your jammies and pick out which bubbles you want for your bath."

Once the crayons were back in their tub, Daisy scrambled out of her chair. "Can I sleep with you again, Mama?" she asked, running toward her bedroom.

"Walk, please," Scarlet called out, wincing as she followed. Not only because her daughter was running, but also because she got next to zero rest when they shared a bed. Her little girl was an active sleeper. But it didn't matter. "Of course, baby. We'll have another slumber party tonight, but I want you to try to sleep in your own bed tomorrow, okay?"

"Okay," Daisy replied, grabbing her pink unicorn night-gown from where it lay on her twin-size bed.

Scarlet opened a dresser drawer and asked, "Do you want unicorn or princess undies?"

Daisy took a few seconds to consider her two options. "Princess. Can we have pancakes for breakfast?"

"You got it." She ushered her daughter into the bathroom with said undies and a waterproof cast cover.

After giving Daisy a bath with lavender-scented bubbles, brushing her tangled black hair out, and helping her brush her teeth, it only took two bedtime stories—and a dose of children's Tylenol—before she conked out. Scarlet glanced at the clock.

Eight thirty on a Friday night.

In her old life, the evening would have been just getting started. Now? She was hitting the shower, changing into her sleep shorts and tank, and falling into bed. Maybe she'd crack the slider and live vicariously through the tourists having a fun Friday night.

Her gaze landed on her sleeping daughter, and her heart ached with guilt. But Daisy was taking everything in stride. Perhaps she could learn a lesson from her child.

A crash had Scarlet's eyes flying open. Disoriented from sleep, she tried to make out the noise that had woken her. It wasn't unusual to hear breaking glass in the middle of the night—unfortunately, the staff at Monty's Tavern tended to dump their empty bottles in the recycle bins at all hours. Tonight, however, Scarlet's racing heart told her that wasn't it.

She grabbed her phone from the nightstand, and the display illuminated.

Three fifteen.

Dread crawled over her skin. At the latest, Monty's closed

at two. The crew was always out of there thirty minutes after they closed their doors.

Her phone's display darkened. Now the only light came from the streetlamp outside, through the sliding glass door's sheer curtain, which billowed gently with the breeze. She could make out her daughter's sleeping form next to her, and she could hear Daisy's soft, steady breath. Otherwise, the apartment was quiet.

What had woken her?

A thump, followed by a muffled curse, sent her gaze flying to her closed bedroom door. Her heart knocked hard in her chest.

Holy. Shit. Someone was in her apartment.

Sitting up in bed, she stared at the door. They were trapped. Her breathing accelerated—until she remembered the billowing curtain. *The balcony!*

As silently as she could, she moved the accent chair from beside her bed to block her closed door, grateful for the carpeted floors. Then, grabbing her phone, she carefully scooped up Daisy, grateful her child was a heavy sleeper, and crept to the sliding door. She prayed it wouldn't choose this moment to squeak.

Luck was on her side as the door noiselessly slid open. She shut it behind her and hustled to the opposite end. With her sleeping daughter tucked in her arms, she huddled down and hid behind the large wicker chair. Her hand shook as she pressed three numbers and put the phone to her ear.

"9-1-1. What's your emergency?"

Scarlet flinched at the woman's loud, sharp voice and immediately turned down the volume. "Someone broke into my apartment," she whispered, tears springing to her eyes. She rushed to tell the dispatcher her address. "Please send someone. My daughter and I are hiding on the bedroom balcony." Her blood turned to ice as she realized she'd further trapped them. "Ohmygod, there's no way down. It's too high to jump."

"Ma'am, please stay where you are. I'm contacting the authorities, and they'll be on their way shortly."

Her apartment was literally across the street from the sheriff's department, but every second felt like a lifetime.

Scarlet squeezed her eyes shut. Still, tears leaked through. *Please, please hurry.*

"Ma'am, are you there?"

It took a few tries, but Scarlet managed to croak, "Yes."

"Good. Stay on the line with me. Now, do you know how many people entered your apartment?"

She shook her head before realizing the dispatcher couldn't see her. "No. I only heard one person, though."

"Can you tell me what you heard?"

"There was a crash," she whispered, mind racing. What else had she heard? "Um, then it sounded like the person ran into something and muttered a curse."

"Could you tell from the voice if it was a male or female?"

"No." Terror had her arms trembling. "Are the police on their way?"

"Yes, ma'am. They should be there any moment."

"Mama?"

"Shhh," Scarlet hushed, willing herself to stay calm. She adjusted Daisy so she was cradled against her chest like a frog, head resting on her shoulder. "We have to stay very, very quiet, baby."

"Like hide-and-seek?"

She grimaced at Daisy's attempt at a whisper. Which wasn't a whisper at all. "That's right. But even more quiet than hide-and-seek. We have to do no talking at all, okay?"

Scarlet felt Daisy nod. Peering down, her frown deepened when she saw her daughter's lower lip jutting out. She ran her free hand up and down Daisy's tiny back. "You're doing great, baby."

"But, Mama, we left Mr. Slothy inside, and he's scared."

Scarlet's pulse picked up speed as she shushed her child. "He's safe. I promise, baby. Mr. Slothy is super brave," she murmured. "I promise we'll get him a special treat tomorrow. But right now, we have to be super-duper quiet."

Daisy nodded again, snuggling even closer, and whispered, "Mr. Slothy wants Otter Pops. The blue kind."

Blinking back more tears, Scarlet pressed a kiss to the top of her daughter's head. The lavender scent from Daisy's earlier bubble bath filled her nose, and the tears broke free, spilling down her cheeks. "You got it, baby girl."

A loud crash sounded inside the apartment. Scarlet jumped, and Daisy let out a tiny whimper. She tightened her arm around her daughter. A split second later, the wail of a siren pierced the night.

She bit back a sob. The phone shook in her hand. "Please say that's the poli—"

Glass exploded. Scarlet stifled a scream as she twisted away from the door, trying to shield Daisy. The sirens grew louder. Blue and red lights lit up the sky. A screech of tires, and then car doors slammed. But all Scarlet could focus on was her crying child.

"Ma'am!"

Scarlet looked around and spotted her dropped phone. "The sliding glass door to the balcony shattered," she explained when she brought it back to her ear. "I think they threw something through it."

"Ma'am, stay with me. The sheriff's department has arrived, and I've informed them where you and your daughter are located." The dispatcher's soothing voice was like a balm over Scarlet's frazzled nerves. "You two need to stay put. The deputies will come find you."

Panic tore through her. "Please don't go!"

"No, ma'am. I'll stay on the line with you until the deputies arrive."

"Thank you." She rocked Daisy, finding comfort in the steady motion. After a moment, Daisy's cries settled into a soft hiccup. "Um, am I allowed to ask what your name is?"

The other woman chuckled. "Of course, ma'am. It's Carol."

Scarlet's throat tightened, and her vision blurred with fresh tears. "Thank you, Carol. For staying with me."

"You're very welcome, ma'am."

She heard the murmurs of the deputies inside her apartment and saw an occasional flashlight beam. Aside from that, everything had gone calm and quiet. Did that mean whoever had broken into her apartment had been caught? Or were they long gone?

A shiver tore through her. She took a deep breath in and slowly released it. Her nerves eased a bit, but her tears kept flowing. "You know, Carol, I can't remember if I told you, but my name is Scarlet. I'm a waitress at Ray's Diner, and if you ever find yourself on Hudson Island, I would love to buy you lunch. I mean, I know it's not much . . . not for everything you've done. I can't thank you enough, though." Her voice broke on the last words.

"That's very kind of you, Scarlet," Carol said, voice unwavering. "It's also unnecessary, but I've heard many good things about Ray's, so I'll come out there sometime soon. I'd love to meet you."

"Me too, Carol. Be forewarned, though. When I meet you, I'm gonna hug the hell out of you."

As Carol laughed, Scarlet saw a man pop his head through the shattered door.

"Hey, Scarlet."

At the familiar face, her shoulders slumped in relief. "Hey,

Chase." Not only was Deputy Patrick Chase part of the Hudson Island Sheriff's Department, but like everyone else on the island, he was also a regular at Ray's Diner.

"I hear they found you," Carol said. "I'll let you go now. Take care, Scarlet."

Swallowing a sob, she nodded, even though the other woman couldn't see her. "Thank you, Carol."

Their call disconnected, and Scarlet gingerly rose from her hiding spot, careful not to jostle Daisy's arm. Her sweet little girl clung to her like a monkey.

"Why don't you stay where you are for another few minutes," Chase said, holding out a hand, halting her. "There's plenty of glass here."

When she nodded, he moved away from the door. Another man took his place. Unlike Chase, who wore his uniform, Sheriff Quinn O'Conner was clad in jeans and a wrinkled T-shirt, and his hair was mussed. Obviously, he'd been asleep when she'd made her call to 9-1-1.

"Let me get you both a pair of shoes before you come this way. Where are they?" Quinn asked in his steady, everything-is-under-control tone.

She wasn't going to lie. That tone helped. Hell, knowing Quinn and Chase were with her helped. Because holy shit, she'd never been so terrified. And that was saying something since she'd been involved in some god-awful situations.

Scarlet blinked as she realized Quinn was staring at her. *Answer the man!* "Oh, sorry. Our shoes are in the closet by the front door."

With a nod, he vanished back inside.

She sighed and shifted Daisy to her other hip.

"Mama? I gotta go potty."

Eyeing the glass fragments on the balcony, she ran a hand down Daisy's back. "Can you hold it for just a little bit?"

Fortunately, Quinn reappeared.

"Here, I'll hold Daisy while you get these on," he said, placing Scarlet's pink Converse at her feet. As he straightened, he held his arms out to her daughter. And Daisy clung even tighter to her.

He held his hands up, and Scarlet shot him an apologetic smile. "How about you put her shoes on"—Scarlet nodded to Daisy's sneakers, which he held in one hand—"while I hold her?"

"Deal," he said, giving Daisy a comforting smile. "Hi, Daisy. I'm Sheriff O'Conner. I'm going to help put your shoes on so your feet don't get cut on all this glass. It's a mess inside too, so make sure you keep your shoes on, okay?"

Daisy didn't say anything, but she tipped her head in a little nod.

Once Daisy's shoes were on, Scarlet stuffed her feet into her Converse and carefully followed Quinn back inside, still carrying her daughter. The crunch of glass beneath her feet turned her stomach.

Upon stepping into her bedroom, she froze. The dresser drawers were hanging open, and the small bin of makeup and toiletries she kept on top was tipped over. She didn't have much, but what she did have was spilling onto the carpet.

"Mama, I gotta go," Daisy whimpered.

Snapping back to attention, she asked Quinn, "Can I take her to the bathroom?"

"Of course," he said. "We'll talk when she's done."

After helping Daisy in the bathroom, Scarlet tried to put her down in her own bedroom—which, thankfully, looked untouched—but her little girl clung on. Not that Scarlet could blame her. It had been a frightening night, and frankly, she wanted Daisy as close as possible.

Draping one of Daisy's favorite toddler blankets around her shoulders, Scarlet went into the living room. She hadn't looked at it when she'd taken Daisy to the bathroom, but now there was no avoiding reality. The living room appeared as though it had been tossed. Like on TV when the bad guy was searching for something. Couch cushions upended, cabinet doors wide open, drawers emptied, Daisy's crayon bin spilled onto the carpet . . .

"There was no one here when we arrived," Quinn began. "However, at the downstairs entrance, there was an obvious forced entry." He gestured to her front door, which looked to be hanging on one hinge. "The apartment next door was also broken into and ransacked. Deputy Chase is over there checking that out. At first glance, there doesn't appear to be any renters staying there, but do you know if there are?"

"Nobody right now," she said, swaying back and forth as she tucked Daisy's head under her chin. "Mr. Wayland shares the rental calendar with me." Quinn's eyebrows lifted in question, and she explained, "For security. He said he feels guilty renting the place out when it's just me and Daisy here alone." She shrugged. "So I know that no one is supposed to be checking in until next Friday."

"That makes sense." Quinn examined her living room. "Can you take a look around and see if there's anything missing? Your purse, electronics, jewelry . . . That kind of thing."

She inclined her head toward the clunky television. "Looks like they didn't want that relic."

He scoffed. "More like they couldn't lift it. They took the flat-screen off the wall at the other place." He scanned the room once more, and his smile vanished. "I'm sorry this happened, Scarlet. Take a look around. I'm going to go check in with Chase."

The second Quinn stepped out of her apartment, she tensed, all her worry and unease returning in full force. What if the person who did this wasn't gone? What if—

No. Focus, dammit!

She blew out a breath, and with Daisy passed out in her arms, she began a slow inspection of the apartment.

It didn't take long for her to determine what was missing. Her place wasn't all that big, and they hadn't accumulated a lot since they'd moved in. *Minimalism* was how she liked to think of it. Because that sounded a whole lot better than *poor*. And now she was even poorer. Because her purse was missing. Her driver's license, debit card, and just over two hundred in cash. Tips she'd meant to deposit in the bank but hadn't gotten around to yet.

She heaved out another sigh, and then her eyes widened.

Her driver's license.

Holy shit. The US Marshals Service had supplied her current Washington State driver's license. Could she just go to the licensing place and get a new one? Was that even possible? Crap. The last thing she wanted was to have to contact them—

"Scarlet?"

She bit back a yelp and spun toward the door.

"Sorry," Quinn said, holding up his hands again. "Didn't mean to scare you."

"That's okay." Heat washed over her face as she glanced between Quinn and Chase. "I'm a little jumpy tonight." When they continued to look at her expectantly, she cringed. "I'm sorry. Did you say something earlier?"

"I asked if you have somewhere else you can stay tonight," Quinn said.

"Oh, um . . ." She considered the question, frowning. Crap. That would be a big, fat nope.

Footsteps sounded, and a man came to a stop behind Quinn and Chase. Her jaw dropped.

"I got here as fast as I could. Are you okay, Scarlet?"

For a moment, she could only stare.

What is Matt Alvarez doing here?

CHAPTER NINE

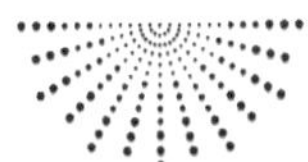

Matt noted the ransacked room, but his focus remained on the woman in front of him. The woman who was holding her sleeping daughter in her arms and staring at him with her mouth agape, her brown eyes wide in borderline disbelief.

He didn't move any closer, didn't want to crowd her space. "Scarlet?"

When she said nothing, his gaze darted to Quinn, who'd moved to stand next to her. The man simply lifted his chin in greeting.

After Chase gave him a nod and made his way toward the other apartment, Matt took a step deeper into her apartment. He kept his hands at his sides to appear as unimposing as possible. "Scarlet, sweetheart," he said, softening his voice. "Are you okay? Is Daisy okay?"

At the mention of her daughter's name, Scarlet jerked like someone had poured a bucket of ice-cold water on her head. "Um, what are you doing here?"

A tiny part of him ached at the way she looked at him. As

if he'd grown two heads or something. But the other part, the larger part, got it. He was probably the last person she'd expected to step through her broken front door.

Gaze locked with hers, he nodded toward Quinn. "He called me. With Poppy and Cade out of town, he thought you could use a friendly face."

Matt didn't think her eyes could get any bigger, but there they went.

"No offense, Matt, but he called *you?*"

Her comment should've stung. But again, he got it.

The corners of his lips twitched up, and he stuffed his hands into his jeans pockets and rocked back on his heels. "What can I say? Quinn's a nice guy. I'm sure he didn't want to wake up Martha and Ray at this ungodly hour." He shrugged. "So you got me instead."

Her face flushed a bright pink as she continued to sway back and forth. "Ohmygod, I'm so sorry. That's totally *not* what I meant. It's just that . . ." She shut her eyes and pinched the bridge of her nose.

"You're fine, Scarlet. And you're right, I'm not exactly someone you'd call a friendly face." He really wasn't—at least not with her. He'd been the exact opposite, in fact.

Shit, maybe this wasn't a good idea after all. But damn, too late now. There was no way in hell he'd leave them in a lurch.

"It's not that, Matt. You are. But . . . you barely know me. It's like four in the morning or something, and yet . . . you're here."

That look of disbelief was back on her face, and frankly, it hurt his heart. "Sweetheart, you're best friends with Poppy."

"Yeah?" she asked, head tilted in confusion.

"And Poppy's basically married to *my* best friend, Cade. They're not here to look out for you, so I am."

Her brow scrunched. "But why?"

Damn, what the hell kind of people had she been friends with before Hudson? "Because you matter to them, and that means you matter to me."

"I called Matt because I know he's part of your circle of friends," Quinn explained, moving to stand beside him. Hell, Matt had nearly forgotten the guy was still in the room. "I didn't call him as the sheriff. I called as a personal courtesy— as a friend to a friend—to let him know you and Daisy needed help."

Scarlet was shaking her head before Quinn finished speaking. "Oh, Quinn, that's not really necess—"

"Do you have a place to stay tonight?" Quinn asked, pinning her with a look that had her squirming.

"Um . . ."

"Exactly." Quinn slapped Matt on the back. "I'm going to see what Chase has found. Check in with me before you take off."

"Thanks, man," he said, nodding at his friend.

Once they were alone, Matt turned to Scarlet. She hadn't moved from the center of the living room, and he could see her mind scrambling. His entire being filled with sadness. He desperately wanted to fix this for her, to make it at least a little bit better.

"You and Daisy can stay with me until your place gets fixed." She opened her mouth, but he didn't give her a chance to protest. "My place has a couple extra rooms, so you two would have your own space. Besides, I was going to call you tomorrow, anyway. To meet up and take Daisy to visit the cats."

Scarlet studied her destroyed living room, and her shoulders slumped. "I don't want us to be an imposition," she said in a small voice.

He shook his head. "You two are the furthest things from that. I know you and I are more like friends of friends . . .

but, Scarlet, that still makes us friends. And it's not safe for you two to be here tonight. If you're not comfortable staying with me, I get that." He was a big guy who'd been nothing but a moody asshole to her, a guy whom she didn't know all that well. "I'm more than happy to crash at Cade's place while you and Daisy stay at my place. Or vice versa. Whatever you're comfortable with."

For a moment, she mulled over his words. Coming to a decision, her shoulders straightened. "If it's truly not an imposition, I'd like to stay with you. I, um . . ." Her eyes shimmered with unshed tears, but she blinked them back. "I'm nervous to . . . Um, I don't really want us to be alone right now."

It took everything Matt had to keep from pulling her into his arms and reassuring her that they would be fine, that he'd take care of them. Instead, he met her gaze and nodded. "That's absolutely understandable. I'm sure tonight was a lot. Why don't you go pack up some stuff for you and Daisy?"

She let out a breath, then gestured to the sofa. "I need to put her down. Could you . . . ?"

Matt took in the upended cushions and pillows, then hustled to the couch and put them back in place. "There you go," he said, grabbing a large throw blanket from the floor and shaking it out.

Scarlet laid Daisy down on the couch, but the instant she let go of her daughter, the little girl's arms flailed. "Mama," she cried out, her big blue eyes filling with tears. "Don't go!"

Matt's chest squeezed tight.

"Oh, sweetie, I'm right here," Scarlet soothed, scooping Daisy up and placing her on her lap.

After a few seconds, Daisy glanced up. Her blue eyes locked with his, and her head tilted to the side in a gesture so much like her mother's. "Mr. Matty?"

A smile pulled at his lips at her sweet squeaky voice. "Hey, Otter Pop."

Daisy's eyes widened, and she glanced around frantically. "Mr. Slothy is still in Mama's room!"

"You sit tight, and I'll go get him, okay?" he said, happy to do this kid's bidding.

She snuggled into her mom's arms. "Okay."

Entering Scarlet's room, he came to an abrupt halt. The pulled-out drawers, the strewn clothes, the shattered sliding glass door . . . Anger surged through him, but he tamped it down. The last thing Scarlet and Daisy needed was for him to lose his cool. But swear to Christ, if they ever figured out who the hell had done this, who'd broken into Scarlet's home —with her and Daisy *in* it—Matt would make sure they paid.

Mr. Slothy sat in the middle of the rumpled queen-size bed. Seeing the blue makeshift cast still on its arm went a long way toward calming him down.

"Here you go, Otter Pop," he said, returning to the living room and handing Mr. Slothy over to Daisy.

"Thank you," she murmured, squishing the fuzzy sloth in a massive hug.

"Sweetie," Scarlet said, running a hand over the top of her daughter's head, "can you sit here with Mr. Matt and Mr. Slothy while I pack us a bag?" At Daisy's nod, she turned to him. "Sorry, do you mind watching her? I'll be fast."

"It's not a problem. Take your time."

"Thank you," she said, setting her daughter onto the couch with Mr. Slothy and Daisy's small fuzzy blanket before hustling to her room.

Matt grabbed the larger blanket he'd shaken out earlier. "How about another one so you don't get cold?" he asked Daisy, holding it up to her.

She shrugged, then perked up. "Mr. Matty?"

"Yes, ma'am?" He draped the blanket over her tiny legs

and sat at the opposite end of the couch, giving her plenty of space.

"When we were hiding, Mama said we could get Otter Pops because Mr. Slothy was so brave. He was all by himself in the bedroom."

"I'm sure you were brave, too." The idea of them hiding on the balcony, terrified out of their minds, fucking killed him. "I'll be sure to pick some up at the store when it opens. Then you can eat as many as you like." He'd buy this sweet girl a fucking truckload of Otter Pops if that's what she wanted.

Daisy's mouth fell open, and she shook her head, hair flying around her face. "But, Mr. Matty, I'm only allowed one a day."

He had to bite the inside of his cheek to keep from laughing. This kid was too damn cute. "Tell you what? How about I talk to your mama? Because I think tonight was a very special case of extra bravery, and I'm pretty sure she's gonna let you have five."

"Five?" Scarlet snorted. "Yeah, right."

He and Daisy turned their heads. Scarlet was leaning against the doorway to her bedroom with a large duffle bag at her feet. There was a smile on her face that was part sweet, part shy, and it had every inch of his body buzzing. He'd do whatever he could to keep that smile on her beautiful face.

"How about four?" he asked.

Scarlet shook her head. She pressed her lips together, but they quirked up at the edges.

"Okay, fine. Three Otter Pops it is," he said, shooting a wink to Daisy. "One for the brave Mr. Slothy and two for the brave Miss Daisy. What do you say, Mama?" He flashed Scarlet his most charming grin.

Just as he'd hoped, she laughed. "Fine. Three." Daisy cheered, and Scarlet approached to drop a kiss on top of her daughter's head. "But only after you have a good sleep and finish all your breakfast."

"Maybe one after breakfast, one after lunch, and one after dinner?" Matt knew he was pushing his luck, but that seemed like a fair and responsible-ish negotiation.

Scarlet rolled her eyes and smirked. "We'll see."

He nodded. Message received. No more pushing.

"I'm gonna have two blues and a red," Daisy declared. Her smile was blinding, and she was positively glowing. "But one of the blues is for Mr. Slothy."

"Of course," he said, holding out his fist to her. When she simply stared at him, he slowly reached out and took her left hand in his. Guiding hers into a little fist, he bumped their knuckles together. Daisy let out a small giggle, and he couldn't stop his grin from growing even if he'd tried. Catching Scarlet's eye, he nodded to the duffle. "That everything?"

"No, not yet. I got sidetracked by your unlimited–Otter Pop conversation."

"It's for bravery." He winked at Daisy. "Right, kid?"

She beamed at him. "Right, Mr. Matty."

Scarlet shook her head and waved down the hall. "I still have to pack some stuff for Daisy." She caught her daughter's eye. "We're having a slumber party at Mr. Matt's place for the next day or two."

"We are?" Daisy's excited gaze swung to meet his. "I've never had a slumber party before!"

His lips twitched. "Maybe later tonight, after the Otter Pops, we'll have popcorn."

She looked at her mom. "Mama, can we? And can Baby Unicorn come, too?"

Scarlet chuckled. "We'll see on the popcorn, sweetie. But yes on Baby Unicorn. I'll make sure she gets in your bag. Now be good for Mr. Matt while I pack, okay?"

As Scarlet disappeared into Daisy's room, he asked, "Do you want to lie down and get some rest while your mom gets your stuff together?"

"Okay," she replied.

His eyebrows damn near hit his hairline when she scooted over to his end of the couch and tucked herself right next to him. She placed the smaller blanket over her lap with Mr. Slothy on top. Then she spread the larger throw blanket over the three of them, leaned into his side, and closed her eyes. "So you and Mr. Slothy don't get cold."

Matt resisted the urge to rub the warmth growing in his chest. "Thanks, Otter Pop."

For a moment, he could only stare at the little girl in wonder. He had no clue what the hell he'd done to earn her trust, but he was going to do everything in his power to not fuck things up. He'd also do everything he could to earn Scarlet's trust. In a friendly way, of course. Because facts were facts, and he was too old for her. But that didn't mean he couldn't look out for her. For them. It's what friends did.

Careful not to disturb Daisy, he pulled his phone from his pocket and sent a quick text to Gavin, informing him about what had gone down. He knew his friend—and now boss— liked to keep a finger on the pulse of what was happening on Hudson Island. Hell, he wouldn't be surprised if Gavin already knew.

Before he could return his phone to his pocket, it began vibrating with incoming texts.

GAVIN

I'm looping in the ladies. I let them know
what you told me.

BEAN

I'll look into what's going on and get back
to you.

ESME

Let me know if I can assist, B.

MATT

Holy crap. Why are all of you awake?

BEAN

If it's any consolation, I'm in my pjs. Pretty
sure Gavin doesn't sleep and $100 says
Esme's working out.

ESME

Yup. Morning PT. Need any supplies or
groceries for your houseguests, Matt?

MATT

Considering I know nothing about kids, yeah.
But I can hit the store in the morning and find
some kid-friendly stuff.

ESME

Tell me.

Riiight. Matt chuckled and typed out a list of groceries.

ESME

Great. You'll have it all in the morning. But
most likely not until 9. 10 at the very latest.

His eyebrows rose. Before he could ask how that was
even possible, his phone dinged again.

BEAN

Esme's like magic. Logistical magic at its
finest. lol

BEAN

I'll let you know what I find out about the
break-in at Scarlet's. Later.

MATT

Wow, thanks. Appreciate both your help.

GAVIN

Welcome to the team, brother.

A smile tugged at his lips as he reread the messages. Any lingering doubts he'd had about joining Hudson Security evaporated. He wasn't sure how Bean and Esme were able to get things done so quickly—and frankly, he knew better than to ask—but he was glad they were on his side.

Pocketing his phone, he made sure to not jostle Daisy, whose warm, tiny body remained snuggled against his side.

"Okay, I think I'm ready," Scarlet said from the hallway. Returning to the living room, she came to an abrupt halt. Her lips parted in obvious surprise.

Matt glanced down at Daisy and shrugged. "Pretty sure she's out cold."

He shifted Daisy off him and laid her fully on the couch, making sure to keep her tucked in the soft blankets. When he straightened, he faced Scarlet. "Lots of excitement, I guess."

Scarlet nodded, and he took her in. Standing there in casual clothes and half asleep, she looked unbearably beautiful. She'd changed from her shorts and tank into black leggings and an oversized T-shirt. Her hair was in a bun on top of her head, and her feet were clad in a pair of pink Converse sneakers. Her stress and exhaustion were apparent. Not that he could blame her. But there was something else in her expression, something he couldn't quite read.

Every fiber of his being wanted to make everything better for her, fix every damn thing. Scarlet was extraordinary— strong and vulnerable, sweet and spunky. And so damn pretty. But she was so damn young. And *that* was something he needed to remember, to actively remind himself of. But regardless of her age, he hoped like hell the woman knew that he'd never do anything to hurt her or Daisy.

Clearing his throat, he gestured to the door. "Let me find

Quinn and make sure he has everything secured. It should only take a few minutes. Then we can get out of here." He strode from the apartment before she could respond.

Cowardly? Sure. But Scarlet stirred up something in him he wasn't sure he wanted to feel. Something protective and . . . possessive. He had no business feeling either way.

God knew he wasn't a good bet. History spoke for itself.

CHAPTER TEN

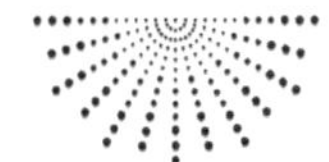

Seeing Daisy curled up against Matt's side had stunned Scarlet. *Daisy.* The girl who took forever to warm up to people. The girl who was so shy that she rarely made eye contact. But there she'd been, sound asleep, practically on top of Matt.

Scarlet knew Daisy recognized him as a friend of Poppy and Cade's, but she was certain that prior to Daisy breaking her arm, they'd only interacted once. That time, months ago, when he'd stepped in when Poppy's ex was being an asshat at the playground. The day that Scarlet's crush on the man had grown to astronomical proportions.

Now here she was, with the sunrise less than an hour away, standing in her destroyed living room waiting for Matt to return. Well, *destroyed* was a bit strong. The front and sliding doors were wrecked, but the rest of the place was just super messy, like a little tornado had touched down.

But that wasn't what had her heart threatening to beat out of her chest. No, that was her agreement to stay with Matt for the next couple of days. At least.

Mr. Wayland wasn't returning from vacation until

Sunday, and she had no clue how long it took to repair stuff, but she did know that getting the rental apartment back in shape before the next guests arrived on Friday would be his priority. It had to be since he charged her so little for rent. Once that was done, he could focus on her place.

"Hey," Matt said, reentering her apartment. "Quinn and Chase have secured the main door downstairs. The back door —which is how they think whoever did this got away—wasn't damaged. The locks are good on that one." He gestured toward her bedroom. "Quinn will get your slider boarded up before he takes off, but he said we're good to go. You ready?"

Was she ready? Probably not, but she nodded anyway.

Giving her living room one last look, she sighed. A part of her wanted to clean up, but the other figured that was a chore for another day. "Do you mind carrying our bags? I can get Daisy."

"No problem." He reached for her bags, then hesitated. "Wait. Daisy's car seat. If you give me your keys, I can transfer it to my truck before you bring her down."

Car seat. Right. She hadn't even thought of that. *You're a shit mom.*

Scarlet rubbed her temples as she scanned the room for her keys. She spotted them on the table by the door and pointed, sending up a prayer of thanks that whoever had done this hadn't taken her car.

"Be right back," Matt said, grabbing the keys and both of her bags.

He returned in under five minutes. She scooped up Daisy and followed him down the back staircase.

"Chase boarded up the main door. So until that's fixed and secure, you'll need to use the back entrance. Also"—he glanced over his shoulder—"I had Quinn double-check to make sure I installed the car seat correctly."

Of course he had. "Thanks, Matt. I really appreciate you taking us in. For being here." She wasn't used to leaning on others, wasn't used to having people to depend on. Hell, in her old life, *she'd* been the dependable one, the one people had gone to for help. Which was a complete joke and absolutely stupid, because her old life had been a train wreck.

Matt stopped and turned. He was standing a couple of steps below her, so they were nearly eye to eye. "You don't need to thank me, but you're welcome. We're friends, remember? You and Daisy are welcome to stay as long as you need."

Until this moment, she'd never noticed how his eyes were a rich chocolate brown. He was staring at her so intently, yet so . . . tenderly . . . that she was having a hard time thinking straight.

"Well, Matt, I still appreciate it."

The corners of his lips lifted. "Well, Scarlet, you're welcome. Now watch your step."

Quietly exhaling, she descended the remaining stairs. They exited into the alley, and he led her to his truck, a burly black GMC Sierra, and opened the back door. With the dome light on, she saw he'd placed Daisy's car seat in the middle.

Scarlet frowned. She claimed she was five-three, and most of the time, people believed her. In truth, she was just shy of five-two. There was no way she was getting Daisy into that truck. From where she was standing, it was logistically impossible. The truck didn't have running boards she could use to boost herself up.

With a soft chuckle, Matt approached. "How about I put her in, and then you can buckle her?"

Carefully transferring Daisy, she muttered, "I'm not even sure *I* can get up there."

"Sure you can. After I get Daisy in, I'll enable the running boards."

"You can *enable* the running boards?" Holy crap, that was fancy.

Matt nodded. "Obviously, it doesn't matter to me, but my mom's short. So, unless I wanted to get an earful—which no son wants—I had to make sure there was a running board option."

He placed Daisy in her car seat, then hustled to the driver's side and pressed a button. The running boards dropped with a low buzz. Scarlet climbed up to secure Daisy, shaking her head. The more she got to know Matt Alvarez, the more the man surprised her.

Twenty minutes later, Scarlet stood in Matt's guest room, her mouth hanging open. She wasn't quite sure what she'd expected, but it hadn't been *this*. The room was opulent—and probably bigger than her entire apartment. There was even a fireplace and a seating area. In the bedroom.

Matt approached the massive king-size bed with a sleeping Daisy in his arms, and she pulled herself out of her stupor to help him.

"She can sleep with me," Scarlet said as she removed her daughter's sneakers—she needed her little girl close tonight —and pulled back the bed covers. Matt placed Daisy down with a gentleness that was at odds with his size.

Pointing out the attached bathroom, he promised to show her more of the house later in the morning. Then he squeezed her shoulder and said, "Get some sleep. We can visit the cats in the afternoon when you guys are rested."

After he closed the door, Scarlet tucked a pillow on either side of Daisy to prevent her from rolling around. Then, unhooking her bra and pulling it through the armhole of her top, she climbed into the opposite side of the bed, not bothering to change out of her leggings and T-shirt.

Comfy in the soft sheets, with the clean scent of laundry detergent filling her nose and the beginnings of the kaleidoscope of sunrise peeking through the window, she sighed and stared at the ceiling. She'd gone from a lazy Friday evening to a night of sheer terror, panic, relief, and everything in between. There was no way she could fall asleep. She was completely wired from all that had happened.

Focusing on her breath, she listened to Matt walking down the hallway, murmuring in his deep voice. He was probably on the phone. She closed her eyes and pictured him in her mind. His handsome face. His impressive and somewhat-imposing figure. His soft smile. She thought of how he'd helped her tonight, how he'd talked with Daisy.

How he'd been there for her. For *them*.

Before Scarlet knew it, she had drifted off into a dreamless sleep.

CHAPTER ELEVEN

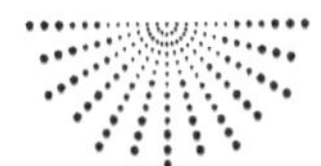

Scarlet rolled over and snuggled deeper into the warm, fluffy duvet, inhaling the sheets' clean cotton scent. Then her eyes shot open. After two panicked heartbeats, she recognized her surroundings.

She was in Matt's guest room with Dai—

Another surge of panic whipped through Scarlet at the sight of the empty space beside her. No Daisy. No Mr. Slothy. No Baby Unicorn. She scrambled up to sitting, then froze, straining to hear . . .

Daisy's faint giggle. Followed by a low rumble and her daughter's full-fledged laugh.

Scarlet flopped back down on the plush mattress and willed her heart rate to return to normal. Glancing at the bedside clock, her eyes widened. Holy crap, it was nearly ten. She couldn't remember the last time she'd slept in this late. No wonder Daisy wasn't in bed with her anymore.

Worry brewed in her belly, and she hoped Matt was okay hanging out with Daisy. It still boggled her mind how her daughter had taken to the man. He seemed to like Daisy as well, but Scarlet knew lots of people could only tolerate kids for so long.

The thought prompted her to get out of bed and pull her bra back on. After a quick stop in the bathroom, she followed the soft voices down the hallway, past another guest room and a cozy sitting room.

In the kitchen, she came to a halt. Daisy sat at the large kitchen table, coloring. Matt was next to her with his own paper in front of him and a crayon in hand. Scarlet's stomach did a little flip at the sight.

How she wished she could give something like this to Daisy . . .

A vise gripped her heart, and she wanted to slap herself upside the head. There was no use yearning for something that wasn't possible.

"Mama!" Daisy squealed, noticing her in the entryway. She scrambled down from her seat and raced over, hugging Scarlet's legs as if they'd been separated for weeks.

Scooping her daughter up, she kissed her noisily on the cheek. "Good morning, baby girl." When Daisy started squirming, she placed her back on her feet and smiled as her daughter zoomed to her seat to resume drawing.

She met Matt's gaze, and heat washed over her face. The man was barefoot and dressed in faded jeans and a white T-shirt. No one should look that good in such plain clothes.

"Good morning," she said, shifting on her feet. She was officially waaay out of her comfort zone. "Um, you have a really nice place. Thanks again for letting us stay here."

"Nothing to thank me for, remember? We're friends." He leaned back in his seat. "And as much as I'd like to take credit for this place, I can't. It's actually my brother's."

"You have a brother?" she asked, desperate for any kind of small talk. She usually excelled at small talk—she was a waitress, after all—but here? Right now? Standing with this man in his kitchen? She was floundering and nervous and at a complete loss.

Matt nodded, seeming unaware of her impending mini panic attack. "Jake. He and his wife live in Seattle."

"Are you guys close?" Scarlet slapped a hand over her mouth. "Sorry. That was rude. And absolutely none of my business." She glanced around the kitchen and spotted the coffee maker. "I think I need caffeine. My brain and mouth aren't on the same page yet."

He chuckled. "Not rude at all, Scar. And help yourself. Cups are above the coffee maker, and there's flavored creamer in the fridge."

"Thanks," she said, grateful for something to do. She filled a mug three-quarters of the way, then topped it off with vanilla creamer.

"Wow," Matt said, amusement in his voice. "I take it you like your coffee sweet?"

Scarlet took a sip, and the sugary deliciousness had her sighing. "My motto is the less it tastes like coffee, the better."

The edges of his lips quirked. "So why drink coffee, then?"

"It wakes me up. You know, the whole gets-the-brain-and-mouth-syncing thing. For as long as I can remember, I used to drink a couple cans of Diet Coke in the mornings. But then"—she pointed at Daisy with her mug—"I didn't want her to think that was okay. I know firsthand how hard it is to stop being a soda junkie."

"So now it's sweetened coffee and no more morning sodas?"

She shook her head and took a larger gulp. She needed the caffeine to kick in as soon as humanly possible. "No more soda *at all*."

His eyes widened. "You gave it up for good?"

"After my morning coffee, I drink *water* now." She

grimaced, and he chuckled. "It's g-r-o-s-s, but supposedly better for me. It also gets the munchkin drinking it, too, so that's a plus."

And water was free, unlike sodas and juices. Ever since Daisy's birth, Scarlet had scraped by on a tight budget. When she'd been in Arizona, the water had tasted nasty, but water filters had still been cheaper than her multiple-cans-of-Diet-Coke-a-day habit. With her apartment in Hudson, she'd lucked out because not only did her fridge have a built-in water filter, but Mr. Wayland supplied her with replacement filters for free. Now, if only water didn't taste so . . . blah.

"If it's any consolation," Matt began, "I didn't drink water as a kid, either. It wasn't until high school, when I got really involved in sports, that I started properly hydrating. Good for you for setting a strong example—and an early example—for the Otter Pop."

"Thanks, but water really is . . ." She finished the thought by scrunching up her face.

Daisy's head whipped toward Matt. "Can I have an Otter Pop, Mr. Matty?"

"Probably later." Daisy's face scrunched up like Scarlet's had, and his brown eyes twinkled with humor. Looking back at Scarlet, he said, "Give it time, Scar. Maybe you'll get used to the taste?"

She winced. "It's been three years."

"Well, at least you're both well-hydrated." He seemed to bite back a laugh. "But to answer your not-rude question, yes. My brother and I are close. Jake and his wife, Carmen, have crazy busy schedules, so we don't see each other as much as we want, but we text and call all the time. We try to get together in person once a month or so. When I got hurt, he offered me this place. Knew the quiet and slower pace would help my recovery. He also knew Cade was here and that he'd watch out for me." Matt shook his head. "Even though Jake's my little brother, the guy's a bit overprotective."

"Of course he is. Didn't you get *shot?*" Again, she slapped her hand over her mouth and grimaced. "Sorry. Gossip train info." She gestured between them with her mug. "I moved to Hudson a few months before you, and let me tell you, when you arrived, there was *lots* of tea going around about you."

Matt frowned. "Tea?"

"Gossip. All the ladies were curious about who you were, what you were doing on the island, and what your whole backstory was. They didn't think anything nefarious since everyone knew you were friends with Cade, but the theories were wild. Small towns, right?" She laughed at the look of horror on his face. "Someone mentioned that you'd been shot—probably for something heroic—and that you were here recovering."

He chuckled, but there didn't seem to be any humor in it. "Shot, yes. Heroic, no. When my brother offered up this place . . . I had a lot going on in addition to the physical recovery thing, so it was a no-brainer for me to take him up on it."

Scarlet sensed he was uncomfortable with where their conversation was leading, so she pivoted. "Did it help?"

He tilted his head in question.

"You said your brother thought the quiet would help with your recovery. Did it?"

Matt remained silent for a moment, pondering his answer. When he finally met her gaze, a soft smile played on his mouth. "Yeah. It took quite a bit of time, but yeah. It did."

That brief, solemn darkness in his eyes had eased, and she was thankful. Seeing it had hurt her heart. "And now you're working at Hudson Security?"

He nodded. "After I recovered physically, I took some time off. Things had gotten . . . complicated over at the

Seattle PD, and the longer I stayed away, the less I wanted to go back."

Oh, to be a fly on the wall of his brain. Because there was a whole story behind that entire *complicated* bit. Scarlet was sure of it. But she didn't know him well enough yet to press.

"Gavin was pushing hard for me to join his crew, and I figured why the hell—" His gaze darted to Daisy and then back to her. Her stomach did that flipping thing again. Stupid stomach. "I mean, why the heck not? Fresh start and all that."

"Mama?" Daisy cut in, still picking through her small box of crayons. "Mr. Matty said we could see the kitty cats today if you said it was okay." She glanced up. "Is it okay? Please?"

Scarlet couldn't help but grin. Her kid was so stinking cute. "Yes, we can go visit the cats a little later this afternoon. But first—"

The doorbell rang, and Matt rose from the table, patting Daisy on the head. "But first, that should be our breakfast."

Scarlet gave him a questioning look, and he winked in response as he left the kitchen. Butterflies took flight in her belly. She tried her best to ignore them.

Seconds later, Matt returned carrying two bags of groceries. "Ladies, how do pancakes and bacon sound?"

"With chocolate chips?" Daisy asked.

Scarlet shook her head. "Daisy, we don't—"

"Yup," he said, pulling a bag of semi-sweet chocolate chips out of one of the grocery sacks. "*And* I have a box of these bad boys." He held up a striped box—Otter Pops—and Daisy cheered. "But these aren't until later, remember? You have to finish all your breakfast."

Scarlet snickered when Daisy nodded. "Ohmygod, she's gonna be in a sugar coma by noon."

"You're one to talk," Matt said with a smirk, gesturing to her coffee. "Besides, they're for bravery, remember?"

She rolled her eyes. "Oh yes, how could I forget?"

"Mr. Matty, look! I drawed you a picture!" Daisy held up a paper with blue, red, and green . . . things on it.

Scarlet had a hard time deciphering Daisy's drawings on a good day. With Daisy using her left hand? Yeaaah, there was no hope.

"Wow, that's beautiful, Otter Pop," Matt said, reclaiming his seat next to Daisy. "Can you tell me all about what you drew?"

Scarlet suppressed a chuckle. Smart man.

Matt shot her another wink, and she grinned. This time, it was harder to ignore the butterflies.

"This is Mr. Slothy," Daisy began, pointing at one of the blue figures on the paper. "And that's me and Baby Unicorn and *you*! We're all holding hands!"

"Oh wow, that's really pretty." Smiling, he touched a lone blob off to the side. "And what's this?"

"Oh, that's just Mama. She's taking a picture of all of us."

Matt laughed. "Well, that's really nice of your mom."

"Mr. Matty, can you put it on your figyator?"

For a moment, he held Daisy's gaze. A look that Scarlet could only describe as wonder flashed over his face. "It would be my honor, Otter Pop." He bopped her on the nose as he stood, taking the picture and placing it front and center on his refrigerator. "What do you say you draw your mama a picture while I make us some pancakes and bacon?"

Daisy got busy with a fresh piece of paper.

"Can I help?" Scarlet asked.

"Any food allergies for you or Daisy?"

She shook her head.

"Then how about you hang out and keep me company?"

Was this guy for real? "Surely there's something I can help with."

"You can measure out how many chocolate chips you

think would be best. I mean, you're probably right that a sugar coma isn't the wisest decision for a Saturday morning."

They spent the next half hour making pancakes and frying bacon and the following half hour gobbling it all up. Matt kept the conversation flowing and light—which Scarlet appreciated. And what she appreciated even more was that he involved Daisy. When he asked Scarlet what shows she was watching, he asked the same of her daughter. He spoke to the little girl like a regular person, never talking down to her or outright ignoring her.

As they finished brunch, Daisy's eyelids were drooping.

Scarlet wiped her mouth and set her napkin down. "Hey, baby girl. How about a nap?"

"No, Mama," Daisy said with a pout.

Scarlet arched an eyebrow, causing her little girl to still. "Excuse me? Try again, miss."

"I'm not sleepy," Daisy grumbled.

She leaned back in her seat and crossed her arms, pinning her daughter with a sharp look. "If you don't take a nap, then you don't get to go with Mr. Matt to visit the cats."

Daisy's lower lip wobbled, and her gaze flew to Matt. "Mr. Mattyyy," she wailed.

"I'm sorry, Otter Pop." The poor guy looked heartbroken. "Your mom's the boss on this."

"What'll it be, Daisy?" she asked. "Take a nap and visit the cats? Or no nap and no cats?"

"But, Mama, I'm not sleep—" Her words died on a giant yawn.

Done with the back-and-forth—because god knew it could go on forever—Scarlet stood. "Let's go wash your hands. But first, please tell Mr. Matt thank you for breakfast."

Daisy looked over at Matt, her blue eyes as big as saucers. "Thank you, Mr. Matty."

He gave her a soft smile. "You're welcome, sweet girl. Have a good nap, okay?"

"Okay." Daisy climbed down from her chair and paused next to him. "Will you be here when I wake up? Will you take me with you to see the kitty cats?"

He twisted in his seat to face her, placing his elbows on his knees so they were eye to eye. "I'll be here when you wake up, and I won't go see the cats today without you."

"Do you promise?"

He nodded and held out his fist. "I promise, Otter Pop."

Giggling, Daisy bumped her fist against his. Then she launched herself at him, wrapping her arms tight around his neck. She pulled away, placed her small hands on either side of his face, and gave him a giant grin. "Thank you, Mr. Matty."

Scarlet's jaw hit the floor. Mostly because of how much her daughter adored Matt, and partially because of the syrupy handprints she'd left on the guy. The guy who had that look of wonder on his face again.

He patted Daisy's back, then dropped a kiss to the top of her head. "Thanks for the hug, Otter Pop. Now go and wash up for your nap."

With a wave, Daisy skipped down the hallway.

"Don't touch the walls! And go straight to the sink and wash your hands!" Scarlet called after her daughter. Turning to Matt, she said, "Sorry about all the . . . sticky."

"No worries, Scarlet. You know, if you don't mind me saying . . . you've got a fantastic kid. You're a great mom." He touched his cheek and chuckled when his fingers stuck to his skin. "You weren't kidding about the sticky, huh? I'm gonna go wash up, too." On his way out of the kitchen, he paused and glanced back at her. "Don't worry about the dishes. I'll take care of them while you put Daisy down for her nap."

Scarlet stood rooted as he left. She knew she should go

make sure Daisy was washing her hands, but she couldn't move. She could only stare at the space where Matt had been. Where they'd all spent the last hour making brunch and eating together. Like a family. Like the lazy weekend mornings she'd seen on television growing up. And holy shit, she'd never experienced anything remotely close to it.

God, what would it be like to have this life? With a man like Matt? Who was thoughtful and considerate? Who made freaking pancakes and bacon for breakfast? She'd never met anyone like him. But that probably had more to do with the company she'd kept than anything.

A tiny part of her desperately wanted to believe she could have this. Well, not with Matt, because there was no way in hell he'd be interested in anything like this with *her*—but something like this. The other part, though—the larger part that was based in reality—knew it wasn't going to happen.

With a resigned sigh, she made her way to the guest room to check on Daisy. After rewashing her daughter's face and hands, she tucked her in with Mr. Slothy and Baby Unicorn. Daisy was out like a light in minutes.

Lying beside her daughter, Scarlet tried to shake off her mood. For as long as she could remember, she'd relied on herself. Granted, with questionable success. But she was still alive and kicking, and Daisy was happy and healthy.

She cringed. Well, minus the broken arm.

She should be satisfied with that. It was pointless to want more.

The problem was that the more time she spent with Matt, the more she liked him.

Before this week, she'd been attracted to him because he was hot and growly. Hell, he'd perfected a smolder that could put romance novel heroes to shame. That kind of crush had been safe. Easy to move on from. But now her crush had transformed into something else entirely. She'd gotten to know Matt and discovered he was . . . kind. And compassionate. And attentive.

He'd gone from giving her short, one- and two-word replies to full-on conversations overnight. Okay, fine. Not overnight, but still . . .

Scarlet wasn't sure what the catalyst was for that change in him, but she wasn't going to question it. She enjoyed talking to him, getting to know him better. But she'd also entered dangerous territory. Because as much as those butterflies in her stomach had her excited to spend more time with him, she knew she was just setting herself up for disappointment. After all, when had any guy ever wanted to be with her for more than an easy fuck? Even as friends?

Her blood chilled.

Yeah. Never.

CHAPTER TWELVE

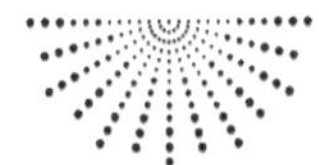

By two o'clock, Daisy was up from her nap and bouncing on her little feet. It was safe to say the kid was ready to visit the cats. Sure, her bouncing might have had a *tiny* bit to do with the Otter Pop Matt had given her when she'd woken up. But whatever.

After Daisy had finished her blue popsicle, she'd asked her mom for a second. Scarlet had given her an emphatic no, and the sweet kid had looked devastated. Her giant blue eyes had welled with tears, but Scarlet hadn't budged.

Honestly, Matt wasn't sure how Scarlet did it. Good god, if Daisy had turned those Disney doe eyes on him, for sure she would have eaten half the box by now. But apparently, letting four-year-olds eat that many popsicles in one sitting was frowned upon. Go figure.

So, with only one popsicle in Daisy's belly, they piled into his truck and made the short drive over to Cade's. He let them in with the spare key he'd been given and disarmed the security system. Scarlet took Daisy hunting for the cats while he put fresh water in their bowls and filled their food dishes. Unsurprisingly, the moment Ripley and Bishop heard their kibble rattling around, they came running. Much to Daisy's delight.

As the cats began eating, the little girl broke away from her mom and made a beeline for them. Matt scooped her up before she could reach them. Fortunately, his reflexes were still on point.

"We don't bother the cats while they're eating, Otter Pop," he said, propping her on his hip.

Daisy frowned. "But they missed me."

"I'm sure they did, but we don't mess with animals when they're eating. They might get angry and try to scratch or bite you."

Her lower lip popped out. "But that's not nice."

"Do you like it when people mess with you when you're hungry?"

"Yes," Daisy huffed.

Scarlet snorted. "Really, miss? What did you do the other day when Miss Martha accidentally took away your french fries because she thought you were done?"

Daisy let out a sad sigh and dropped her head onto his shoulder. "I cried."

Goddamn, this kid was too damn cute.

"I'm sorry you cried," he said, resting his cheek against her head. "But that's why we don't mess with animals when they're eating. Sometimes, instead of crying, they get angry. Let's just wait until they're done before you say hi, okay?"

"Daisy, sweetie, why don't you go find the cats' toys while they're eating? That way, when they finish, you'll be ready for them to play."

Daisy perked up and began squirming. Matt put her down, and she dashed to the living room.

"I take it she knows where the cat toys are?" he asked.

"Oh yeah," Scarlet said, puttering around the kitchen.

"You know, it's really nice of you to look after the cats while Poppy and Cade are gone."

He shrugged. "It's the least I can do. The poor dude is one giant ball of stress."

"Is Cade nervous about his fighters? About their chances of winning?"

"Nah, he has every confidence in his guys. He was a wreck over propos—" He slammed his mouth shut. *Fuck!* "Uh . . ."

"Ohmygod!" Scarlet's face lit up as she clapped her hands together and bounced on her feet. "Is Cade gonna propose to Poppy while they're in Europe?"

He grimaced, then chuckled. Well, in for a penny and all that shit . . . He pointed a finger at Scarlet and mock-glared. "You *cannot* let on that I told you. Got it?"

Her grin was magnetic. And the way she mimed locking her lips and tossing the key over her shoulder? Holy shit, she was fucking cute.

"When we were talking at the beginning of the week, he hadn't quite figured out when or where, but he was thinking maybe at the Eiffel Tower."

"Ohhh. Poppy would love that!"

Matt smiled. "I know, but Cade's overthinking everything and making himself a nervous wreck."

Scarlet pursed her lips, and he struggled to tear his gaze from them.

"You know," she said, tapping a finger to said lips, "as romantic as an Eiffel Tower proposal would be, I don't think Poppy will care where it happens. So long as she's with Cade, that's all that matters. Oh, and the twins will be there with them, too! I think *that* would be her perfect proposal."

"I believe I may have said those exact same words." His smile grew. "Great minds think alike, huh?"

"Right?" She beamed at him. "We could be, like . . . Team Marlet."

He scrunched his forehead in confusion.

"You know, Matt and Scarlet. Marlet. Like Bennifer?" She shook her head, and a flush of color stole over her cheeks. "Never mind, it's dumb. Ignore me."

Yeaaah. She was fucking cute. "Nah, it's a good team name."

"Oh, look," Scarlet said, pointing at the cats. She rounded the kitchen island and hopped up on one of the stools facing the living room.

He knew she was blatantly changing the subject, but he'd go with it. The cats had finished eating and indeed found Daisy. The little girl was sitting cross-legged in front of the living room couch with Ripley on her lap as she dangled a feather on a stick in front of Bishop.

Matt pulled out a stool for himself, making sure to leave an empty one between them. Scarlet had her eyes glued to her daughter, so he used the opportunity to take her in.

After Daisy's nap, Scarlet had seemed a little subdued, and he wasn't sure why. Granted, they were only beginning to get to know each other, so she could have simply been tired. But when they'd talked about Cade and Poppy's pending engagement, she had returned to being the animated woman he'd witnessed countless times at the diner. Now the anxious air was back around her, and he was clueless as to why.

He thought they'd all had a nice, relaxing time this morning. However, he'd been wrong before, and frankly, he knew jack-shit about women. He just hoped he hadn't fucked anything up by inadvertently crossing any lines or insulting her somehow.

"You doing okay, Scarlet?"

She startled, and he wanted to kick himself. "Yeah. Sorry. Just distracted, I guess."

"There's nothing to apologize for. Last night was rough." And he was an idiot who'd thought their nice breakfast had been enough to take her mind off what had happened. He racked his brain for anything he could do to help. "Do you need a hand replacing anything?"

"What do you mean?" She swiveled on the barstool to face him, her right arm coming to rest on the island.

Shit. What *did* he mean? "You mentioned to Quinn last night that your purse was stolen. I assume that means you don't have a driver's license. Do you need me to drive you anywhere? Maybe over to one of the big box stores over on Whidbey Island if you need to replace anything?"

Her shoulders slumped. "That's kind of you, but no. When Daisy was napping earlier, I called the bank and put a freeze on my checking account. The Hudson branch's machine that makes debit cards is getting repaired and won't be working until at least Tuesday, so I have to wait until then."

"I'm more than happy to pay for whatever you and Daisy need." Matt held up his hand when her mouth opened. By the glint in her eyes, he knew she was going to protest. "You can pay me back later." No way in hell was he taking a dime from her.

"Um, you know, I think we're okay. They only took my purse. That was it. But . . ." She shifted in her seat, looking anywhere but at him.

He placed his hand on hers, and she stilled. "But what, Scar?"

Her brown gaze shot to his, then down to their connected hands. "This makes me sound so dumb, but how do I get a new driver's license? I've never . . . lost one before."

Matt refused to let that comment slide. "Look at me, Scar," he said, squeezing her hand. He waited until she complied. The doubt and uncertainty in her expression riled up something in him. Something protective. Something that was borderline possessive. "Don't call yourself dumb, sweetheart. You're the furthest thing from that. Hear me?"

A tiny smile tipped the corner of her lips, but her eyes remained dejected. "You're really sweet, Matt."

It killed him that she didn't believe him. Didn't believe in herself.

Releasing her hand, he ran the backs of his fingers down her jawline before clasping his hands together in his lap. He had to stop touching her before he hauled her into his arms. He'd never seen anyone who looked like they needed a hug more. "Scarlet Miller, don't sell yourself short. You're not dumb. In fact, you're pretty damn amazing."

She shook her head. "Like I said, you're sweet. But I don't even know how to get a new driver's license."

Matt shrugged. "You said it yourself: you've never lost one before. *And* you're fairly new to the state. Cut yourself some slack."

It was on the tip of his tongue to call her kid again. To remind himself how young she was. But that bullshit needed to stop. It was time to accept he was stupidly attracted to her. He was a damn adult and could deal with it. Scarlet needed him to *help*. Not push her away because he feared lusting after her.

"I assume you had a Washington driver's license and not one from Arizona?"

She nodded.

"I'm pretty sure you can just do it online, then."

"I won't need to go into a driver's licensing office?"

His eyes narrowed as he tried to recall how the Department of Licensing's system worked. "I don't think so. We can hop on my computer when we get back home to double-check, but I'm pretty sure you can just fill out a form and print out a temporary license, and then they mail a new one to you in a few weeks."

Her exhale was long and slow, her relief apparent. "Oh, okay. Great. Thanks."

"No problem," he said, but the intensity of her reaction raised the hairs on his neck. Something was off, and it made worry crawl up his spine like tiny spiders.

Matt had been a detective for over eighteen years. He knew when someone was keeping secrets. And though he hated to admit it, he suspected Scarlet was doing just that. But he also knew he couldn't pry whatever she was hiding out of her. He needed to gain her trust if he wanted to be privy to her full story. To do that, he needed to be a friend.

He gestured to the love seat near the island. At her small nod, he stood and extended his hand. He held his breath as he waited to see what she'd do.

Only when her smaller hand settled in his did he remember to breathe. They settled at the opposite ends of the love seat, but just half a cushion separated them. From their spots, they could see Daisy playing with the cats across the room, but they were still far enough away for a private conversation.

"Tell me a little bit about yourself, Scar."

She smiled, but he could see the strain behind it. That was the last thing he wanted.

"Oh, there's really not much to tell."

Slow and steady, Alvarez. "Well, you know I have a brother. What about you? Any siblings?"

"I'm an only child. At least, as far as I know, anyway. I never met my dad, so . . . who knows?"

Shit. This conversation was not going according to plan. "Did you grow up in Arizona?"

Again, she shook her head. "I grew up in this tiny little nowhere town in South Dakota."

"I was not expecting that," he said, laughing at himself.

Her lips curved up the tiniest bit. "Things were tough when I was a kid, and I ended up moving out on my own when I was fourteen."

Holy fuck. *Fourteen.* Thank god he'd had years of practice controlling his expressions. He remained quiet, afraid that if he said anything, she'd stop speaking.

Scarlet studied her nails. "I dropped out of school in ninth grade and moved in with some friends. I got a job . . . waitressing, and . . ." She shrugged. "I've been doing that ever since."

Again, his intuition blared at him. He believed she was telling the truth, at least partially. But there was a whole lot more to her story . . .

"Then you moved from South Dakota to Arizona?"

She nodded, and he could see the hesitation in her eyes. As if she were debating how much to tell him. "After a few years, things didn't work out with those friends. I ended up in San Diego for a few months and found out I was pregnant with Daisy. Then I moved to Arizona and got a waitressing gig, had Daisy, and ended up staying there for a few years. I moved here just before her third birthday."

"Of all the places in the world, what brought you to Hudson Island?"

Scarlet grinned, and relief coursed through him at the sight. It was a real smile. One that had her eyes twinkling. "The diner I worked at was owned by this really nice older couple, Walt and Rita. They were just the sweetest people and kinda took me and Daisy under their wing."

"Kind of like how Ray and Martha have?" It was no secret that the couple considered Scarlet and Daisy their adopted grand- and great-granddaughters.

Scarlet's grin grew. "Funny you should say that. See, Rita had a best friend growing up who she'd kept in contact with for their entire lives. But the way things worked out with their marriages and such, they ended up living in different states. So, when I talked with Rita about . . . wanting a change for me and Daisy, she called up her best friend. Who, coincidentally, also owned a diner with her husband . . ."

Matt knew he was sporting the sappiest smile, but he didn't care. "Martha and Ray."

She clasped her hands together over her heart. "Martha and Ray. And they've been absolutely wonderful to us."

"You and Poppy are pretty close, too, right?"

Nodding, she moved her clasped hands to her lips. "I've been so lucky since I arrived here. Poppy has been a godsend. Truly."

"How so?"

Scarlet smiled. How hadn't Poppy been a godsend? That was the better question.

"Poppy's like my role model. When I first met her, she was really intimidating. I mean, she had her business, she's gorgeous, and it seemed like she had the perfect family." Matt scowled, and she held up her hand. "I know. *Seemed* was the operative word there." Poppy's ex-husband, Eli, was a cheating, gaslighting piece of shit. "I quickly found out that things weren't quite how they appeared, and I think that made her an even bigger inspiration. Not only was she a young single mom like me, but she had Carter and Dylan at *sixteen*. Three years before me, and they're freaking *twins!*"

Scarlet shuddered. In comparison to most other kids, Daisy was super mellow. But that didn't mean her daughter couldn't be a handful. The kid definitely had her trying moments. No way could Scarlet even begin to imagine two.

"Poppy shared some of her struggles with me," she

continued, "and I was just so impressed that she not only ran a successful business, but at the same time, also raise two amazing sons basically on her own—because we can all agree that Eli was worthless."

Matt snorted. "Very true."

Watching Daisy play with the cats, Scarlet was grateful that her daughter was blissfully unaware of all the adult stressors in life. "I don't know," she said, letting out a breath. "Poppy has kind of become my big sister, and her friendship and support mean a lot."

Her friendship and support meant everything. She'd never had someone like Poppy. Someone she could count on. Someone who truly cared about her. Someone who wouldn't fuck her over the second it was beneficial to them. "Poppy gives me hope that I can do right by Daisy. Like if she could make a good life for two kids, then I can do the same with one."

A couple of seconds ticked by in silence, and her face flushed with embarrassment. Damn. She was pretty sure the last thing Matt wanted to hear was all this. Before she could backtrack and make some quip to lighten the mood, he reached over and took her hand. She froze.

"It kills me that you doubt yourself."

She dared to peek at him, and the care in his eyes stopped her breath.

"You're a wonderful mom, Scarlet." Without releasing her gaze, he nodded toward Daisy. "She's a wonderful kid. That's all you."

This man made her want to spill her guts. He was so calm and steady, and she didn't know why, but she felt like no matter what she said, he wasn't going to judge her. "I worry about her. She's so shy and quiet. I'm so scared kids are going to bully her or hurt her or try to take advantage of her."

Squeezing her hand, Matt shook his head. "Yeah, she's shy and quiet for sure. But she's also a tough little cookie. Cade told me that the summer program at the day care is a whole new crew with double the kids. Yet, shy and all, she wanted to be there the day after she broke her arm, wanted to participate in all the things. And she hasn't been shy or quiet at all with me."

"Well, not to pump up your ego or anything," she said with a smirk, "but you're definitely the exception to the rule."

"Yeah?"

"I think it took meeting Cade at least a dozen times before she spoke to him. Same with Four. Mind you, when she does talk to them now, it's only one- or two-word replies." She narrowed her eyes at him. "Kinda like how you used to be with me."

Matt slapped a palm to his chest. "Ouch."

She laughed. "Am I wrong?"

"No," he said, grimacing. "I'm an idiot. But idiot or not, I'm obviously much cooler than Cade and Four. So that's a bonus, right?" He grinned, and she couldn't help but notice that he was still holding her hand. "So not only is Daisy a tough cookie, but she obviously has great taste in people, too."

"Cookie?" Daisy said, head popping up like a gopher. She ran toward them, cats long forgotten. "Can we get cookies, Mr. Matty?" She climbed onto the couch and snuggled in between them.

Scarlet tried not to be disappointed when Matt let go of her hand.

"Uhhh . . ." He tossed Scarlet a flustered look before returning his attention to Daisy. "You know, I don't think I have any. But don't you have some more bravery Otter Pops coming your way?"

"I do." Daisy spun toward Scarlet. "Mama, we need to go to Mr. Matty's so I can have more Otter Pops. Can we bring the kitty cats with us?"

Matt's eyes widened, and she bit back a laugh. Yeah, Daisy's ping-ponging brain took a little getting used to. "No, baby. Ripley and Bishop need to stay here. This is where they live."

"But they can come visit like how me and you are visiting Mr. Matty."

"Sorry, Otter Pop. No can do. The cats stay here." Matt rose to his feet. "How about we have a movie night? You like movies, right?"

Daisy was eagerly nodding before he'd finished speaking.

"Great," he said as Daisy scrambled off the couch. "We'll have an early dinner, and you can have a bravery Otter Pop after. Then we'll pop some popcorn and mix in some M&M's."

Scarlet's heart stuttered when Daisy took Matt's hand, tugged him closer, and reached up with both her arms.

Grinning, Matt picked her daughter up and settled her on his hip. "Have you ever had popcorn and M&M's together?"

Daisy shrugged, and the sweetest smile graced her face, like Matt was the most fascinating person she'd ever met. It was the same way she looked at Ripley and Bishop, which said a *lot*.

"Movie night it is," Matt said. "Otter Pop, I'll even let you pick the movie . . ."

As Scarlet followed them down the hallway, she couldn't bring herself to complain about the sugar coma she was sure Daisy would fall into tonight. Because her heart was too full. Aside from herself, she'd never, *ever* seen Daisy this comfortable with anyone.

She knew she shouldn't be looking deeper into it.

Shouldn't be imagining this scenario turning into reality, the three of them forming a little family . . .

But as stupid as it was, as impossible as it was, as setting-herself-up-for-disappointment as it was . . . she couldn't stop daydreaming about a future with Matt Alvarez.

CHAPTER THIRTEEN

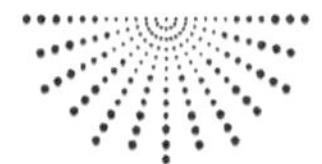

As usual, Matt woke at five. No noises came from the guest room that Scarlet and Daisy shared, so he changed into his running clothes and slipped out of the house. He planned on a short run, but at five miles, his mind was still turning, so he picked up the pace and kept going. After another five, he called it quits. A half-mile cool-down walk and multiple rounds of burpees, planks, and sit-ups later, his thoughts had finally settled enough for him to face the day—a Sunday with Scarlet and Daisy.

Not that the pint-sized woman and her adorable kid were wreaking havoc on his mind or anything.

Damn. He wasn't about to start lying to himself again. Both ladies made him nervous—in totally different ways, of course. Scarlet because . . . well, because she was funny and beautiful and strong and so damn off-limits. And Daisy because she had him completely wrapped around her little finger. She was beyond precious, and he didn't know the first thing about kids.

Yeah, he could hang with Poppy's boys but they were teenagers, technically adults, so it wasn't the same. He'd never understood the baby-talk thing, so he spoke to Daisy like he would anyone else—with fewer curse words, of course—but he wasn't sure that was what he was supposed to do.

But Matt was resolved to go with the flow. He didn't know what the fuck he was doing with either of them, so he would just take everything as it came. He would be a good friend to Scarlet. Get to know her better and help her in any way that he could.

But he would have to be careful. Because the last thing he wanted was to put pressure on her. He knew he'd initially come across as an asshole with all his grunted replies, and he hoped to make up for that. However, he didn't want her to think she *had* to be his friend because he was helping her out.

Quietly letting himself into the house, Matt checked his watch. It was almost seven. He would make his customary protein shake, shower, and whip up some breakfast for his houseguests. After last night's junk food fest, maybe he'd make some eggs and bacon to combat all the sugar.

Wiping his brow with the T-shirt he'd taken off at mile seven, he turned the corner to the great room and kitchen and stopped dead in his tracks. The sight before him made his breath catch, his chest clench tight.

"Hi!" Scarlet said, a pink flush brightening her cheeks. She stood at the island, dressed in loose rainbow pajama pants with a blue tank top. Her long dark hair was piled atop her head in a bun. "I hope you don't mind," she said, indicating the items she had laid out in front of her. "I saw you working out in the front yard and thought that maybe you'd like eggs, bacon, and some toast for breakfast?"

Damn, she was gorgeous. *Shit. Focus, Alvarez!*

"That sounds perfect, thank you. I was just thinking the exact same thing, actually." He glanced at the table. Daisy sat there, still in her unicorn sleep dress, with crayons and paper spread out in front of her. A cartoon played on the great room television—featuring some blue Australian-sounding dog—but she paid no attention to it. Instead, she stared at him with twinkling eyes. "Good morning, Otter Pop."

"Good morning, Mr. Matty. Did you know someone drawed all over your arms and top?" she asked, patting her chest.

"What?" he exclaimed, rotating his arms in front of him.

She giggled, as he'd intended. "Mr. Matty, you're silly."

"My friend Slash is a tattoo artist, and he drew all these on me. He even drew on my back, too." He grinned, twisting so she could see the ink that ran across the top of his back up to his neck. When he faced her again, he asked, "What are you up to?"

"I'm drawing you another picture for your figyator."

"Well, I can't wait to see what you come up with." He shot her a wink, then looked at Scarlet. "If you don't mind, I need to hop in the shower. I'll be quick."

"No problem. I'll get the bacon going, so take your time."

"Five minutes. And thanks, Scar," he said, throat growing thick with emotion.

Rein it in, Alvarez. Right. Easier said than done, though. Because damn, this moment—Scarlet and Daisy relaxing in his kitchen, completely at home—hit him square in the fucking chest. He didn't want to admit it. Wasn't comfortable acknowledging it . . . but they had him itching for something he had no business wanting.

Friends, dammit. You need to be her friend.

Scarlet tried with all her might to concentrate on the bacon. Admittedly, she was doing a shit job, because the splatter had already gotten her twice. Her mind would *not* stay on the task at hand. Instead, it kept filling with visions of Matt.

Shirtless.

Thick, corded muscles glistening with sweat.

His ridiculous eight-pack tapering down to a delicious *V*.

And holy shit . . . the tattoos.

She'd known about the ink on his forearms, but damn, the rest of it was downright mouthwatering. The all-black designs looked like some sort of tribal art. One tattoo covered his entire left pec, continuing down his left arm and across his back. And oh, what a freaking glorious back it was—

Another searing splatter of grease landed on her arm. *Ah! Focus, Scarlet!*

Transferring the cooked bacon to a paper-toweled plate, Scarlet carefully added more to the frying pan. A fresh wave of the comforting bacon-y aroma filled the kitchen as the meat sizzled. She got a pot of coffee going, and when it started percolating, she wanted to pat herself on the back for not spilling the grounds everywhere. Because yes, she was still that distracted.

She spun back to the stove and—

Slammed into a large, hard body.

"Whoa, there," Matt said, hands clamping down on her waist to steady her.

She sucked in a breath. Wrong move. His woodsy, soapy scent filled her nose, and every nerve in her body became a live wire. Good god, this man . . .

He cleared his throat and stepped back. She immediately missed the feel of his strong hands at her waist. God, what it would be like to have his hands all over—

Slow your damn roll, girlfriend!

The bacon popped, and she used the excuse to step

around him. "Sorry," she murmured. She knew her face was flushed, so she busied herself with breakfast.

"Can I help?" he asked, making her jump.

When had he moved to stand beside her?

Ohmygod. Get. It. Together!

Plating the last of the bacon, she grabbed the carton of eggs. Basically, looking anywhere but at him. "Um, can you help Daisy clear the table?"

"You got it." Her pulse picked up when he gently squeezed her shoulders. "Thanks again for breakfast."

Scarlet cracked half a dozen eggs into the pan and scrambled them. Lowering the heat, she popped four slices of sourdough into the fancy toaster.

Matt had changed into a plain black T-shirt and dark jeans, and while she returned to stirring the eggs, she couldn't help but appreciate how the simple shirt accentuated his chest. How the jeans showed off his mighty fine—

The toaster popped. *Holy crap, girl. Stop ogling the man!*

With a shake of her head, she cut the toast into triangles and placed them on a plate. Turning off the stove, she scooped the eggs into a large bowl. She brought both to the table and smiled. Matt had apparently shown Daisy how to fold the paper napkins into rectangles, and he was placing their forks atop them.

Scarlet set the food in the center of the table and shot Matt a nervous grin. "Now, who's hungry?" Her smile turned genuine when her daughter's hand shot into the air.

"Me!" Daisy scowled at Matt. "Mr. Matty, raise your hand."

He dutifully complied, giving Daisy a sheepish smile and a murmured, "Sorry, Otter Pop."

Damn, he was cute.

CHAPTER FOURTEEN

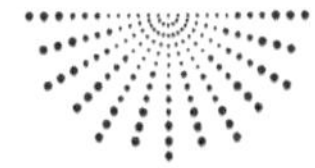

Scarlet's anxiety settled as they enjoyed a relaxing breakfast. It helped that Matt and Daisy carried the conversation, discussing various Disney movies and their favorite playground equipment. Swings for Daisy and slides for Matt. Once they finished eating and loaded the dishes into the dishwasher, Matt showed her his home office and the Department of Licensing website where she could replace her driver's license.

When it appeared that he planned to stay in the office with her, she asked him to check on Daisy. To see if she wanted to color instead of watch a movie. A ridiculous request, since they'd *just* set her up with her stuffies and one of her favorite movies, *Monsters, Inc.* Which they'd watched the night before. By the wary look Matt gave her, she knew he wasn't quite buying what she was trying to sell. However, he gave her privacy.

When Scarlet had decided to move to Hudson Island, she hadn't been sure of the protocol, so she'd contacted her former handler to find out what the steps were. Deputy Marshal Bateman—or Bates, as he'd preferred—had simply told her to call him after finding a place to live. He'd said he would handle everything for her. So she had, and within a week of moving, she'd received a package from Bates with her new Washington State driver's license and a stack of information about the state-provided discount healthcare program he'd signed her and Daisy up for. However, now that her driver's license was missing, she—again—wasn't sure of the protocol.

As she typed her information into the online portal, her fingers shook. She knew her documents were legit—they were from the US Marshals Service, after all—but what if there was a glitch? What if the system didn't recognize her social security number? The last thing she wanted was to contact Bates again. Though she remained eternally thankful for all his help, she needed to put that entire chapter of her life behind her.

Progressing through the online form, she held her breath every time she clicked Next, convinced some sort of alarm would sound. The last screen was a payment portal. She entered her banking information and sagged into the office chair when her confirmation number and temporary license appeared on the monitor. While the document printed, she scrubbed her hands over her face. She'd come a long way since arriving on Hudson Island. But these last few minutes? Yeah, they'd proven she still had a long way to go before she could call her past buried.

Scarlet snagged her temporary license off the printer and went in search of Matt and Daisy. She found them on the couch with Mr. Slothy, Baby Unicorn, and two other stuffies between them. Sully and Mike Wazowski cracked jokes on the television.

Catching Matt's gaze, she held up the paper. "Got it. A new license should be arriving in seven to ten business days.

Do you mind swinging me by my place so I can pick up my car?"

"Not a problem." He reached over and patted Daisy on the leg. "Let's pause the movie, okay?" Daisy frowned, so he rushed on, "You need to change out of your pajamas because we're going to go visit the cats. How does that sound?"

"Yay!" Daisy cried, scrambling off the couch and bolting down the hallway.

Scarlet chuckled. "Good save."

"I don't know how you do it, Scar. Once that bottom lip of hers pops out, I just can't . . ." He shook his head as he rose from the couch and moved to stand beside her. "Hope you don't mind, but it looks like we're going to check on the cats before we head to your place."

"I figured," she said with a laugh. Then she patted his bicep and went to follow her daughter. "But you've got to be strong, Matt," she said over her shoulder. "Don't give in to the pouty lip."

"Sorry, Scar." He grimaced. "I don't think I can."

They'd only been at Poppy and Cade's for twenty minutes when Scarlet's phone rang. Answering, it was Mr. Wayland. He'd just returned to town and was at her apartment. After agreeing to meet with him and disconnecting the call, she eyed her daughter who was lying on the living room floor. Ripley was sprawled on Daisy's chest, and Bishop was tucked in the crook of her good arm, purring loudly. And Matt was taking a picture of the blissed-out trio.

Battling a cringe, Scarlet called out, "Daisy, we have to go. I have to meet Mr. Wayland, so I need you to say goodbye to the cats."

"But, Mama," she whined as she sat up, her expression

crestfallen. "I didn't get to play very long with the kitty cats. They still miss me."

By the way the cats circled Daisy, nudging her for attention, her daughter wasn't wrong. "Sorry, sweetie. We'll stay longer tomorrow. I promise. But we do have to get going."

The second her daughter's lower lip began to tremble, Matt made a strangled noise.

Glancing at him, Scarlet had to bite her cheek to keep from laughing.

"Hey, Otter Pop. How about I take you to the playground while your mom has her meeting?"

Daisy's head shot up, her eyes wide. Before Scarlet could blink, Daisy wiped her tears on her good forearm, shouted a hurried goodbye to the cats, grabbed Mr. Slothy off the couch, and ran to the front door.

"Uh . . ." Matt's forehead scrunched. "What just happened?"

She chuckled and grabbed her purse. Ensuring the lights were turned off, she motioned for him to follow. "The playground is one of Daisy's most favorite places."

As they neared the front door, Matt stopped dead in his tracks, mouth agape. "She's waiting by my truck?"

Scarlet snickered. Sure enough, her daughter was standing in front of Matt's passenger door. With a giant smile, Daisy hopped from foot to foot as she clutched Mr. Slothy to her chest. "Like I said, the playground is her favorite. Pretty sure she'd already be in the truck, but she's too short to reach the door handle."

"Holy shit, she's so fucking cute," he murmured, before ushering Scarlet outside. "Let's go, slowpoke, we can't keep her waiting, can we?"

Scarlet laughed. Yup, the man was definitely a sucker for Daisy's pouty lip.

The drive downtown was quick, and now they stood in

front of Hudson Island Antiques. Well, technically, they stood in front of the boarded-up door next to Hudson Island Antiques that led to her second-story apartment, but whatever.

"Are you sure you don't mind?" she asked Matt.

He peered down at Daisy, then crouched so he was at her eye level. Scarlet's heart pinged at the small gesture.

"What do you say, Otter Pop? You sure that you and Mr. Slothy want to go to the playground with me while your mom meets with Mr. Wayland?"

Daisy nodded in excitement, practically bouncing in her sneakers.

Thank you, Scarlet mouthed to Matt before eyeing her daughter. "Same rules, miss. You need to listen to Mr. Matt, *and* you have to hold Mr. Matt's hand on the way to the playground. Okay?"

"Yes, Mama," Daisy said, still nodding. She turned to Matt, and with Mr. Slothy clutched tight in her good hand, held up both arms.

It was on the tip of Scarlet's tongue to remind her daughter that she could walk, that Matt, in fact, was not her personal carrier. But her words died when he immediately scooped Daisy up.

"I have my cell," he said, settling Daisy on his hip. "Text me when you're about to wrap up, and we can meet you back here."

"Oh, that's okay. I can just meet you two at the playground when I'm done."

He shook his head. "Depending on how long it's going to take to fix your place, you may need to pack more stuff for you and Daisy. I don't want you to have to lug everything to your car by yourself."

She cleared her throat, smothering a chuckle. "My car is just down the stairs from my apartment, Matt."

"I know you're a perfectly capable person, Scarlet, but I'd still like to help. Humor me. Please."

The chuckle won out, and she nodded. "I'll text you. Daisy can pick out a few more things to bring over, too. And remind me to pack her headphones."

"Headphones?"

"They're pink with sparkles," Daisy chimed in. "They have a unicorn horn on it!"

"Wow," Matt said, awe in his voice. "That's the fanciest headphones I've ever heard of."

"They sure are." Scarlet grinned. "But trust me, Matt, you're not going to want to listen to *Bluey* for the next however many days we're with you."

His brow furrowed. "That's the blue Australian dog cartoon?"

"I love Bluey," Daisy said. "She's so funny, but my favorite is Coco. She's pink and Bluey's friend."

"Okay, sweet girl," Scarlet said, stepping toward them. "I'm going to meet Mr. Wayland. You be good for Mr. Matt and be careful with your arm, okay?" She popped onto her tiptoes and kissed Daisy's cheek. A glance up had her heart thudding in her chest.

Matt was *right* there. She'd never noticed how his brown eyes, the color of dark chocolate, were framed by the thickest and fullest lashes. She was close enough to catch his woodsy, soapy scent again, and it did something to her insides. His jaw clenched at her attention, but she couldn't tear her gaze away. For a split second, she wondered what it would be like to nibble on that spot . . .

Holy shit, the man is potent.

Daisy tucked her head into Matt's shoulder, and Scarlet's attraction only increased. Her ovaries were threatening to explode at any moment.

Dropping down from her tiptoes, her face heated, and she

cleared her throat. "Thanks again, Matt. I'll text you when we're wrapping up." She ran a hand over her daughter's casted arm. "Have fun and be good, sweet girl."

"Bye, Mama."

She watched them stroll down the sidewalk, chest squeezing tight.

Matt Alvarez was completely unexpected. Who knew that behind the growly one-word answers was this wonderful man? One who lit up all her senses and grew more appealing by the second?

A loud creak had her spinning toward the door, which she'd thought was boarded up.

"Scarlet, perfect timing," Mr. Wayland said, stepping onto the sidewalk. Somewhere in his sixties, he was a multi-generation Hudson Island local and one of the kindest people she'd met. His troubled expression had her frowning.

"I'm so sorry about what happened, Mr. Wayland," she said. "I hope the damage to the apartments wasn't too extensive."

"Don't be ridiculous. *I'm* the one who's sorry." He awkwardly patted her shoulder.

Scarlet suppressed a smile. Mr. Wayland was definitely one of those this-is-*my*-personal-space-and-that-is-*your*-personal-space kinds of people, so his gesture was beyond sweet.

"I'm sorry that happened to you, and I'm just so thankful you and little Daisy weren't hurt."

"Thanks, Mr. Wayland. Me too."

They went upstairs and entered her apartment. "I don't know if you've ever met my son, Jim?"

She shook her head.

"Well, you just missed him. He's a contractor over on Whidbey Island. He said he can get the front doors to your apartment and the rental changed out today and the main door downstairs by this Friday. Unfortunately, he checked around at multiple places, and your bedroom slider, since it's not a standard size, is on backorder. Jim says the delivery is about two to three weeks out, but once it comes in, he can install it immediately."

Two to three weeks? She closed her eyes in defeat. She'd known the repairs would take time, but she hadn't expected them to take *that* long.

"I'm so sorry, Scarlet."

Opening her eyes, she shrugged. "It is what it is, Mr. Wayland."

He sighed. "In the meantime, why don't you pack up? While we're waiting for the new slider, I'd like to get a professional cleaner in here. At no cost to you, of course."

"Oh, that's okay. That's not necessary."

"I insist, Scarlet. There's so much glass in your room, and after the door installations, there will be even more debris. Pack up what you and Daisy need, and I'll take care of the rest. You do have a place to stay, right?"

"We're staying with Matt Alvarez." But holy crap, would it be okay for them to stay with him for two to three *weeks*?

"Good, good." He nodded. "Former detective, and I hear he's just joined Hudson Security. Solid guy."

Her eyebrows lifted, causing Mr. Wayland to smile. "News travels fast around here. Besides, you know Martha's my aunt, right?"

Scarlet chuckled. "Enough said."

CHAPTER FIFTEEN

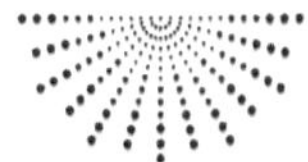

The playground was nearly empty, which surprised Matt since it was a sunny Sunday morning. Only two other kids were playing—two boys on the large climbing structure, who looked to be a few years older than Daisy. They were screaming their damn heads off while their mother stared at her phone, completely ignoring them.

Glaring at the boys behind his sunglasses, Matt carried Daisy to the opposite end of the play area. "Do you want to swing?"

"Yes!" she squealed.

He set her down and helped her climb onto the swing. "Here," he said, taking Mr. Slothy from her and shoving half the stuffed animal in his back pocket. "You have to hold on really tight with your good hand, okay?"

He looped her casted right arm around the chain so it was snug in the crook of her elbow. Then he frowned. Shit. This had *bad idea* written all over it.

With a gentle push, he set the swing in motion. Daisy wobbled and let out a little yelp, and he swore his damn heart stopped. He scooped her out of the swing and had her back on his hip in under a second.

"Sorry, Otter Pop." He ran a hand over her hair as she clung to him. "Swings aren't a good idea when you have your arm in a cast, huh?"

"I almost falled down," she whispered, eyes wide.

He met her bright-blue gaze. "I won't let you fall."

"Promise?"

The center of his chest ached, and he rubbed his fist against it. Damn, this kid . . . "Do you know what a pinky promise is?"

She shook her head.

"Do this," he said, holding out his pinky.

She imitated him with her left hand.

"Now, a pinky promise is one of the most important promises. Ever." He hadn't thought her eyes could grow any wider, but they did. Biting back a smile, he hooked his much larger pinky with hers. "I promise, Otter Pop, that I won't ever let you fall. Not on my watch. Now we shake."

Daisy giggled as they shook pinkies. "Pinky promises are funny, Mr. Matty."

"They are, but they're also a pretty big deal. And you know what? You can just call me Matt from now on. You don't need to call me mister."

"Okay, Matty."

He couldn't help his grin. *Matty it is.*

Pulling Mr. Slothy from his back pocket, he gestured to the playhouse behind the swings. Given the shorter slide and the structure's lower height, it seemed geared toward smaller kids. "Want to take Mr. Slothy and play over there?"

She nodded, and he handed the stuffy over as he placed her on her feet.

At the playhouse, he stood to the side of the structure. His position provided a visual on Daisy no matter which part she played on. "I'll be right here, okay?"

Waving, she took off to explore the playhouse with Mr. Slothy.

"Uh, hey. What's going on, dude?"

Matt glanced to his right and saw Four walking toward him. He lifted his chin in greeting. "How's it going, Four?" He shifted to face his friend, but he still had Daisy in his sights. "Wait, what the hell are you doing here?"

Four smirked. "I'd like to ask you the same thing. I mean, there I was, driving down the street and minding my own damn business, when I spotted you. At the *playground*. I'll ask again, dude. What's going on?"

Matt motioned toward the playhouse.

Four's eyes narrowed. "Is that Scarlet's daughter?"

"Yup."

"Ahh. Rumor has it they're staying with you. I didn't quite believe it, though."

Matt shrugged. The gossip train in this town was often scary accurate.

Four scanned the playground, then dropped his voice. "I heard about the break-in at Scarlet's. Are they doing okay?"

"I think it shook Scar more than she's letting on, but she's hanging in there. I don't know if she's talked much with Daisy about what happened, but the kid hasn't brought it up. Thankfully, neither of them was hurt." He ground his molars together as a surge of anger washed over him. "They had to hide out on her fucking balcony."

Four cursed under his breath. "Man, that's totally fucked up."

"Tell me about it." He had seen the outdoor chair they'd hidden behind. It was fucking tiny. God, he couldn't imagine what would have happened if the sirens hadn't scared off that asshole . . .

"Where's Scarlet?" Four asked, looking around the play area.

"She's meeting with Wayland at her place. Figured while Scar was doing that, I'd take the little Otter Pop over here and let her burn off some energy."

"'Otter Pop'?" Four laughed, elbowing him in the side. The fucker.

"What? The kid loves Otter Pops." Matt knew his comeback was lame. But whatever. It was the truth. The nickname fit.

"Sure, bud." Four snorted. "You keep telling yourself that."

It was on the tip of his tongue to tell his friend to fuck off—nicely, of course—but Daisy came running up. "Matty, I gotta go potty."

He froze. "Uhhh . . ." His gaze swung to Four. Who burst into laughter.

"Don't look at me, dude," Four said, holding his hands up. "I know less about kids than you."

Fuck.

Daisy began hopping from foot to foot, her cute little face scrunched up. "I gotta go bad."

"All right, let's go," he said, scooping her up and scanning the nearby buildings. His eyes landed on Ray's Diner. "Oh, thank fu—"

He slammed his mouth shut. *Shit, that was close.*

Taking her stuffed animal from her hands, he tossed it to his friend. "Four will watch Mr. Slothy while we get you to the bathroom," he said, striding toward the diner with Four on his heels—laughing like a damn hyena.

Matt burst through the diner's front door, knowing he looked like a crazy person. "Martha!" He hustled to the older woman. "Daisy has to go to the bathroom. Bad. Can you please take her?"

Setting a dish towel down on an empty table, Martha reached for Daisy.

The little girl shook her head and burrowed into his chest. "No, Matty. You!"

Fuck. He patted her back. "Sorry, Otter Pop, but I'm not allowed to go into the bathroom with you." Nor did he think it was appropriate. As much as he adored the kid, no way was he helping her in the bathroom without explicit permission *and* instruction from Scarlet.

Daisy's lower lip popped out, and panic rushed through him. *Shit.* "I'm not a lady, sweet girl. I'm not allowed to go into the ladies' room."

"But I'm not a lady. I'm just a little girl," Daisy whined.

He shook his head and tapped her nose. "No, you're a little lady. Now please go with Martha."

Heaving out a giant sigh, Daisy turned in his arms and reached for the older woman.

"We'll be right back," Martha said in a singsong voice.

Matt grimaced at the shit-eating grin she flashed him on her way to the bathroom.

"Don't look now," Four murmured, elbowing him in the side. "Gossip train. Ten o'clock."

Matt peeked over his friend's shoulder and bit back a groan. Mrs. Abbot, Mrs. Yoshida, and Mrs. Green—the head honchos of Hudson Island gossip—sat together at a table with their attention glued to him. They all had matching knowing smiles. *Damn.*

Four held out Daisy's stuffy. "Mr. *Slothy*? Creative."

The fuck? Matt's hackles rose, and he snatched the stuffed animal from Four. "Don't be a dick, man. Daisy's *four*, and the name's fucking cute."

There were three seconds of absolute silence before Four howled and the women at the nearby table tittered in delight.

"Shit, that was too fucking easy," Four said, slapping him on the back. He glanced at the women. "You ladies catch all that?"

"We sure did," Mrs. Yoshida said.

"Oh yes, we did," Mrs. Abbot chimed in.

Matt swore they had hearts in their damn eyes. *Christ.*

"Little ears are coming back," Mrs. Green warned, nodding toward Martha and Daisy. "Watch those mouths of yours, boys."

"Yes, ma'am," Four said, suppressing a smirk.

"Yes, ma'am," Matt echoed.

"Matty, I went potty and washed my hands," Daisy said, standing in front of him. She raised her arms, and he picked her up.

"Feel better?" he asked, handing her Mr. Slothy.

She nodded, then placed her head on his shoulder. "Matty, I'm hungry."

He glanced at his watch and frowned. "We just had breakfast not too long ago."

"I'm hungry."

Before he could respond, his phone buzzed.

SCARLET

We're just about done here. Probably another ten minutes or so.

He tapped her name and held his phone to his ear. No way could he text her back while he was carrying Daisy.

"Um, hello?" He could hear the surprise in Scarlet's voice. Apparently, she wasn't a phone talker.

"Hey, Scar. Daisy and I are at Ray's. Daisy's hungry—"

"I want Miss Martha's nuggets, Mama."

Scarlet chuckled, obviously hearing her daughter. "Why don't you guys stay put, and I'll meet you there. I'm almost done here."

"Daisy and I can come get you at your place, and then we can all come back here for lunch."

"Matt, you know the diner's, like, two blocks away, right? Maybe two and a half, if you're gonna get technical."

Matt looked around and noticed all eyes staring at him. Everyone was listening to their conversation. He stepped away from the group. "I do. But—"

"Oh, look at that," Scarlet interrupted. "Mr. Wayland said he's heading to the diner, too, so I'll just walk over with him. When we're done eating, we can come back here and load up my car. How does that sound, Mr. Overprotective One?"

He pressed his lips together and fought a smile. Smart-ass. "Do you promise he's walking with you?"

"Yes, I promise, Matt." She chuckled, and he was pretty damn sure she'd just rolled her eyes.

"Okay, then. See you soon." Hanging up the phone, he sighed. Four and the ladies were beaming.

What was that saying . . . ? *If you can't beat them, join them?* Yeaaah.

He pointed at the table next to the ladies. "Martha, can we sit there?" He met Four's gaze. "You eating with us?"

Four barked out a laugh. "Nah, man. I've got to get to the restaurant. But it has been a fucking pleasure witnessing these lovely Hudson Island mavens in action."

"Ahem, young man," Mrs. Green said, glaring daggers at Four.

He cringed. "Sorry."

Mrs. Yoshida tsked. "It's not us you need to worry about."

"That was a very bad word," Four said, looking at Daisy. "You shouldn't say it, sweetie."

"What word?"

"The f-word I just—"

Mrs. Abbot smacked him on the head.

"I was only joking," Four said with a laugh, rubbing the spot she'd hit. "I wasn't actually going to say it."

"What's an f-word?" Daisy asked, head still on Matt's shoulder.

Covering Daisy's exposed ear with his hand, Matt mouthed *fuck you* to his friend, who simply grinned back at him. "Don't worry about it, Otter Pop. Four was just leaving."

CHAPTER SIXTEEN

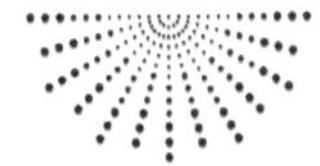

Matt pulled into an open space along the street, put his truck in Park, and cut the engine. A glance at the dash showed he was twenty minutes early. Gavin was meeting with Quinn this morning to go over a couple of their upcoming cases, and he'd asked Matt to sit in.

The two men had been friends long before Matt's arrival in town, and Gavin tried to keep Quinn in the loop on cases that directly involved Hudson Island. Gavin claimed it was out of professional courtesy. Matt figured the true motivation was staying on the sheriff's good side in case Hudson Security stirred up shit for the island.

Matt glanced down the street, and when his gaze landed on Ray's Diner, he smiled, thoughts drifting to the past weekend. It had been . . . different. That was for damn sure.

He rarely had people over to his place, and when he did, it was either Cade, Four, or his brother. He'd been enjoying his solitude this past year—he winced. *Enjoying* was a bit of a stretch. Regardless, he'd grown accustomed to his house being quiet. If he wanted noise, he went to the gym or Monty's Tavern.

However, with Scarlet and Daisy staying over, it had been anything but quiet. Not that they were obnoxiously loud or anything. They just went about their lives, filling his home with the sounds of children's television shows, padding feet, and joyful laughter. It was a good kind of different.

The junk food–fueled movie night on Saturday had been great. He couldn't remember the last time he'd indulged like that. Definitely not any time this past year, and not even when he'd been married. High school maybe?

Similarly, he couldn't remember the last time he'd stepped foot on a playground. But yesterday had been a good time. He'd enjoyed spending the morning with Daisy. And part of him had taken pride in the fact that she wasn't shy with him—but she was with Four. And Mrs. Abbot, Mrs. Yoshida, and Mrs. Green. The only other person Daisy had interacted with at the diner was Martha, but the woman was practically her grandmother. Or was it great-grandmother? Didn't matter. What *did* matter was that Daisy felt safe with him. It filled his damn heart.

While eating lunch at Ray's, Scarlet had updated everyone on the break-in and the upcoming repairs to her apartment. When she'd mentioned that the final repairs were still two to three weeks out, Matt had told her that she and Daisy were welcome to stay as long as they needed. She'd worried aloud about them being an imposition, but he'd simply stated that they weren't. That there was more than enough space for them.

For the rest of their meal, Matt had done his best to ignore the stares and sly grins sent his way by the gossip train ladies.

If he were being completely honest with himself, he would admit he'd just had the best weekend in . . . Shit, he didn't even know. But a fucking long time. Being with

Scarlet and Daisy was so relaxing, so normal, so fucking comfortable . . . like it's what they had always done.

It worried him, though. Because he really liked having them in his home, in his space, and it was getting harder and harder to imagine them leaving.

This morning, when they'd gotten ready for work? Yeah, they'd bumped into each other a couple of times in the kitchen—he'd gone for the drawer to get a spoon while she'd reached into a cabinet for a glass—but it had been nice. And he certainly hadn't minded grabbing on to her slim waist to balance her. Not one bit.

Then, on their way out the door, when Scarlet had shot him that shy smile and Daisy had called out, "Bye, Matty!" his heart had just about stopped.

Yeah, he was in trouble.

Matt blew out a noisy breath and glanced at the clock on the dash again. Still fifteen minutes until his meeting with Gavin and Quinn. Enough time to call someone and hash this out, but . . . that wasn't what he did. For better or worse, he'd never been one to talk about his feelings and shit. Even with his therapist, he usually relayed the bare minimum.

No, he preferred to hit the gym and pound on a heavy bag instead. Or spar with some guy who wanted to take his head off. It wasn't exactly the healthiest way to handle his feelings —or *not* handle his feelings—but it's what he knew.

However, there was one person he knew he could always count on. Granted, he could count on Cade, too. But there truly was only *one* person who Matt swore could read his damn thoughts.

His phone rang, and he answered without looking at the display. It wasn't necessary. "It seems our twin-telepathy shit is alive and well."

"How ya doing, big brother?"

Matt chuckled. As in shape as he was—and he was in

damn good shape—he still didn't hold a candle to his "little" brother. They were identical twins, and Matt was eight minutes the elder, but Jake was definitely the bigger guy. "I'm doing okay. You?"

"Cut the shit, bro. What's going on?"

He grinned. Yup, just like Jake to get to the point. "I've got fifteen minutes to kill before I need to head into a meeting, and I'm sitting in my damn truck thinking about the best fucking weekend I've had in forever."

Jake whistled long and low. "I'm intrigued. Spill."

Letting out a breath, he told his brother about Scarlet and Daisy. About being tongue-tied. About the break-in. About their breakfasts and visiting the cats and watching movies with M&M popcorn and playing at the playground. He ended with their very public lunch at the diner, and when he finished speaking, Jake remained quiet.

"Shit," Matt groaned. "I bored you to fucking death, didn't I?"

"Don't be stupid. It's just I . . ."

His eyes narrowed at the hesitancy in his brother's voice. "You what?"

"You just sound . . . happy." Jake cleared his throat. "I haven't heard you sound like this in a really long fucking time, bro. You know I'm the sappier of the two of us, so you gotta give me a minute." It was his brother's turn to blow out a breath. "Carm and I have been so damn worried about you. You don't understand what a relief it is to hear some excitement in your voice."

Matt closed his eyes. He knew he'd been struggling this past year. Getting shot, being away from the force, and then the clusterfuck of his divorce . . . Life had been rough. He just hadn't realized how much his misery had affected those around him. His throat grew tight. "I'm sorry, little brother. I didn't know that—"

"No, Matt. There's nothing for you to apologize for. I'm just so damn thrilled to hear you happy. So what's the problem?"

His forehead scrunched. "Why do you think there's a problem?"

"Our twin-telepathy shit, remember? So, again, what's the problem?"

"Scarlet," he said in a growl.

"The same Scarlet whose name sounds like fucking rainbows shooting out of your mouth when you talk about her? *That* Scarlet?"

He chuckled. He couldn't help it. "Yes, asshole, that Scarlet."

"Aaand?"

"And she's young. A lot younger than me."

"Holy shit, Matt. Is she legal?"

He scoffed. "Fuck you, dude. Of course she's legal." Barely. *Fuck!*

"How old is she? And how old's her daughter?"

"She's twenty-three. Daisy's four."

"Well . . ." Matt could practically hear Jake's grimace. "I mean, it could be worse. Twenty-three is young, but she could be, like, nineteen."

Matt sighed and dropped his head against the headrest. "Not helping, man."

Jake laughed. "Dude, I'm just fucking with you. Look, you and I both know that age does *not* determine maturity. It doesn't determine how kind someone is or whether you're compatible with them. She's an adult. You're an adult. Period. Are you attracted to her?"

"Yeah." *Attracted* was an inadequate word for how drawn he felt to her. She was fucking beautiful, but truthfully, it wasn't just her looks that pulled him in. She was so much more than her appearance . . .

"Okay, then. So she's young. But you know what, big bro? I like how you sound when you talk about her. *That* is what matters to me."

That's what was beginning to matter to him, too. Still . . . "She has her whole damn life in front of her, Jake. Why the hell would she want to saddle herself with a fucking forty-year-old divorced guy?"

Jake scoffed. "Because you're all washed-up and decrepit?"

He rolled his eyes. "You know what I mean."

"I take it nothing has happened between the two of you yet?"

Matt scowled. "I invited her and Daisy to stay with me so they have a safe place to live while their apartment is getting repaired. *Not* to take advantage of Scarlet. I'm not a *complete* asshole, Jake."

"You're right. You're just a little bit of an asshole. Kidding. Kinda." Jake chuckled. "So, have you at least asked her out, then?"

Matt said nothing.

His brother heaved out a sigh. A sigh Matt was very familiar with. It meant *you're a complete moron.* "You know what one of the most important things I've learned from Carmen is?"

"She's way smarter than you, so it could be any number of things."

Jake snorted. "You're not wrong. But the most important thing I've learned is that I don't know shit."

"I could have told you that."

Jake continued as if Matt hadn't spoken, "Particularly about anything having to do with women. So, my advice is to talk to Scarlet. Be a fucking adult and ask her if she'd be interested in going on a date with you."

Matt opened his mouth to reply, but nothing came out.

Damn. His brother's advice was so much easier said than done.

"Look, man, I don't know what went down with you and Krista . . . but I have my theories."

Matt blocked out the hurt and bitterness that swelled at the mention of his ex-wife's name. "Oh yeah?"

"Yeah. But guess what? Not every woman is like Krista. And from what you've told me about Scarlet, she's nice. She's a good person, right?"

"She is." He had no doubts about that.

"So be honest with her."

Matt ran a hand over his jaw. Again, so simple. Yet . . . not. "Thanks, little bro."

"Always. By the way, Carmen and I are heading to the island either next weekend or the one after. We're waiting for a couple calendar things to set before deciding. Carm wants to stay at the resort, so you don't have to worry about us being in your hair."

His lips quirked. "It's *your* house, dude."

"Whatever. But I want to meet Scarlet and Daisy. Make it happen, okay?"

"What exactly am I making happen?" Matt asked, arching an eyebrow even though his brother couldn't see it.

Jake snickered. "At this point? Anything. This overanalyzing bullshit you're doing is stupid. So stop it and man the fuck up. Oh, and on a random full-transparency kind of note, I'm setting up a meeting with Gavin when I'm in town. He's interested in these new cameras I came up with."

Matt grinned. His brother—bless him—was a bona fide nerd. A workaholic, brilliant-in-all-things-tech nerd, to be exact. The man ran a gaming empire, was a co-owner of a wildly successful Irish pub in Seattle, and in his limited downtime, he loved to tinker with shit and had designed an entire line of miniscule superspy-type cameras. Jake was fucking awesome.

"Speak of the devil," Matt said as he saw Gavin walking down the sidewalk. "I have a meeting with the guy now, so I gotta go."

"Cool. I'll catch you later, bro."

"Hey!" he called out before Jake could hang up. "Thanks for checking in, man. I didn't realize how much I needed to talk to you today. Give Carm my love."

"Will do. Love ya, bro."

Climbing out of his truck, a sense of calm, of rightness, settled over him. He was so damn glad he'd spoken with his brother. Jake had a way of putting things into perspective, and he loved the guy more than words could express.

He pocketed his phone and walked across the street to where Gavin waited for him. Greeting the man with a chin lift, he fell in stride as they turned the corner toward the sheriff's department.

"How was your weekend?" Gavin asked. "Are Scarlet and Daisy doing—" He held up a hand as he brought his ringing phone to his ear. After answering, the troubled look on his face had Matt's gut tightening. "Okay. We'll be right there."

Gavin hung up, then spun around and headed in the direction from which they'd come. Matt kept up, unease building with each hurried step.

"That was Martha," Gavin said, voice low. "She says something's going on at the diner and we need to come in and act like regular customers."

Matt's stomach dropped. Shit. Scarlet was working this morning . . .

Picking up their pace, they walked through the front door of Ray's Diner in less than a minute.

"Well, hello, you two," Martha called out, waving them

over to where she stood on the opposite side of the diner. "I have your usual table ready for you."

The hairs on the back of Matt's neck rose. They didn't have a usual table. But he kept his expression neutral and followed Gavin to the booth along the far window.

Martha seated them with a tight smile. "Be right back with your usuals, boys."

She returned moments later, placing a large omelet in front of Matt and a breakfast-sandwich-and-hash-brown combo in front of Gavin. Neither were their usuals. The older woman remained standing at the end of their booth, and Matt studied her.

Martha was beautifully round. Her dark-brown eyes always twinkled with mischief, and her heart-shaped face was usually filled with laugh lines. But not today. Today, tension emanated from her frame, and deep, worried grooves cut the planes of her face.

She caught Matt's gaze, and her eyes widened the smallest amount as they darted to the man seated at the table behind her. "Enjoy your food now. I'll be back to check on you soon."

"Thank you, Martha," Matt said, nodding.

"You're very welcome." She turned and moved on to the man she'd indicated.

After years as a detective, it had become second nature for Matt to memorize the details of his surroundings. As such, he'd noted all the patrons upon entering the diner. But nothing special had stood out about the man Martha now served.

White male. Mid-thirties to late-forties. Blue eyes and closely cropped, borderline buzz-cut light-brown hair. Though the guy was sitting, Matt pegged him to be roughly six feet tall and around two-twenty. He'd been in shape at some point but had since gone soft, and he had the look of someone who hadn't lived an easy life.

The dingy white T-shirt he wore showed off the shitty tattoos on his right forearm. Well-worn jeans and scuffed black motorcycle boots completed his attire. He was clean-shaven, but Matt would bet his life savings that the guy had recently sported a full beard. The tan lines on his face were a dead giveaway.

In a tone that was a million times more casual than he felt, Matt said to Gavin, "Man, I'm starving. Chow down. Then we'll talk."

Gavin grabbed his fork and scooped up some hash browns, but he didn't eat.

"I'm sorry, honey," Martha said to the man, handing him back a photo. "I don't recognize the girl. We've had a number of different waitresses over the last few years, but none that look like her. I can show my husband if you want, but his memory's not so great these days."

Matt caught Gavin's stare and knew the hard look on his friend's face matched his own. Ray's Diner had *not* had a number of different waitresses over the last few years. Aside from Scarlet, the six other members of the waitstaff had been employed here for years, some for decades. As for her comment about Ray? Eighty-plus years and all, the man's mind remained a steel trap.

"Are you sure?" the man asked, waving the photo. "This was taken seven or eight years ago, so she'd be in her early twenties now. She's blond in the photo, but she used to change her hair color a lot."

"No, sorry," Martha said. "She looks like a sweet girl, though. I hope you find her."

"You're *sure* you haven't had anyone working here that looks like her? Five-two? Petite?"

Matt's eyes tore across the restaurant, but there was no sign of Scarlet. Who stood five-two and had black hair liberally streaked with pink, teal, and purple.

What the hell does this fucker want?

"Well, of course I have a petite little waitress who works here." Martha chuckled, taking the man's empty plate. "But I've known little Scarlet since she was an itty-bitty girl."

The hairs on Matt's arms rose. Another bald-faced lie.

"Are there other diners on the island?" Frustration laced the man's tone.

Martha shook her head. "Not on Hudson. However, I know there are dozens over on Whidbey Island next door."

The man frowned. "Is Whidbey the same size as this island?"

"Lord no!" Martha chortled. "Whidbey's easily three, maybe four times the size of little ole Hudson. Like I said, they have dozens of diners. Your best bets on the south end would be in Clinton and Langley, then Coupeville in the middle of the island. If you head north, there are a bunch in Oak Harbor by the naval station." She pointed at the photo. "You'll probably have better luck over there, though it will probably take a while since Whidbey's so big."

Rising from his table, the man grumbled something Matt couldn't hear but had Martha nodding. He stuffed some bills in the guest check holder and handed it to her. "Thanks. Keep the change."

"Safe travels," she called out after him.

The instant the front door closed behind the man, Martha returned to their booth. Concern strained her features.

"Where is she?" Matt demanded.

Martha motioned with her head. "In the back. The guy sat in her section, but she was on break in the office, talking with the bank. Paula was covering the table and said the guy showed her the photo and started asking a bunch of questions. She said he made her twitchy. And that the photo kind of resembled Scarlet, so she came and got me. I told Scarlet to stay in the back and took over her table just in case. Then I saw the two of you walking down the street, so I called Hudson Security's main number, and they patched me through." She patted Gavin's shoulder.

"What exactly was the photo of?" Matt asked.

Martha pressed her lips into a tight line, and her eyes filled. "My little teenage Scarlet all gussied up. Sitting and carrying on with a bunch of older biker men. She was bleached blond, heavy makeup, and all leather and denim, like a mini biker hussy." Her sigh was sad. "If that man was right and that photo was taken when he said it was, she couldn't have been more than fifteen or sixteen."

Matt's stomach soured at the thought. Bikers and teenage girls were a dangerous combination. And always to the detriment of the girls. Shaking his head, he tried to picture Scarlet in that situation, that kind of life. It was difficult to fathom. The woman he knew was too kindhearted for that lifestyle. Then again, she'd told him nothing about her past.

Matt took Martha's fidgeting hand in his and squeezed. "Thank you, Martha." He glanced at Gavin. "I need to check on Scar."

"Hang on," Martha said, looking around. She let go of his hand and slid into the booth next to Gavin, forcing the man to scoot farther in. Lowering her voice, she said, "We have security cameras. I don't think they're anything fancy because you know Ray doesn't like to spend money on that kind of thing, but if you need to take a look at them to do all that . . . stuff your group does, just let me know. I don't know how to work any of it, but Paula can show you."

"Thank you. I'll take a look." Gavin nodded to Matt. "Go. I'll call Quinn and—"

Matt didn't wait to hear the rest of what Gavin said. He assumed his friend would take care of shit because that's what the man did. His priority was Scarlet. Making sure she was okay.

Knocking twice on the closed office door, he opened it and stepped inside.

Scarlet, who'd been seated at the desk, shot to her feet. "What's going on? Is everything okay?"

"I don't know, Scar," he said, shutting the door behind him.

"Why did Martha want me to stay back here? Did something happen out there?" Her brown eyes were terrified, and she was trembling.

He crossed the room in three strides and pulled her into his arms. She melted against him. The feel of her quaking limbs hurt his heart.

"What's going on, Matt? Please tell me."

Guiding Scarlet to the office's small couch, he sat and pulled her to sit beside him, wrapping an arm over her slim shoulders. "Someone was looking for you."

She went utterly still, and the blood drained from her face. Her sudden gray pallor told Matt what he'd already known: something was terribly wrong.

He ran a hand up and down her spine. "A guy was showing an old photo around, asking if anyone recognized the girl in it. Paula told Martha it resembled you, and Martha was certain it was you when she saw it."

Scarlet gasped and moved to stand, but he placed both hands on her shoulders, stopping her. He pulled her against his chest, holding her in place. "Sweetheart, they both told him the girl in the photo didn't look familiar. They said they didn't recognize her at all. Breathe, Scar." He pressed his lips to the top of her head. "You gotta breathe, sweetheart."

She sucked in a breath and pulled slightly away to look at him. The fear and uncertainty in her dark-brown gaze shredded him. Before his very eyes, her trembling intensified. He vowed to put a stop to whoever it was that made her this scared. No matter what it took.

"I don't understand what's happening," she whispered.

He ran a hand along her back again. "We'll figure it out. I promise."

She covered her face and shook her head. "No, you don't understand . . ."

Dread curled in his belly. "Then tell me, sweetheart. I can help you. Gavin and our entire crew at Hudson Security have your back. But what is it that I don't understand?"

Dropping her hands, she locked her gaze on her lap.

Matt tilted her chin up with his finger and waited until she looked at him. "Scarlet, what don't I understand?"

She went silent for so long, he wasn't sure she'd even heard him.

Shaking her head, her eyes filled with tears, but she blinked them away. "How could they have found me?"

CHAPTER SEVENTEEN

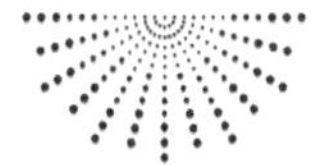

Holy shit. Someone was looking for her. How the hell was this even possible?

Panic bubbled in her chest, and she tried to tamp it down. Dammit. No luck. Her lungs burned, and her heart pounded painfully hard.

"Breathe, Scar."

Not realizing she'd been holding her breath, Scarlet exhaled and slammed her eyes shut. Her mind whirled, but she concentrated on Matt's soothing voice. It was almost as comforting as his touch. Part of her brain recognized that she was cocooned in his arms, practically glued against his chest. That while he had one hand soothing along her back, his other arm was draped over her lap, his large hand clutching the outside of her thigh.

On any other day, butterflies would have taken flight in her belly.

But it wasn't any other day. No. It was a day that had started so promising and taken a terrifying turn.

One thing at a time. She needed the facts. Because none of this made sense. "Can you tell me what you know?"

He relayed the information he'd witnessed firsthand, along with what he'd been told by Martha. Including the description of the photo.

Scarlet's stomach rolled. Bleached-blond hair, leather, and denim? A gussied-up teenage wannabe biker chick? That described the old her to a *T*.

She pinched the bridge of her nose. "Matt, I don't—"

A knock at the door made her flinch, and again, Matt's hand was there, moving along her back in soothing circles. The door opened, and Martha entered, followed by Gavin.

The older woman crossed the room to the couch, bent down, and wrapped Scarlet in a hug.

Her throat clenched tight and her nose tingled as she returned the embrace, taking in the comforting lemon scent that always lingered on the older woman, no matter how many hours she spent at the diner. If Poppy was the sister Scarlet had never had, then Martha was her mother, favorite aunt, and grandmother all rolled into one.

"Oh, sweet girl," Martha murmured, kissing her forehead. "You take the rest of the day off, okay?" Before Scarlet could protest, Martha rushed on, "Naomi's coming in to cover your shift."

"Are you sure?"

Martha nodded, then cupped her face in her hands. "I know what you've told me, sweetie. You need to figure out what's going on, because I love you like my own and *nothing* is going to happen to you. You hear me, missy?"

Warmth filled her chest as she nodded.

Martha was her greatest ally. Because of the circumstances of her arrival on Hudson, Scarlet had shared what she could with the older woman. It had only been fair that she and Ray knew what they were getting themselves into. Not only had Martha stuck by her side, but she'd showered her and Daisy with so much love and support—something

Scarlet had never had. And though Martha was an enthusiastic member of the gossip train, she had been a vault with Scarlet's secrets. And Scarlet would be forever grateful for that.

"Now, you take as long as you need. Don't you worry about work. We'll cover you." Martha placed one hand on Matt's shoulder and her other on Gavin's arm. "Your job is to let these boys do what they do. They'll figure out who that man was and what he wants."

"Thank you, Martha," she said, voice hoarse with emotion.

"Of course, sweet girl. Taking care of my family is what I do."

Standing, Scarlet hugged Martha once more and squeezed. There was no stopping the tears from pouring down her face this time. "You're my family, too," she whispered.

Martha pulled away and wiped her eyes, then turned to Matt and Gavin. "You boys take care of my girl." She pinned Matt with a look as he rose from the couch. "And you. *Nothing* happens to my girl. You hear me?"

Matt wrapped an arm around Scarlet's shoulders and pulled her into his side. "Yes, ma'am."

A short drive later, Scarlet followed Matt into a large conference room at the Hudson Security office. She'd never been inside the building and had to admit she was one thousand percent intimidated. There were screens and gadgets everywhere, and she didn't have the first clue as to what any of them did.

"Can I get you anything? Something to drink?" Matt asked, pulling out a chair for her at the end of a long conference table.

Settling into the surprisingly comfortable chair, she shook her head. "I'm good, thanks."

She was probably as far from good as anyone could get. The mystery stranger from the diner had fear and worry spiking through every single one of her nerves. The only consolation she had was the knowledge that her daughter was safe. Gavin had told her he'd sent one of his Hudson Security team members, Xander, over to Rebecca's to keep an eye on Daisy. Just in case.

Nausea turned her stomach.

She hoped Gavin was just being exceptionally cautious. Because if he truly believed Daisy was in trouble? Believed the stranger looking for her was also looking for her daughter? Holy shit, that was terrifying . . .

"Scar?"

She startled at her name and looked up. It wasn't her and Matt alone in the room anymore. He sat to her right and Gavin to her left. Next to Gavin was a petite brunette with an open laptop in front of her. The woman's fingers flew over the keyboard, and she kept glancing back and forth between her computer and the giant monitor-looking thing on the wall that had numbers and images flickering on it.

Scarlet had no idea what the other woman was doing or what any of the information on the big screen was. All she knew was that the other woman was totally getting added to her ever-growing things-to-be-intimidated-by list, despite looking perfectly nice.

"I didn't know you wore glasses, B," Matt said.

"I don't," the woman replied, pushing her glasses up by the bridge. Her attention never wavered from the screen in front of her. "They give me a headache. Unfortunately, an eye infection left me no choice but to break out the nerd frames."

The corners of Scarlet's lips lifted. Nerd? Right. The woman was projecting some serious Felicity Smoak vibes, only with brown hair. From her fancy blouse and blazer to the dark-rimmed glasses, *nerd* was the last thing Scarlet would call this woman.

Suddenly, the woman's bright-blue eyes were staring at her, and Scarlet swallowed hard. "Hi, I'm Bean. I handle the tech stuff around here."

Gavin snorted. "Tech stuff? That's what you're calling it now?"

Bean rolled her eyes at Gavin, then peered back at Scarlet. The intensity of the woman's stare was . . . a lot.

A warm hand enveloped hers, and she looked at Matt. His brown gaze was steady as he squeezed her hand. Taking strength from his presence, she relaxed her shoulders.

"As I mentioned at the diner," Gavin began, "Xander is one of our PSOs and—"

"A PS-what?" Scarlet asked.

"Personal security officer. He's good with kids and is actually familiar with Rebecca's place." She must have shown her confusion, because Gavin clarified, "When all that shit went down a few months ago with Cade, Dante, and their gyms, Xander was in charge of Rebecca's protection. He stayed with her while she was working. Xander just checked in and said everything's good over there."

A weight lifted from Scarlet. *Everything's good. Daisy is okay.*

"As you know," Gavin continued, "Martha has security cameras around the diner. She gave us access to them. Bean?"

"This is the guy looking for you," Bean said, gesturing to the screen on the wall. "Unfortunately, there's no audio."

A number of low-quality black-and-white videos appeared on the big screen. The man talking with Paula. Eating. Speaking with Martha. But it was the video of him outside the diner, climbing onto his motorcycle, that had Scarlet's breath catching in her lungs.

Lots of people ride motorcycles, dammit. It's just a coincidence. Hell, there's a whole motorcycle retreat going on! A shiver racked her frame. *But that damn photo . . .*

"I have my facial rec program running. So far, no hits." Bean grimaced. "The video quality is shit, though, so even if the guy is in the system, it'll be nearly impossible to get a match. The good news is that I picked him up on the ferry cameras. He has his helmet on, but both the bike and his arm tattoos are a match. He left Hudson on the last ferry that went out and just made it to the Coupeville dock. The guys said Martha told him there are a bunch of diners on Whidbey he should check out. Hopefully, that'll keep him occupied for a while. Regardless, I pulled his license plate number—"

"Were you able to get a name?" Matt interrupted.

Bean shook her head. "The person the bike's registered to doesn't match this guy's physical description—like, at all— but I have another program digging into that. There are a number of cameras on Whidbey, so I can track the bike there. I'll also get a notification if he drives onto any Washington State ferry—whether it's heading to Hudson or not— or if his motorcycle plates cross Deception Pass to the mainland."

"His mistake was coming to the islands," Gavin said. "Unless he's traveling by private boat, we can track all the ways out."

Bean cleared her throat—loudly.

"*Bean* can track all the ways off the islands," Gavin corrected, rolling his eyes.

The woman flashed a smug grin. "Long story short, Scarlet? If this guy comes back, we'll know. Anyway, if I get a ping off facial rec, I'll contact everyone. In the meantime, this is as clear a pic as I could get."

An image from the diner's security footage appeared on

the screen. The man sat at his table and seemed to look directly into the camera.

Scarlet frowned.

"I know," Bean said on a sigh, leaning back in her chair. "The quality is shit. Hell, Martha's security cameras are shit. But that's the best I can enhance it."

The photo wasn't enhanced all that much. It was still super grainy. You could tell the guy had a light-colored buzz cut and was clean-shaven, but that wasn't anything she hadn't already been told.

"Does he look familiar?" Matt asked.

She continued studying the man, then shook her head. "No." He truly didn't. There was maybe something vaguely familiar about him, but honestly, he just looked like every biker she'd ever known. An average guy with that rough-around-the-edges bit. Even in the still images from the security camera, he projected that wannabe-tough-guy persona. Yes, some of the biker men she'd known were legitimately tough and scary. But this guy? Nope.

What could he possibly want with her?

Scarlet released Matt's hand, leaned forward, and propped her elbows on the table. "None of this makes any sense," she muttered, closing her eyes and pinching the bridge of her nose. "My handler said—"

She froze.

Holy. Shit.

She had *not* just said that out loud. But the complete silence in the room told her otherwise.

Peeking out at the table, she glanced from Matt to Gavin to Bean, then back to Matt. The men looked at her intently; Bean's head cocked to the side, her eyebrows pulling high in surprise.

Scarlet's insides began to tremble. Her mouth opened and closed, but no words came out. *Fuck.*

"What about your handler?" Gavin asked, voice calm and controlled, soothing even. But Scarlet knew that was bullshit. He was like a shark who'd just scented blood in the water.

Sitting back in her seat, she fisted her hands in her lap. Her nails dug crescents into her palms. Not knowing where to look, she studied the table. "Um . . ."

In her peripheral vision, she noticed Matt reaching over. Her gaze shot to him when he pulled her chair closer to his. Without saying a word, he took her fisted hands and pried them open. Ran his thumbs over the grooves made by her nails.

"Breathe, sweetheart," he murmured, attention fixed on her palms.

Some of her tension eased at his touch. When she met his eyes, she let out another breath.

He squeezed her hands. "We can't help you unless you tell us what's going on. And, Scar, I will do *everything* I can to keep you and Daisy safe."

Her heart warmed, and she laced her fingers with his, holding on tight. *He included Daisy.*

A flush heated her cheeks as she realized what she'd done. "I'm sorry," she said, attempting to pull away.

But Matt held on. He gave her a slight nod, his gaze never leaving hers, as he prodded, "Your handler?"

For a moment, she could only stare at him. Then she focused on their connected hands. What was she doing? Hell, was she even allowed to talk about this? *Fuck it.* "I don't know where to begin."

His hand was gentle as he tipped her chin up. The small gesture brought tears to her eyes, and she swallowed past the lump in her throat. No man had ever treated her this tenderly.

"Start at the beginning, Scar," he murmured.

Nope. No way did Matt need to know her background.

She loved how he talked to her, looked at her. Like she was a regular person, someone he found interesting. If he ever knew about her past, about who—*what*—she'd been, that would all change.

But the recent past would be okay, right? After all, she'd already screwed up by letting the handler part slip.

The fingers beneath her chin slid along her jaw until they cradled the side of her face. She gulped, and her racing pulse had little to do with the topic at hand.

"It's just us, sweetheart. You can tell me."

She glanced at Gavin and Bean—but they weren't there. Surprise had her mouth falling open. When had they left the room?

"So long as it doesn't put your safety or Daisy's at risk," Matt said, "I promise that I'll only share with Gavin and the team what you want me to. Trust me."

She did. More than she should.

Scarlet sucked in a deep breath for bravery. And as she let it out, she prayed this man was true to his word. "When I lived in South Dakota, I was the sole witness to a triple murder."

CHAPTER EIGHTEEN

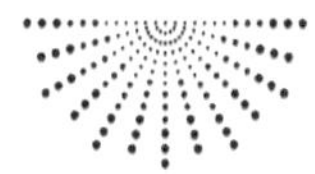

Of all the things to come out of this beautiful woman's mouth, that was the very last thing Matt had expected.

A myriad of emotions flickered over Scarlet's face, none of them good. Worry, sadness, doubt. Without second-guessing himself, he plucked her from her chair, settled her on his lap with her back to his chest, and wrapped his arms around her. He knew that sometimes it was easier to talk if no one was looking directly at you. But he'd be damned if he wasn't going to support her and comfort her while she shared her story.

After a heartbeat, she leaned back into his arms.

Matt pressed his lips to the top of her head and just held her. He didn't know how long they sat there like that before she finally spoke.

"I told you that I grew up in a tiny town in South Dakota," she began, her quiet voice loud in the otherwise silent room. "It was just me and my mom. I didn't have the best upbring-ing. Like I said before, I dropped out of school in the ninth grade, and then she and I went our separate ways."

It took everything he had to not tense beneath her. Because holy shit. A person didn't just go "separate ways" from their fourteen-year-old child. Or rather, they weren't supposed to. Not legally, and sure as fuck not morally. But he had to ask . . . "Didn't anyone come looking for you? The school? CPS?"

She scoffed. "Yeah, right. Even if they did, my mom probably reported me as a runaway. At least, that's what she'd always threatened to do. Said it would make her life so much easier."

"Where did you go?" he asked, impressed that he'd kept his voice calm. He was so pissed at her piece-of-shit mother. And because he was pretty sure he knew where Scarlet had ended up.

"There was a girl a couple years older than me who lived a few trailers over that kind of took me under her wing."

He frowned. Blind leading the fucking blind.

"She hung out at the local motorcycle club, and so I tagged along. A lot. Until she and I were basically living at the clubhouse."

"How old were you?"

She flinched, and he wanted to kick himself. He ran a hand down her arms to comfort her. And himself.

"Almost fifteen."

Matt closed his eyes. He'd expected the answer, but hearing her say it out loud . . .

Holy fuck. He knew what went on in most MC clubhouses. The idea of her living in one at fourteen years old would haunt him for the rest of his life.

He dropped a kiss to the top of her head. "And then?"

She went quiet for a moment. He imagined she was gathering her thoughts. Deciding what she should and shouldn't reveal. Which was fine. Because he knew he hadn't fully earned her trust. Yet.

"I was a fixture there for a few years . . . and then one night, after a really wild party, I witnessed the club's vice president shoot and kill three club members for disrespecting him."

Ice slithered down his spine. There was more. He knew it in his gut, but he wouldn't push. Not now, anyway. "Holy shit, Scar," he whispered, tightening his arms around her.

She let out a deep breath, then shifted on his lap to face him and tentatively met his gaze.

"What happened after that, sweetheart?"

"The cops came the next morning for something totally unrelated. I can't even remember what. Steele, the club's VP, and a couple other guys were moving the bodies when they showed up." She chuckled, but there was no humor in it. "Shitty timing, right? But long story short, I was the only witness to Steele shooting the guys. The feds swooped in—the club was apparently running drugs and guns—and I was placed in witness protection."

"Are you still in WITSEC?"

She shook her head. "Steele's trial was about four months after the arrest. I stayed in the program for just over three years. Then Steele was killed in prison, and around the same time, the MC disbanded."

Awfully convenient timing, he thought.

"A month after all that went down, it was decided I didn't need protection anymore. There was no longer a threat. Bates, my handler, said I could either go back to my old life or keep the identity they made for me and start fresh. It was a no-brainer, really, so here I am."

"Fresh start," he murmured, tucking a lock of hair behind her ear. His eyes narrowed as a thought occurred to him. "Was that why losing your driver's license had you acting—"

"Totally freaked out? Panicked enough to kick you out of your own office?" A sad smile tipped her lips. "Yeah. I wasn't sure how it all worked. When I moved here from Arizona, Bates took care of the details for me. Driver's license, health insurance . . . That kind of thing. Truthfully, I think he felt sorry for me. It's safe to say I was a nervous wreck."

"That's completely understandable, Scarlet. Give yourself some grace."

She shrugged, and her face flushed. "Anyway, that's why I kinda freaked when my license was stolen. Because I wasn't sure if the new identity they gave me was actually in the system or not."

"Again, understandable, sweetheart. Obviously, Bates did his job and everything checked out. Must've been a relief, huh?"

"You have no idea." She smiled, and it almost reached her eyes. Almost. "Are you regretting coming to my rescue yet?"

He tilted his head in question. "What are you talking about?"

"All of this"—she waved her hand between them—"started because I was freaking out over Daisy breaking her arm. You came to my rescue then, and again after the break-in."

He shook his head. "Please don't paint me as some kind of hero. I'm far from it."

She scoffed. "You're kidding, right?"

"I'm not, Scar." He was dead fucking serious. "I didn't *rescue* you. I helped out a friend. A friend who has become very important to me. And you can't say you wouldn't do the same for me."

"I would. But this is a lot, Matt. Like *a lot* a lot. I get it if it's too much. I mean, if you don't feel comfortable with me and Daisy staying with you, I one thousand percent understand. We can—"

"Listen to me, and listen good, sweetheart. Everything you just said about your past? It changes nothing." He frowned. "No, wait. It does. I knew you were strong before.

But now? You're the strongest fucking woman I know." She looked at him like he was crazy, and he couldn't let it stand. He was going to make her believe him. No matter how long it took. "I can do the math, so I know you had Daisy somewhere in the middle of that chaos. Going through all that shit by yourself? You leave me in absolute awe, Scarlet You blow my fucking mind."

She blinked, and something that looked a lot like hope flickered over her face. Or maybe that was just wishful thinking on his part. After a moment, she asked, "Blow your mind in a good way?"

Matt wanted to pump his fist in the air. He hadn't been wrong. Hope now shined bright in her eyes, and it made him feel ten feet tall.

He framed her face in both his hands, and her mouth dropped open the tiniest bit. It took all his willpower to not kiss her. Time and place—neither was right. "Yes, Scarlet Miller. You built yourself into the incredible woman before me, and it blows my mind in the best damn way possible."

"Oh," she said softly, breath whispering over his lips.

Matt's gaze dropped to her mouth. And when he looked back into her eyes, something deep within him rejoiced at the heat he found there. They might not be on the exact same page, but at least they were in the same chapter.

Running his thumb gently over her lower lip, he laid a chaste kiss to where her cheek and mouth met. "You are so damn special to me. Don't ever doubt that."

Behind them, someone cleared their throat. He let go of her beautiful face and scowled at the intruders in the doorway.

"Sorry," Gavin muttered at the same time Bean pointed at him and said, "Blame him, not me."

Helping Scarlet back onto her chair, Matt ran a hand over his jaw. "Oh, don't you worry, Bean. I'll always blame Gavin."

"Hot damn." Bean retook her seat and opened her laptop. "I *knew* having you join the crew was going to be awesome!"

"Zip it, B," Gavin grumbled.

"Sure thing, boss," she said, giving them a wide grin. "Now, what do we know?"

Matt looked at Scarlet. The ball was in her court. However much she decided to share, he would support her.

Nodding, Scarlet blew out a breath and reached for his hand.

He linked their fingers and squeezed. "I've got your back."

"*We've* got your back," Bean chimed in.

Scarlet's mouth opened, then closed.

"Just so you know," Bean said, expression turning serious, "whatever you tell us doesn't leave this room unless you say so."

"And if you do give us the okay to share your info, then it would be on a need-to-know basis only," Gavin said. "We want to help you. Even if you just tell Bean the basics, with your permission, she can dig deeper into everything. See what the connections are."

"But we don't even know this guy's name." Disbelief tinged Scarlet's words as she gestured at the image on the conference room's giant Smartboard.

Gavin shrugged. "Yeah, but it's Bean. She's like . . ."

"Magic, boss," Bean said, that smug smile on her face. "The word you're looking for is *magic*."

Scarlet chuckled, seemingly put at ease by their banter. She caught Matt's gaze and mouthed, *Thank you*, then turned back to the others. As she retold her story, pride surged through him. The woman was fucking amazing. Tough. Resilient. Courageous.

Matt knew he was falling in deep with her. Knew that fact should give him pause.

Should.

But it didn't. Not any longer. Because the more time he spent with Scarlet, the more he got to know her, the more right this thing between them felt. Sure, part of him still worried he'd get burned like before. That this time around, the heartbreak would be even more devastating. However, the more sensible part knew down to his marrow that Scarlet was nothing like his ex-wife, that she'd never do what Krista had done.

He took in the woman beside him and calm settled over him.

For once, Matt was going to put the doubt and second-guessing away. He was going to trust her, and in turn, himself. He wanted to see where they went.

CHAPTER NINETEEN

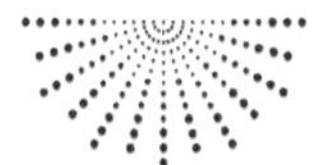

Something had shifted. Scarlet didn't know what. But sometime between being sequestered in the diner's office, not knowing what was going on in the restaurant, to now, listening to Bean, Gavin, and Matt discuss their next steps, something had changed between her and Matt. There was a newfound ease she couldn't quite describe. A familiarity that warmed her heart.

Scarlet wasn't a touchy-feely person. In fact, aside from a very select group of friends that she could list on one hand, she strived to keep her personal bubble intact. After a lifetime of that bubble being disregarded, it was something she was actively conscious of.

But with Matt? It felt as if holding his hand was the only thing keeping her from flying off a cliff of anxiety. Every time he laced their fingers together or laid his hand on her back or squeezed her shoulders or tucked a lock of hair behind her ear, she felt . . .

Protected. Cared for. Safe.

Minutes ago, he'd cupped her face in his hands, kissed her

cheek, and stunned her with the sweetest words she'd ever heard. Her stomach still fluttered from the thought, along with . . . something else. Beneath that sweetness and comfort was a simmering heat that was both unexpected and breathtaking.

"So, that's basically the gist of it," Bean said, pulling Scarlet from her musings.

She glanced between Bean, Gavin, Matt, and the giant screen, not wanting to admit she'd tuned out the conversation. Rehashing her past with them, even the bare-bones version of it, had been exhausting. So, when they'd begun discussing the technology they were using to track the mystery guy, her mind had wandered. She barely had a ninth-grade education—she wasn't putting herself down, just stating the facts—and she didn't understand a tenth of what they'd been talking about.

Scarlet waved at the screen with her free hand. "I'm not familiar with all the jargon and stuff—"

"We can go over it again," Bean offered.

She shook her head. "Oh no. That's okay. I trust you guys know what you're doing. I'll just have Matt give me a summary of the highlights later." Hopefully, in English.

Peeking over at Matt, she was met with a grin, as if he knew exactly what she was thinking. "I can do that, sweetheart."

Gavin's phone dinged, drawing everyone's attention. After reading the message, his gaze locked on Scarlet's, and she did her best to not squirm. There was no other way about it. The man was intense.

"Quinn found your purse near one of the dumpsters at the ferry dock. All the cash and cards were gone, but your driver's license was still in it." He gestured to the screen. "I let him know about what happened earlier today, and he doesn't think it's related."

"So it was a random break-in?" Matt asked.

Her mind spun, and her eyes ping-ponged between the two men. She had no idea if the news was a good thing or a bad thing.

Gavin nodded. "There was some drug paraphernalia dumped near her purse, too. And he said that a handful of rental properties over by the wineries have been broken into over the last couple weeks. With the electronics that were taken from Wayland's other apartment, he thinks it was most likely a grab-and-go—"

"A grab-and-go?" she asked.

"It's also called a smash-and-grab robbery. Basically, a crime of opportunity where someone quickly grabs whatever they can sell fast for cash," Gavin explained, then glanced at Bean. "Quinn's going to send you what he has. I'd like you to double-check things."

"Of course, boss," Bean replied, her fingers already flying over her keyboard.

Letting go of Matt's hand, Scarlet leaned back in her seat and crossed her arms over her chest. "Why are we ruling out the crimes being related? Couldn't the mystery guy have broken into my apartment while he was looking for me?"

Gavin pursed his lips, then shook his head. "I don't think so. If the mystery guy already knows where you live, then why bother with the photo at the diner? He'd be more likely to watch your place, learn your movements, then make his move. Not break in and go around asking about you afterward. Truthfully, the fact that he's showing your photo around is sloppy."

Gavin's explanation made sense. But that meant they were no closer to finding out who the mystery guy was or who had broken into her apartment. Which was terrifying. A shiver ghosted down her spine, and she rubbed her hands over her arms.

"Scarlet, are you okay with me digging into your past?" Bean asked.

No. Not at all. That was the very last thing Scarlet wanted.

Even with the basic information she'd provided everyone, she was certain the other woman's cyber skills were indeed magic. She worried what Bean would find. But if it kept Daisy safe, Bean could dig all she wanted. Because Daisy was what mattered most. "Go ahead. But please keep what you find need-to-know."

"Of course," Bean said, giving her a reassuring smile.

"Ready to get out of here?" Matt asked, laying a hand on her shoulder.

She nodded. "Please."

After saying thanks to Gavin and Bean, Scarlet followed Matt out to his truck. He passed through the security gates and turned in the opposite direction of his house, where she'd assumed they were going. After a few miles, she realized they were heading back downtown, and she suppressed a sigh. She really didn't want to return to work, but she still had a few hours until she had to pick up Daisy, so whatever. Might as well. Besides, she was certain Matt had other stuff to do.

She frowned as they passed Ray's Diner without slowing. Okaaay.

Spotting Hudson Island Antiques, everything clicked into place. Of course. "I appreciate the ride back to my car . . ." Her frown deepened as they passed her apartment. She pointed behind them. "Um, Matt, my car is . . ."

"I'll have one of the guys bring your car to the house later today."

She stared at him, but he kept his focus on the road. "Matt, where are we . . ."

He pulled up in front of Rebecca's and put his truck in Park. "I don't know about you, Scar, but I could sure use a quiet afternoon at the house. Especially after hearing Bean explain all the tech she's implemented. My brain is damn near fried. What do you say we pick up Daisy and do another early dinner and a movie night?"

Her jaw dropped. God, this man was wonderful. "That sounds gre—oh wait! We have to get Daisy's car seat from my car first."

"Nah, we're good," he said, cutting the engine.

Scarlet spun around, jaw dropping again when she saw the back bench. In the center was a car seat. Swinging her gaze back to Matt, she noticed the slight flush on his cheeks. "How . . . When did you get that?"

"I can't take credit for it."

Her eyebrow arched. She'd beg to differ.

"I don't know if you've met Esme?" When Scarlet shook her head, he continued, "She's Hudson Security's go-to person for anything they need." He shrugged, and the pink tinge on his cheeks deepened. "I may have mentioned that you and Daisy are staying with me for the next few weeks. I told her about Daisy—how even though she's four, she's a tiny little thing. I also gave her the brand of car seat you use. It's no big deal. This way, we don't have to switch the clunky thing back and forth between our vehicles."

She bit the inside of her cheek to keep from smiling. No big deal? The man was wonderful *and* delusional.

"Let's go," he said gruffly, reaching for the door handle.

She grabbed his arm, stilling him. She waited until he met her gaze, until the heat in his eyes gave her courage. Then she trailed her fingers down his forearm and caught his hand. Bringing it to her lips, she pressed a kiss to his knuckles. "Thank you, Matt."

His jaw clenched, and she swore he let out a low growl. His voice was like gravel when he whispered, "You're welcome, sweetheart. Now let's get Daisy."

When they met on the sidewalk, he reclaimed her hand. Scarlet's heart expanded, and she couldn't have stopped her grin if she'd tried. Who would have thought she'd actually be able to smile after the last couple of hours?

Katie let them in the front door, and two seconds after walking inside, an exuberant "Matty!" greeted their arrival. Her daughter, hot-pink cast and all, shot across the room and threw herself into Matt's arms.

"Hey, Otter Pop," he said, catching Daisy with ease. He swung her in a circle before setting her on his hip.

Scarlet's heart threatened to explode. Ohmygod, this man . . .

"Hi, Mama!" Daisy shouted with her arms outstretched and lips puckered.

Taking her daughter from Matt, she gave Daisy a noisy kiss.

Matt gestured across the room to where Flora and Xander stood. "I'm going to talk to Xander before we take off. I'll be quick, though."

"Take your time," she replied, squeezing Daisy extra tight and inhaling her fruity scent. A lump formed in her throat. No one was going to hurt her little girl.

"Mama, you're squishing me."

"Sorry, baby," she murmured, softening her hold. "We're going to go home early today. We'll make some dinner, and Matt was thinking of maybe doing another movie night."

"Mmm-kay." Daisy burrowed her face into Scarlet's neck. "Do you think Matty will make me popcorn and M&M's again?"

She ran her hand over her daughter's hair. "I'm sure if you ask Matt nicely, he can put a small bowl together for you."

Daisy sat up in her arms, and her bottom lip wobbled. "A *small* bowl?"

Her eyebrow arched. "A small bowl or no bowl at all."

Daisy grinned before resting her head back on Scarlet's shoulder. "Small bowl."

CHAPTER TWENTY

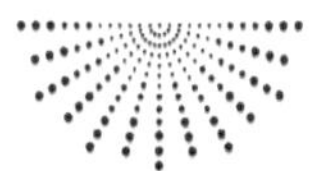

Scarlet plopped down on the sofa and let out a weary sigh. *What a day.*

After picking up Daisy, they'd swung into the grocery store to grab supplies for dinner. Matt had prepared grilled chicken, roasted potatoes, and steamed broccoli, and then he and Daisy had put together their popcorn-and-M&M mixture, set all her stuffies on the couch, and watched *Kung Fu Panda* together.

Scarlet had been more than happy to leave movie night to the duo since she'd seen the film nine million times. But rather than head to bed early, she'd busied herself cleaning the kitchen and folding laundry. Her reasoning had been that if she was going to drive herself crazy overanalyzing every little thing that had happened today, she might as well be productive while doing it.

Once the movie had ended, Daisy had gotten an extra-long bath and three stories. Now she was out cold in bed, surrounded by her array of beloved stuffies. And Scarlet was still unable to sleep, hence her plop on the sofa. Though she was utterly exhausted, her mind wouldn't settle.

"It's been quite the day. Can I get you a glass of wine or something?" Matt asked, sitting at the other end of the sofa, a lowball glass of amber liquid in his hand.

She gestured to her mug of tea on the end table. "I'm good, thanks. Did you like the movie?"

After taking a sip of his drink, he grinned. "You know, it was actually pretty good."

"There's like four of those movies, so be prepared."

"I'm looking forward to it. Are you sure I can't get you anything?"

She shook her head.

"You don't drink much."

To Scarlet, his words seemed more like an observation than a question. She shrugged. "Not really."

"Any particular reason?"

He seemed genuinely curious. Not judgy. That's the only reason she chose to answer. "For one, the cost. I mean, I could get a couple drinks at Monty's, or I could use that money to buy Daisy a dress, a little toy, or a special treat." She pulled her legs up to sit cross-legged, facing him. "But mostly because it's just me."

"What do you mean?"

She fiddled with a lock of her hair. "What if Daisy wakes up in the middle of the night with an emergency? If I'm wasted, I can't drive her to the hospital. I'm a lightweight, so even a couple drinks would put me over the legal limit. I'd rather not take that risk. It isn't worth it to me."

"That's admirable. Does it bother you that I drink?"

"Not at all. Honestly, it's been so long since I've had alcohol that I think I've lost the taste for it. Not that I used to drink the good stuff or anything." She nodded to his glass. "What is that?"

"Whisky." He held it out to her. "It's my brother's, so it's the *really* good stuff. Want to taste? Smell?"

She took the glass, brought it to her nose, and sniffed. "Yikes, no, thank you," she said with a grimace, handing the glass back.

Matt laughed. "I've been told it's an acquired taste."

"I'll stick to my chamomile tea, thanks. And I wouldn't call not drinking admirable. It's just me trying to be responsible."

He studied her for a moment. "Why do I feel like there's more to your reasoning?"

"What do you mean?" Holy crap, was she that transparent?

"Like there's a story behind why you don't drink."

Yup. She *was* that transparent.

Scarlet didn't know what it was—the quiet night, the comfortable couch, the company—but something had her wanting to open up. Had her wanting to tell Matt things she'd never told anyone. "You could say I didn't have a really great childhood."

He nodded. "I figured as much when you mentioned you and your mom went separate ways. In ninth grade, right?"

"That's right," she said, a little surprised that he'd remembered. "But even before that, things weren't . . . Our home wasn't very stable." Understatement of the year. It had been utter chaos, and she'd lived in a constant state of fear. Of being taken away, of having to stay, of . . . everything. "Like when I was in third grade, I remember waking up in the middle of the night with the most horrible stomach pain. My mom was in the living room, but I couldn't wake her up."

She recalled the crushed beer cans and empty jug of tequila that had littered the floor. Recalled her mom passed out on the couch, a bottle of vodka clutched in her hands. Bile turned in Scarlet's belly. It was as if the stench of stale cigarettes, sour beer, and spilled liquor still lingered in her nose.

"I stumbled to the trailer next door, and I swear, I thought old Mrs. Hattery was going to slam the door in my face. But thankfully, she didn't. I was doubled over in pain and ended up puking all over her floor. I was an absolute mess, but she loaded me into her car and took me to the ER." Cursing Scarlet's drunk of a mother the entire time. "I had kidney stones."

"Holy shit, Scar," Matt murmured, sorrow and anger flashing over his face.

"CPS was called while I was in the hospital, and my mom got in trouble. I was put in foster care for a couple months until she 'cleaned up her act.' Then I went back to living with her. That was our merry-go-round for years."

Seeing the empathy in his gaze, Scarlet straightened her shoulders. What was done was done. She might not know what a good mother was, but she knew firsthand what an awful one was. "I *refuse* to let that be Daisy's life."

The empathy in his gaze morphed into something that looked like respect. But, no, that couldn't be right. Could it?

"You are so damn strong, Scarlet. I hope you realize that. And I also hope you know that you've raised an amazing daughter."

"Thank you." Warmth bloomed in her chest. Daisy *was* pretty damn amazing. "What about you? What was your childhood like?"

Matt chuckled. "Boring."

"I highly doubt that."

He took a sip of his drink. "My brother and I are close, but we're very different. Growing up, Jake was the really smart one, and I was the athletic one. Unfortunately, our dad is a bit of an ass who only values athleticism and 'manliness.'" He air-quoted the last word with a scowl.

"He would try to pit us against each other, showing obvious favor to me. It was so stupid, and thankfully we saw it for what it was and stayed close. To this day, I truly don't understand our dad. My brother is a great fucking guy and *beyond* successful. I mean, look at this place." He gestured at the room with his glass. "This house is his. And he's got a handful more scattered around the globe. He even paid off my parents' house. Yet our dad is still an ass to him."

"That must be hard. Not just for your brother, but for you, too."

He shook his head. "It's hard for Jake."

"And not you? You obviously care about your brother, so it must have sucked—it must *still* suck—to see him being treated that way."

"It does." Matt's brown eyes held a wealth of sadness, and the sight tore at her heart. "When we were kids, my brother was smaller. He had a heart condition that slowed his growth. And in middle school, he was super lanky. He got picked on a lot. So we teamed up. He helped me with school, and I helped him in the gym, helped him get bigger. Now? The guy's a freaking beast."

"Uh, you're not exactly scrawny, mister."

He grinned. "Oh no. Jake's *way* bigger than me. He's like The Rock with a full head of hair."

Scarlet chuckled.

"He'd like to meet you."

Her smile faded. "What?"

"My brother. He'd like to meet you." An amused glint sparked in his eyes, but she was too shocked to appreciate it. "Jake and his wife, Carmen, are going to be over sometime in the next few weeks, and he wants to meet you."

"You told him about me?"

"Of course I did. Told him about Daisy as well. Jake says Carm wants to stay at the resort while they're here, so what do you say? Want to have them over for dinner? Throw some steaks on the grill or something?"

Meet his brother and sister-in-law? "Um, if you're sure. I mean, I wouldn't want to impose on your brother time."

"Trust me, you're never an imposition."

He studied her for a moment, and she watched him back. Seeing this relaxed side of him was nice. Beyond nice, actually.

"So, we've discussed our childhoods. What else should we talk about?" She tapped her finger against her chin playfully, enjoying how talking with Matt took the edge off her nerves. "Are you dating anyone?"

His grin was ridiculous. "You know I'm not."

"Hey," she said, holding up her hands. "You never know."

"I haven't dated anyone in a long, long time."

"How is that even possible? You're . . ." She waved her hand at him in a circular motion.

His brow scrunched. "I'm what?"

"'What?' You're fishing for a compliment is what." She rolled her eyes. "You're a ridiculously good-looking man, Matt. And you know it."

He scoffed. "I know no such thing. I moved to Hudson right after I got divorced, and as you're aware—firsthand, I might add—I'm not exactly amicable. To anyone."

She snorted. "'Not exactly amicable'?"

"Hey, it's nicer than saying I'm an asshole, right?" He threw her a wink.

"You were never an asshole," she said, laughing. "Just kind of . . . grumpy. Growly. Broody." She shrugged. "Not gonna lie though, it also kinda worked for you. The growly thing you do is superhot."

His smile was blinding as he placed his drink on the coffee table. "Is that so?"

"Maybe . . ."

"Well," he said, scooting over a cushion. Now he sat right

beside her. "What would you say if I told you the only reason I was grumpy and growly—"

"And broody," she added with a smirk.

"Right. Then what if I said I was grumpy and growly and broody with you because you tied my tongue in knots?"

She chuckled. "Sure."

"I'm dead serious, Scar. You can even ask Cade."

Scarlet pursed her lips as she studied the man. The earlier melancholy in his eyes was gone, replaced by a lightness she'd never seen. And she liked it. A lot.

She also liked how his gaze lingered on her mouth.

"Are you flirting with me, Matthew Alvarez?"

"Mateo."

She tilted her head in question. "What?"

"It's Mateo, not Matthew."

Her grin widened. "I'll rephrase, then. Are you flirting with me, Mateo Alvarez?"

"Maybe." He shot her that brilliant smile—the one that never failed to make her stomach flip. "Is it working?"

The corners of her lips kicked up. "Maybe."

"In that case . . ." He crooked a finger at her.

Every nerve in her body tingled with anticipation, and she leaned closer. How could she not?

With the same finger he'd used to beckon her closer, he lifted her chin. "I think I like flirting with you," he murmured, lowering his head until his lips were just a whisper away from hers.

Scarlet's heart thumped rapidly in her chest, and her skin tingled. She'd never wanted anything—any*one*—more. "Then you should probably do it more often."

Her next breath was cut off by his lips. And holy crap, the kiss was better than her wildest imaginations.

Matt's lips were soft but demanding. One hand wrapped around her waist and pulled her close, while the other tangled in her hair. It was pure heaven. And she desperately wanted more, wanted to climb the man like a tree.

She lost all concept of time. The only thing she remained conscious of was Matt. How his solid chest felt pressed against hers. How he tasted like sin. How he set her on fire.

They could have kissed for a minute or fifteen, she didn't know or care. She pulled at his shirt and snuck her hands under the material. His skin was hot and firm. He was all solid, chiseled muscles.

With a groan, he pulled away. "Hang on, Scar." His hands enveloped hers, and he brought them to his lips, kissing her knuckles. "We have to slow down."

Her breath locked in her chest. What was going on? Did he not want . . . ?

Reality crashed over her like a bucket of cold water.

Holy shit. He wasn't into it, wasn't into her.

Mortification heated her face, and she tried to pull her hands from his grasp.

"Nope," he growled, gripping both her hands in one of his. Tipping her chin up, he crashed his mouth down on hers.

Surprise had her lips parting. In an instant, he was there, licking and nipping. She moaned when their tongues tangled and couldn't stop herself from grabbing on to his biceps.

They were both breathless when he pulled away. "Whatever you were thinking was wrong, Scarlet."

"How did you—"

"I've been watching you for a while. I can read some of your expressions. I can see when the doubt starts creeping in. Hear me, sweetheart. When we're together for the first time, it's not gonna be a quick fuck on the couch. Don't get me wrong, at some point I'll fuck you on this couch—hard and fast, for sure."

His eyes burned with desire, and heat pooled between her thighs. *Ohmygod. Yes, please.*

"But the first time we make love, we're gonna take our time. I'm planning on tasting every inch of you. And it's gonna be on a bed."

A thousand times yes. I'd—

Wait. What had he just said? She pulled away so she could look him fully in the face. "Umm . . ."

His grin was more smirk than smile. "It was the 'make love' comment, wasn't it?"

Shaking her head, she chuckled. "A little bit, yeah."

"I want to be absolutely clear, Scarlet. When we finally come together, we'll be making love. To me, this isn't going to be a casual, meaningless fuck. So I don't want to go too fast."

Her eyes widened. Wow. Okay. The man wasn't playing games. Hell, he was putting it all out there. And that made her heart melt a little more for him.

"I'm not taking getting involved with you lightly. For one, I need you to be sure—"

"I am." She was. God knew she'd never desired a man as much as Matt. He was sweet and thoughtful—two things she'd never really experienced. Not to mention outrageously handsome. Hell, the guy was flat-out crazy hot. She'd be a fool to not want him.

"I mean more than just sex."

Confusion had her stilling. Did he actually want to date her? Like long term?

He ran his fingers along her jaw, then leaned in and gave her a soft kiss. "Sweetheart, you're so much younger than me. You have your whole future in front of you. I need you to be sure that you want to be with me." She opened her mouth to tell him he was ridiculous, but he kept on talking. "And second—this is the most important—there's Daisy. I think the world of that little girl, and I want to be in her life. But I need you to decide if you're okay with that. Because

I'm in this for the long haul, Scarlet. As long as you'll have me."

Holy shit. He really did want to date her. Wanted a *relationship* relationship. Like what Poppy and Cade had.

She could only stare at him as she absorbed what he'd said. It had been a lot. And not at all what she'd expected.

Yeah, she really liked him. And yeah, she'd dreamed up little happily-ever-after scenarios with the three of them. But she'd never thought those scenarios could come true. How was this even real?

Guys didn't want more from her. She wasn't girlfriend material. She was good enough to fuck, but nothing more. She'd never been good enough for *anything* more. Her dear, drunk mother had drilled that into her brain. And the guys at the motorcycle club had proven it time and time again.

"Shit," Matt said on a sigh, taking her hands in his. "Did I just fuck this all up? Did I freak you out by jumping the gun?"

"I don't . . ." Her heart twisted. She wasn't worthy of this man. He just couldn't see it yet. "I don't think you really know me—like, the *real* me."

"That's my point, sweetheart. As much as I love kissing you, as much as I want to bury myself deep inside you . . . I want to get to know you more first."

Scarlet took him in. His hopeful brown eyes, his handsome face, his hulking frame that made her feel so fragile yet protected . . . *Damn.* She needed to be honest with him. He deserved that. "I really like you, Matt."

He winced. "I sense a *but* coming."

She looked at him apologetically. "But . . ." *God, this sucks.* "I don't think I can give you what you're looking for."

"I think you can," he countered with a stubborn lift of his chin.

The corners of her lips twitched. "I think you have this

idea of who I am, and it's really sweet." No one had ever described her the way he had. "But it isn't accurate."

"I think you're strong and brave and smart and beautiful. What's inaccurate about that?"

Her stomach dropped. She was none of those things. *Honest. He deserves honest.*

"I was a club whore, Matt. For *years,* I lived in an MC clubhouse and fucked whoever wanted to fuck." She dropped her gaze to her lap, battling a sudden flare of nausea. "I'm not good enough for you. Not by a long shot."

His hand cradled her jaw, and she tried to ignore the offered comfort. But after a moment, she leaned into his touch. She was weak like that.

"Scarlet, sweetheart. Look at me."

She took a deep breath of courage, then complied. Her eyes widened in disbelief. Because he wasn't looking at her with revulsion. He wasn't looking at her with judgment. No, he was looking at her like he always did. Like she was important to him, like she mattered.

"Your past is your past. Neither one of us can change it."

"Yeah, but—"

He pressed a finger to her lips, silencing her. "When I look at you, I don't see a club whore. I see a woman who's fought tooth and nail to provide a loving and stable home for her daughter. A woman who's strong and brave and smart and beautiful, but also generous and kind and so damn special to me." He kissed her, slow and tender, then pulled back to meet her gaze. "Scarlet, sweetheart, your past is in the past. I want your now. I want your future."

Tears prickled her eyes, and she blinked them away. The man absolutely destroyed her with his words.

"But like I said earlier, Scar, I want you to be sure. So let's get to know each other better. Take our time."

A giant lump formed in her throat, rendering her speech-less. She managed a nod.

He pressed another soft kiss to her lips. "Can I walk you to your room?"

The lump in her throat expanded. *Too sweet. This man is too damn sweet.*

Again, she nodded.

Matt held his hand out to her, and together, they rose from the couch. He intertwined their fingers as they made their way down the hallway.

At her closed bedroom door, he brought their linked hands to his lips and dropped a kiss on the back of hers. Then he simply held her in his arms. "We're going to make this work, Scar," he murmured. "I have a good feeling about us."

Her heart clenched. So did she. She was absolutely scared as hell, but so did she.

CHAPTER TWENTY-ONE

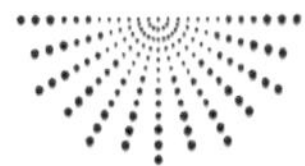

It had been nine days since the incident with the mystery man at the diner. Confident in Hudson Security's capabilities, Scarlet had gone back to work the very next morning. Though she didn't understand the full scope of their plan, she trusted them to keep her and Daisy safe. Gavin had called Xander off Daisy duty, but he'd also made everyone at Rebecca's day care aware of the situation. Which had gone a long way toward putting Scarlet's mind and nerves at ease.

Now here she was, Thursday night, spooning with Matt on the couch, her mind in a whirl. Just thinking about the long day she'd had made a fresh wave of exhaustion wash over her.

They were coming up on the Fourth of July weekend, and the island was packed. Hudson celebrated the holiday in a big way and had an extravagant fireworks production scheduled for the main event on Monday. The holiday weekend coincided with the final week of the motorcycle retreat at the Pacific View Resort, and it seemed as though everyone who rode a bike had stopped by the diner at least once.

The tourists who'd come in had been lovely, but Scarlet

was ready for all of them to be gone. Motorcycles had over-ridden the town. Every loud rumble had her wincing. Every rev of an engine frayed her sanity a little more. She struggled to keep the paranoia at bay. She knew Bean was tracking the man who'd asked about her, but she still felt like she was being constantly watched. It was unnerving.

She expected the mystery man to pop out at every turn, expected him to . . . Well, she didn't know exactly what, but definitely nothing pleasant. Of course, that hadn't happened.

For nearly a week, the mystery man had driven up and down Whidbey Island, stopping at countless restaurants and diners. There were still no clear shots of his face. It was as if all small, mom-and-pop diners were required to have crappy surveillance cameras—that is, if they had any cameras at all.

However, for the last couple of days, there'd been noth-ing. No movement. No notifications. Absolutely nothing. And no updates on the person who had broken into her apartment, either.

The not knowing was driving her crazy.

However, one thing that steadied her—as ridiculous and cheesy as it sounded—was coming home to Matt.

Initially, she had thought things between them would be awkward after her I'm-a-club-whore declaration. But they weren't. If anything, Matt had stepped up his sweetness. Or maybe she was just noticing it more.

They'd fallen into a pretty amazing routine since that conversation. Every morning, Matt ran an ungodly number of miles while she and Daisy got ready and had breakfast. When he returned all sweaty and flushed and delicious, Scarlet had his protein shake makings laid out on the island for him. She'd tasted one once, and yeah . . . no, thank you. She would stick with pancakes and syrup like her four-year-old.

The three of them then spent some time together, talking

about whatever, before she and Daisy headed out. She would drop her daughter at Rebecca's, who was now back from her family's month-long stay in Seattle—Daisy was over the moon to have her BFF, Rocco, back—and go to work.

After her eight-hour shift, she would pick up Daisy and head home. Well, Matt's home. But the more time they stayed there, the more it felt like hers and Daisy's, too. In fact, the weekend before, Matt had surprised Daisy by redecorating the other guest room for her. Pink bed linens, unicorn throw pillows, and a little flower night-light that projected shapes onto the ceiling. He'd even bought her two Squishmallows to add to her stuffy collection: a pink cat and a popcorn bucket. Because of course he did. To say Daisy had been more than happy to move into her own room was an understatement.

After work, she and Daisy got dinner going so it was ready when Matt came home. She wasn't the best cook in the world, but she could do the basics. Except grilling. In that case, she would prep everything and leave it for him to take care of. Then they'd all sit down together and eat.

Meals had always been bonding time for her and Daisy, but now, with the three of them together, sitting around the table talking about their days—or rather, Daisy telling Matt the minute-by-minute breakdown of her days—they were that much more special.

But Scarlet knew her apartment would be fixed in the next couple of weeks, and they'd have to head back home. It was something she'd gently reminded Daisy of. Her daughter was growing more attached to Matt by the hour, and she knew going back to their apartment would be a tough adjustment.

For both of them.

Still, she would cherish their shared dinners for the rest of her life. Their movie nights, too.

Much to Daisy's delight, they'd even had Four, Gavin, and Xander over last Saturday night to watch Cade's fighters win their first UFC title belts. She and Daisy had unapologetically squealed when the cameras had panned to Poppy and the twins celebrating the dynamic wins. Granted, Scarlet didn't know much about MMA fighting, so it had all looked dynamic to her.

As for bedtimes, a new routine had been adopted for Daisy. Apparently, Matt did the character voices better than Scarlet, so she had been demoted to bath time and teeth brushing while he read the nightly stories.

After they got Daisy settled each night, Scarlet and Matt stayed up talking in the living room. Those few hours meant the world to her. Not only did she get to decompress and have some adult time, but getting to know the man was simply amazing. They'd talked about everything—their interests and hobbies, the shenanigans of their mutual friends and other Hudson locals, funny stories from their younger years, and some not-so-fun stories of their childhoods.

In between all the talking, they'd make out on the couch. So far, clothes had remained on, but their hands had, for sure, wandered. The fire Matt lit in her was nothing short of glorious. And he put zero pressure on her to go further. She knew without a shadow of a doubt that if she called a halt to things, he'd stop. No questions.

She had slowed things down a few nights before, and he'd complied without question. He hadn't made her feel guilty or acted all put out. No. He'd just stopped, cuddled her close, and resumed their conversation. It was equal parts shocking, comforting, and . . . freeing.

Her heart had been bruised and battered over the years, but Matt—with one little comment here and one small gesture there—was slowly healing it.

His arms tightened around her, pulling her from her thoughts. She sank into his chest and sighed. The television was playing some movie she'd paid zero attention to.

"Would you like to go out to dinner with me?" he asked, sneaking a hand under her shirt to trace lazy circles on her stomach. "Just me and you?"

She craned her neck to look back at him. "Just me and you?"

He nodded, and a sly grin played on his lips. "I may have run into Rebecca earlier this week and asked if she'd be okay watching Daisy one evening."

"Did you now?" Well, that explained Rebecca's teasing over the last couple of days.

"How does dinner Saturday night sound? I figured Daisy would enjoy some extra time with Rocco."

Scarlet's mouth popped open and her eyes narrowed. She twisted, pushing Matt onto his back and climbing on top of him so they lay chest to chest. Chin propped up on her hands, she asked, "Is this why Rebecca offered to have Daisy spend the day with them? She claimed they were going to have a lazy Saturday playing in their backyard, followed by a movie night. 'Rocco would just *love it* if Daisy could hang out with us.' Was that your doing, mister?"

Chuckling, he framed her face in his hands. "Maybe." He pulled her down for a quick but thorough kiss that had her toes curling. "You can't deny that Daisy and Rocco would have a great time."

A smile crept over Scarlet's face as she recalled Daisy's excitement over the news of the potential playdate. She couldn't deny anything. Including this man. "You've thought all this out, haven't you?"

He shrugged. The casual gesture was at odds with his fiery gaze. "Well, we *are* dating. And I've been a complete asshole and haven't taken you out anywhere yet."

Planting her forearms on his chest, she reached up and traced her thumbs along his jaw. "You aren't an asshole, and I don't like it when you call yourself one. Joking or not. Besides, we've had countless meals together."

"You're sweet, Scar." He turned his head to kiss both her palms. "But you know what I mean. I want to take you *out* out. Where neither of us has to cook or clean. Don't get me wrong, I love all the time you and I have spent here at home. And you know I love everything about Daisy. But I've been looking forward to just me and you going out."

Home. Love. Daisy. You.

The combination of those words had her practically swooning. Maybe she was reading way more into them than he'd meant, but she didn't think so. With every breath, this man claimed a bigger and bigger piece of her heart.

She took in Matt's handsome features. His warm brown eyes, his jaw cut like granite, his five o'clock shadow . . . Then she took in the rest of him. His T-shirt perfectly hugged his broad shoulders and arms. And his hard bulge pressed against her in a way that was impossible to miss.

"You keep looking at me like that, sweetheart, and I'm gonna have to rethink the fucking-on-the-couch thing."

She trailed a finger down his neck and along the collar of his T-shirt. In the near-silent room, her nail made a soft scratching noise against the cotton. "Would that be such a bad thing?"

Before she could shoot him a grin, she was on her back with Matt lying between her thighs.

"You're so damn tempting," he said. Holding her face in his hands, he simply stared at her.

The look in his eyes had her core clenching. "I want to be with you, Matt. Not just tonight. And not just our bodies. I want . . ."

"What do you want, baby? Tell me."

Her heart thudded in her chest. The passion and affection shining in his eyes gave her courage. "I want to be yours. And . . . I want you to be mine."

Matt crashed his mouth to hers, and she gasped. Their tongues met, and she moaned into his mouth. Just as the last coherent thought vanished from her mind, he pulled away.

"I'm yours, Scarlet. I've been yours for longer than you know." Slipping his hands under her shirt, he squeezed and molded her breasts. "You're mine, Scarlet. Mine."

"Yes," she whimpered as he ground his hard erection against her. "Make me yours, Matt. Take me. Please."

He pressed another kiss to her lips before standing and pulling her up. Without a word, he linked their fingers and walked her down the hallway. In front of Daisy's room, he paused and released her hand. Quietly opening her daughter's door, he peeked inside. He nodded in satisfaction and pulled her door nearly closed.

Retaking her hand, he whispered, "She's out cold, spread out like a little starfish. But we'll lock the door, just to be safe."

Oh god, this man . . . Even in the throes of passion, he cared enough to check on Daisy.

Once they were in his room, Matt indeed locked the door behind them. He whipped off his shirt and dropped it on the floor. For a moment, she could only stare. He was breathtakingly beautiful. He'd probably balk at that description, but it was true. He truly, truly was beautiful.

Her fingers trembled as she reached out and traced the lines of his chest tattoo. "Do these have significance?"

"Yeah," he said, voice raspy. "But fuck if I can remember what."

Scarlet glanced up at him, and desire stared back at her. Need consumed her, but she managed a flirty grin. "Why would that be?"

"Sweetheart, I've dreamed of you touching me. And, baby, the reality is so much better than I imagined."

Heaving out a breath, she dropped the flirty smile and gave him honesty. "I'm so nervous, Matt."

He covered her hand with his. "We can stop whenever you want. You call all the shots with us. Always."

She erased the tiny bit of space between them, and he wrapped an arm around her waist, holding her tight. His skin was like an inferno, and she soaked up his heat. Tilting her head back, she met his gaze. "I want you so much. I'm just . . ." She blew out a breath. "Nervous."

Which was stupid. It's not like she'd never done this before.

"But you've never done this with me," he murmured, caressing the side of her face.

She should have been embarrassed about speaking her thoughts aloud, but his gentle touch alleviated the awkwardness.

"I've never felt this way before," she confessed.

"Me neither." He snagged her hand and guided her toward the bed. Sitting on the edge, he pulled her between his legs.

She draped her arms over his shoulders. They were almost eye to eye now.

"You matter so much to me, Scar. I want to know everything about you. What your dreams are. What your hopes are. And I want to help you get every damn thing you want." He ran his hands up her sides, lifting her shirt as he went. When it cleared her head, he tossed it aside. "I want to know what scares you and what makes you soar." His eyes roamed over her, and he pressed a kiss to the center of her chest. "I want to know what makes you tremble. What makes you sigh."

She did both those things, and wetness flooded her pussy. "Matt . . ."

He unhooked her bra and tossed it away. A second later, his hands were back on her ribs, thumbs caressing the undersides of her breasts. "These beautiful nipples, I've fantasized about them. I want to know how sensitive they are. I want to suck on them and make you come from that alone."

Her eyes closed as he pinched the sensitive buds between his fingers, rolling them. His mouth descended on her left breast while he continued to work her right with his hand. She groaned when he sucked, and her pussy clenched.

"Shhh," he murmured. "We have to be quiet, sweetheart."

"Make love to me, Matt. Please."

"Soon," he said, moving to her other breast. "There's still so much to explore." He flicked her nipple with his tongue, and she threw her head back. Then he sucked it deep into his mouth.

"Please, Matt," she begged, biting her lower lip.

"Tell me what you want," he murmured against her breast.

"Touch me. Please."

"Where?" His hand moved to her stomach, his touch soft and fleeting. "Here?"

"Matt . . ." She squirmed, in desperate need of his touch.

His hands drifted lower, and he pushed her pajama pants and panties past her hips. They fell, pooling at her feet. His thumbs skimmed up her inner thighs.

"Here?" he asked, his fingers slipping through her wet folds.

"God, yes."

"Oh fuck, baby," he groaned, his clever fingers exploring and teasing. "You're so fucking wet for me." He spread her lower lips and found her clit with his thumb, rubbing tight circles over the nub.

She ground down on his hand. "More, Matt . . . please."

His thumb picked up its pace, and her hips began moving. He caressed her slit, then sank two fingers deep inside her.

"Yes!" she cried out.

"That's it, baby. Ride my hand. You're so fucking beautiful."

His fingers pumped inside her. The wet noise of her pussy, of her desire, filled the room.

"More," she begged. She was so, so close.

In one smooth motion, he turned and pushed Scarlet onto the bed. Hovering above, he spread her legs wide and fucked her with his fingers until she was moaning. The tension in her body built. And the second his mouth found her breast, she detonated. Her thighs locked around his hand.

"That's it, baby," he murmured. "Milk my fingers with that sweet pussy."

A fresh wave of excitement flooded through her.

Heaving out a breath, she met his gaze. His pupils were blown. "More, Matt. Please. I need more."

"Yeah?" His smile was triumphant. "You want my cock, sweetheart?" Her core clenched around his fingers, and he chuckled. "I'll take that as a yes."

She grinned. "I knew you were a smart man."

He withdrew his hand from between her thighs and reached for his nightstand. Passing her a box he'd pulled from the top drawer, he said, "Get one out, please."

She tilted her head at him.

He shrugged. "I'm gonna be a little busy."

Scarlet's jaw dropped as he sucked her juices off his fingers.

"Yeaaah . . ." He gripped her knees and pulled them wide. "You grab the condom. I'm gonna be a little more than busy."

She lurched off the bed when his mouth met her molten

center. He clamped an arm over her stomach to hold her down, and she slammed her lips together to keep quiet.

Matt ate her out like a starved man. His tongue moved from flicking over her clit to fucking her deep. She was a writhing mess, and when he sucked her clit between his lips and pressed his fingers inside her, she exploded again.

"Fuck, you're delicious," he growled, rising to kneel between her thighs. He grabbed the condom from the bed and rolled it on.

Scarlet's mouth watered at the sight of him towering over her. His long, thick erection was straining up, almost hitting his belly button. God, what she'd do to swallow that down . . .

"Later, sweetheart," he said. "I want to see how good you take my cock."

She smiled and opened her knees wide. "Yes, please."

"Fuck, you're spectacular." Lining himself up, he paused and caressed the side of her face. "Thank you, sweetheart. Thank you for trusting me."

The tender words and touch were unexpected. Tears rushed to her eyes.

"You mean everything to me," he murmured. "*This* means everything. But know that even if we fuck like mad rabbits, we're still making love."

Scarlet pulled his lips to hers. She tasted herself on him, and a new wave of desire washed over her. But their kiss remained slow and sweet and tender.

He pushed into her, and they both groaned. He was thick and long, but she was so wet from her orgasms, from *him*, that he bottomed out with ease.

"Ohmygod," she moaned. She'd never been so full. "You feel amazing."

"Fuck, Scarlet. I have to move."

"Yes," she said, hiking her legs up.

He set a fast rhythm, hitting so deep that the sated tension within her quickly built back up.

"Harder, Matt," she whispered. "I'm almost there."

"Get there, baby," he demanded, pistoning his hips.

She reached between them and rubbed her clit. That's all it took for her body to tense and shatter. She flew over the edge again.

He pumped inside her once more before stilling with his release.

Collapsing onto his forearms, he pressed their foreheads together. "I think you may have killed me, sweetheart."

"Same." She placed a kiss on his lips, then sank into the mattress. "Not a bad way to go, though, right?"

CHAPTER TWENTY-TWO

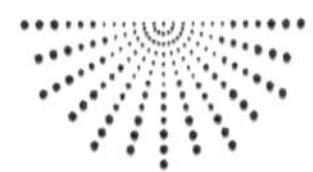

Matt couldn't remember a time when he'd been more content.

Content. What an inadequate word. *Happy* seemed better, but even that didn't do the moment justice. *At peace*, then?

All Matt knew for sure was that he felt quiet and sure. Settled. Like having Scarlet wrapped in his arms—with her head resting on his shoulder, her arm draped over his chest, and one of her legs tossed over his—meant he was home. He wasn't sure when exactly it had happened, but sometime between Daisy breaking her arm and now, he'd fallen in love with her.

Little by little, as they'd gotten to know each other, Scarlet had opened up to him. Relaxed. Become herself. Not the chipper waitress with the ever-present smile, but the real her. Yes, she was often chipper and smiling, but she could also be frustrated and tired and crabby. And the fact that she let him see all sides of her meant the world to him.

She was sweet and funny and sarcastic. She teased and laughed and warmed a part of him that he'd thought died after his divorce. Hell, in truth, it was a part that he'd thought died long before his divorce.

He wasn't sure Scarlet would ever fully understand how much she meant to him. But he'd damn well make it his duty to show her. Because as far as he was concerned . . . his heart was hers. Hopefully forever.

She shifted in his arms and pressed a kiss to his pec. "What's got you thinking so hard over there?"

He smiled. "You."

She propped her chin on his chest. "Thinking good things, I hope?"

"Always, baby."

She rolled her eyes. "Riiight."

He was pretty certain she wasn't ready to hear she was it for him. That he was hers. So, to keep things light, he asked, "Where do you want to go to dinner on Saturday?"

"I thought you had it all planned out?" she teased.

Running a hand up her spine, he felt her shiver. "Only who's watching Daisy. I didn't want to take you somewhere you don't like."

"I'm not super picky. What were you thinking?"

"We can go fancy like the Watermark at the resort or as casual as you'd like. We can even head over to Port Townsend or Whidbey Island. Whatever you're in the mood for."

"Not the Watermark," she said, scrunching her nose.

His eyebrows lifted in surprise. The Watermark was an amazing Michelin three-star restaurant with a months-long wait list. However, his buddy was the chef there, so he had an in. "Not a fan?"

"Oh, I've never been. It's just that it's *fancy* fancy. Thinking about stepping foot in the place makes me uncomfortable."

He tipped her chin up with his finger. "Sweetheart, you have nothing to feel uncomfortable about." Scarlet opened her mouth to protest, so he hurried on, "But we can go somewhere else."

She kissed his pec again, then lowered her chin back to his chest. "I'm high maintenance, I know."

He snorted. "Hardly."

"Taking the ferry to Port Townsend or Whidbey for dinner sounds stupidly romantic . . ."

"But . . ." he prodded, tucking that little nugget away in his brain.

Her nose scrunched again. "But it seems a bit extra, you know?"

She was so fucking cute.

Tapping a finger to her lips, she asked, "How about Monty's? We know the food's good, and it's right in town."

He grinned at her. "Sounds like a plan. Besides, I think Daisy would like to join us if we took a ferry somewhere. Something tells me she'd get a kick out of it."

The smile Scarlet treated him to was blinding. "She would. We don't leave Hudson all that often."

Daisy's sweet little face popped into his mind, and his chest ached. Scarlet wasn't the only one he'd fallen in love with. That was for damn sure.

The question that had swirled in the back of his mind for as long as he'd known Scarlet shoved itself to the forefront. Before he could second-guess himself, he said, "Can I ask you a really personal question?"

The hand tracing his chest stilled. "Of course."

He pulled her tighter to him. "You don't have to answer if you don't want to. I'm just curious . . ."

She shifted to meet his gaze. Her eyes narrowed as she asked, "You want to know about Daisy's dad?"

Shit. Was he that obvious? "I do. But you don't have to tell me anything. I was just wondering—"

She pressed a finger to his lips. "It's okay, Matt. It's not something I talk about, but . . . it's okay. It's you."

Who was Daisy's dad?

Dammit. Scarlet had known this conversation was inevitable. She'd just stupidly hoped it would never come up. Like, ever. Panic bloomed in her belly, and she tried to squash it down. Without much luck.

She just really, really hoped that what she and Matt had shared minutes before would make her next words less likely to drive him away. Because their connection was beyond sex. It was beyond making love. She couldn't exactly define it, but she prayed it was enough.

However, she was a realist. She would not be surprised if Matt told her to leave his bed after this conversation. She wouldn't blame the guy. Not one bit, because come on . . .

Taking a deep breath, she aimed for a calm expression and a casual shrug. Unfortunately, she had a feeling her calm expression was more like a cringe.

"Well . . ." *Holy shit, never mind.* She'd been wrong. She couldn't do this.

Scarlet closed her eyes and concentrated on Matt's touch. The soft up and down of his hand on her back took the edge off her nerves. She reminded herself to have faith in him. After all, she trusted him with Daisy. So she could trust him with her secrets, too. Right?

She met his steady brown gaze. "I left that spot on her birth certificate blank." Which wasn't a lie.

Chuckling, he shifted them into spooning positions, then

kissed the top of her head and pulled her close. "You know that's not what I'm asking, baby."

With a sigh, she ran her hands over the coarse hair on his forearm and relaxed against his chest. "I know."

"Let me rephrase. Does the guy who fathered Daisy know about her?"

Scarlet wanted to say no, but in truth, she wasn't sure. She'd been just over four months along when she'd testified against the club, so someone could have noticed. However, she'd taken extra precautions to hide her pregnancy. The last thing she'd wanted was for any of them to realize she was carrying one of theirs.

Instead of saying anything of that, she remained silent, savoring the feel of Matt's arms around her. It could very well be the last time he held her like this . . .

"The reason I'm asking is because I want to keep you and Daisy safe. If there's even a remote chance her biological father knows about her, then I'd like to keep an eye on him."

Scarlet's earlier panic resurfaced and twisted her belly.

Truth. He deserves the truth. No matter how much she didn't want to tell him.

"I don't know who her dad is," she whispered. "There are a few possibilities."

Matt tensed, and she could practically feel his confusion.

"The highest probability and most likely person is Steele."

"He was the club's VP that you testified against?"

She nodded. "But like I said, he died in prison."

"And the low probabilities?"

Bile crept up her throat. "There were the three guys who had a go." Dash, Zip, and Jester. Newly patched club members who had thought they were hot shit but hadn't fully understood the rules.

"'Had a go'?" Matt's icy voice chilled her blood.

"I wasn't Steele's old lady or anything, but still, he didn't like to share. He had me on the side for a few months, and no one was allowed to mess with me. But these guys . . . they either didn't get it or didn't care. They cornered me at a party and did their thing. Steele found me after." She'd been a bruised and bloody mess, barely hanging on to consciousness. "And he made them pay."

Matt's arms tightened around her. Otherwise, he gave no response.

Scarlet closed her eyes in an attempt to block out the vile memories of that night. The rough hands and fists. The terror and burning pain as they'd forced themselves on her. But it didn't work. Goosebumps claimed her skin, and she shivered. "So it doesn't matter. All of them are gone now. Anyone who could have fathered Daisy isn't a concern."

"What do you mean they're all gone?" Matt asked, rubbing her arms.

"Steele killed them."

"For raping you." It wasn't a question.

She scoffed, and a bitter smile lifted her lips. "Yeah, right. Steele didn't care about that. Those guys disrespected him. They were newly patched members who took what was his without permission. Steele's exact words."

Matt remained silent for a moment, as if contemplating what she'd said, but his hands continued warming her arms. "Steele killed those fuckers in front of you. That's what he went to prison for. That's what you testified against him for."

"Yes," she whispered, memories of that night playing in her mind. "After the three of them . . . took their turns . . . I was really messed up. Steele found me and made me rat them out. He waited a few hours for me to get my bearings and then took me to the club's basement."

Once she'd managed to stand without toppling over, he'd thrown a dirty towel at her, told her to clean the fuck up, and dragged her with him to the basement. A place she'd never been allowed to go.

She could still smell the musty, coppery scent that had grown heavier with every step down. Could still feel the fear that had skittered over every inch of her skin. No one had been allowed in the basement unless they'd been fully patched in. No old ladies, no prospects, no hangers-on. Just club members.

Steele had led her into a windowless cement room with bare walls and a lone drain in the center of the floor. Kneeling in a line behind the drain, Dash, Zip, and Jester had waited. Their hands tied behind their backs and their faces pummeled in.

"Three counts of first-degree murder," she said. "Steele got three consecutive life sentences and was fine with it. Proud of it, even. He'd been a prominent member of the club, but after that, he reached god-like status. Because he proved to everyone that disrespect wouldn't go unpunished."

"That's so fucked up." Matt's arms once again tightened around her. "But you know what, Scar? Regardless of why he killed those fuckers. I'm glad he did. They deserved it for hurting you."

Tears filled her eyes, and she held tight to his forearms. "Thanks," she whispered.

"I have one more question. If you don't mind, that is."

"Ask it," she said, even as dread swirled in her stomach.

His arms remained locked around her. She prayed that meant something.

"Did your handlers ever tell you how Steele died in prison?"

Scarlet closed her eyes in relief. It was a question she could handle. "He was just over three years into his sentence when he apparently mouthed off to the wrong guy. He got jumped in the cafeteria." She shrugged. "I didn't believe it—

Steele always seemed so invincible—but Bates showed me the autopsy photo. Within days of Steele dying, Bates said the club broke up. Apparently, there was some sort of sting. A lot of the guys were busted for selling guns to undercover cops. Shortly after that, they released me from witness protection."

"Do you really think they disbanded?"

"I don't know. It's doubtful, but if most of them were hauled off to prison . . . who knows? What I do know is that Bates gave me a generous stipend and let me keep my new identity, so there's that." She'd been beyond petrified. But she'd made it, dammit. Through grit and a whole lot of luck, she'd made it. And she would continue working her ass off for as long as it took to keep her daughter secure and healthy. "I think I mentioned Rita and Walt before?"

She felt him nod. "They're Ray and Martha's friends who own the diner you worked at in Arizona, right?"

A grin split her lips. It still boggled her mind that this man remembered all the things she'd said. "After I got out of witness protection, I told them about my past. I wasn't quite ready to make another change, so they helped me for a few months. And then they helped me with the move here."

Matt guided Scarlet onto her back so they could see each other. Her heart thumped painfully in her chest as she tried to read his expression.

"I know I've said it before, Scar, but I'll say it again. You're so damn strong." He touched the side of her face, pushed her hair off her forehead. "It kills me that you've suffered some of the greatest atrocities a person can suffer. I want to dig up those assholes who hurt you and kill them all over again."

She reached up and cradled his jaw. "It's over, Matt. It's in the past."

"That's right. And we're looking to the future." He kissed her palm. "But please know that I will help you in any way I can."

Scarlet pulled his face down to hers. "Then make love to me again." She pressed a soft kiss to his lips. "Because you make everything better. It's like you're my prize. I had to go through hell, but it's okay because I got you and Daisy out of it all."

"You have me," he murmured, settling between her thighs. "Forever, sweetheart."

CHAPTER TWENTY-THREE

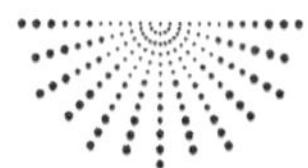

Matt had been wrong. He'd thought lying in bed with Scarlet in his arms after making love for the first time was the most content he would ever be.

Nope. It was *this*. It was waking up with her snuggled into his side after a full night of not only savoring her body, but being entrusted with her secrets. *This* was the most content, the happiest, and the most at peace he'd ever be. Surely.

Glancing at the clock, he saw it was just before five. He should get out of bed and go for a run. Instead, he buried his face in Scarlet's hair and inhaled. Running was off the table this morning. He'd rather lie here with her for the next hour and enjoy this moment. Enjoy her.

Trailing his hand over her arm, gently so as not to wake her, he stared at the ceiling and grinned. He wanted to pinch himself, not quite believing that this, that *she* was real. That they were going to give this a shot.

Oh, who the hell was he kidding? He wasn't giving this a shot. He was all in. Completely.

And yet . . . doubts lingered in the back of his head. With his history, how could they not?

Matt was terrified that she would change her mind. That after a few weeks, months, years, or even longer, she'd decide he wasn't what she wanted after all. He knew there were no guarantees in life, but the mere thought of that possibility gutted him, hollowed him out in the most devastating way.

He couldn't lose her. He couldn't lose Daisy. They'd quickly become his world.

"Good morning," Scarlet said, her voice raspy. "What time is it?"

Glancing down, Matt met the most beautiful pair of brown eyes. She'd pulled one of his T-shirts on before bed last night, and yeaaah . . . Seeing his woman in only his shirt, with that sleepy gaze and rumpled hair, made his cock twitch. He kissed the top of her head. "It's not even five. Go back to sleep. You have another hour."

"Are you going for a run?" she asked, toying with the hairs on his chest.

"I think I'll skip today."

Her head lifted off his shoulder, and she looked at him in obvious surprise.

He let out a quiet chuckle. "What can I say? I'm comfortable."

"Me too," she said with a soft grin, lying back down. She resumed caressing his chest, then paused at the top of his right pec.

Matt went absolutely still as she touched his most recent scar—a raised circular mark. From the bullet he'd taken.

"Does this hurt?" she asked.

Remembering to breathe, he shook his head. "No. You know, funny enough, I'd kinda forgotten about it."

For so damn long, he'd been consumed by his injury. Not so much the actual bullet through his chest, because even now, he'd take a bullet for his brother any day of the week. Rather, he'd been consumed by the aftermath of the shooting. The implosion of his marriage. His subsequent divorce. Leaving the force.

Recently, however, he hadn't given any of those things much thought. He could say it was because he'd started working with Hudson Security. That reason held a small grain of truth. But the fact was, his thoughts and emotions were now consumed by Scarlet and a tiny little four-year-old. Both ladies had stolen his heart and mind.

"Can I ask what happened?"

He tugged her closer until she lay half on top of him. "You can ask me anything, sweetheart," he said against her forehead. "In a nutshell, it was a case of mistaken identity."

Scarlet tipped her face toward him, and questions swirled in her brown eyes.

He tucked a lock of hair behind her ear and eased her head back to his chest. "My sister-in-law, Carmen, had this sick fucker who was stalking her. She and I were walking to get some food, and the asshole shot me, thinking I was my brother."

Scarlet gasped. "Oh, Matt . . ."

"I'm okay." Now.

Her fingers still lingered over the scar, so he covered her hand with his, flattening her palm to his chest. Not because he wanted her to stop touching it, but because he wanted to feel her entire hand on his skin. "The guy shot me in the back and the bullet exited here. I'm just so damn thankful that Carm was standing next to me and not in front of me, or else it would have hit her, too."

She pulled free from his grasp and wrapped her arm around him. Squeezing, she asked, "Do you promise you're okay?"

God, this sweet woman . . .

"I promise, Scar."

After holding him for another moment, she loosened her

grip and propped her chin on his chest once more. "Your brother and sister-in-law are okay, too?"

Recalling everything that had transpired with Jake and Carmen, Matt sobered. He'd been so damn helpless.

"Yeah. They're good now. Granted, they went through hell, but they came out on top. They were instrumental in my recovery, actually. I wasn't in a good place after all that, but they were both there for me."

"Talk to me," she whispered, caressing the side of his face.

Matt leaned into her touch. This woman had trusted him with the dark secrets of her past. The least he could do was trust her with his own. And to his surprise, he *wanted* to share this part of himself with her, even though he'd never told another soul. Not his brother, not Cade, not his department-assigned therapist . . . No one.

He moved Scarlet fully on top of him, spreading his legs so she could settle comfortably between them. She tucked her head under his chin, and he pulled the sheets over them before wrapping his arms around her.

"I'm not sure where to start," he admitted. Taking a deep breath in, he took comfort from Scarlet's hand tracing gently back and forth along his rib cage. "I guess . . . Long before I was shot, things hadn't been going well in my marriage. When Krista and I got married, I'd already been a detective for a couple years, but I was still the newest one in the department and out to prove myself. Things were fine for a while."

Until they weren't.

"I don't know," he continued as Scarlet remained silent. Her steady touch kept him grounded, let him know she was still there and listening. "I could play the blame game, but with hindsight, I know I wasn't faultless. I put my job before her a lot. I worked really late hours, and that wasn't fair to her. For the last nine or ten months of our marriage, we were in couple's therapy, and it looked like we could maybe work things out, but then . . . I got shot."

Matt remembered waking up in the hospital and being flooded with panic about Jake and Carmen. And then he remembered the agonizing pain. The difficulty breathing. The concern on Krista's tear-streaked face.

"When I came to at the hospital, Krista was there. She was obviously upset and scared. She told me I had to keep fighting. I had to get better. For her. For us. For our baby."

Scarlet gasped. She lifted her head off his chest, and her surprised eyes locked with his.

Unable to hold her gaze, he looked at the ceiling and swallowed past the boulder in his throat. "I remember being so fucking happy. So goddamn thrilled. She and I had talked about having kids someday, but the pregnancy was a surprise. The best fucking surprise . . ." His voice grew hoarse, but he continued, "I wasn't out of the woods yet, and I'd gotten a nasty infection. I drifted in and out for a couple more days. When I woke up again, I was still in the ICU, but things were clearer. I remembered exactly what Krista had said. We were having a baby, but . . ."

He screwed his eyes shut. The grief was a tangible pain in his chest, like someone had reached through his ribs and yanked out his fucking heart. He ground his teeth together until his mouth ached and a low growl left his throat.

Warm hands cupped his face. Soft lips pressed gently against his.

"Breathe, baby," Scarlet whispered into his ear. "Breathe. I'm here."

He hugged her tighter. It took two tries, but he finally managed to say, "The baby wasn't mine."

Scarlet pulled away, and again, her hands framed his face. "What do you mean?"

Whether it was the scent of her floral shampoo, her

comforting touch, or having finally said the words out loud, he felt steadier. But his heart was still broken over something that had never been his.

"When I came to and looked at Krista, I realized I wasn't the father. I couldn't have been. She and I hadn't been intimately involved for at least six months. And there was no way she was that far along." Their confrontation replayed in his mind. His yelling, their tears, her denial . . . "She insisted the baby was mine, but I knew she was lying. I had the hospital staff bar her from seeing me. Hell, I basically tried to have everyone barred from seeing me."

He let out a bitter chuckle. "The next day, my old partner came to visit. Even though Davidson and I didn't work together anymore, we were still close. We still hung out. He was one of my closest friends. But he came to apologize. Said it was a lapse in judgement. That he'd never intended to get involved with Krista and that it was all a mistake. Like anything he said would make any of it better."

Disappointment sat like a sour rock in his gut.

"Oh, Matt, I'm so sorry." Scarlet scooted up his body and placed a tender kiss on his cheek.

"To this day, I still don't know what hurt more—my wife cheating with my friend or my friend cheating with my wife."

"Neither one of them deserved you."

The corners of his lips tipped up at her fierce declaration. "Thank you, sweetheart."

"I'm serious, Matt," she said, capturing his gaze. "You're the most amazing man I've ever met. You're kind and honorable and loyal. You didn't deserve to be treated like that and lied to. *They* are assholes and you're a million times better off without them in your life. Good riddance."

His heart warmed at her words, and he stretched up to kiss her. "Thank you."

Scarlet ran a finger along his jaw and stared at him for a moment. "You know I trust you with Daisy, right?"

His breath caught.

"Daisy's the most important person in my life, and I trust you with her. I know that you'll protect her and look out for her. That you'll always try to do what's best for her."

"Scar . . ." He was speechless. Holding her face in his hands, he kissed her lips. She didn't realize she'd just given him the greatest gift. "I swear to you, I will protect that wonderful little girl with my life. You and Daisy . . . You two . . . I just . . ."

He closed his eyes. *Honest, Alvarez. Be honest.*

When he'd collected himself enough to meet her gaze, the hope staring back at him had all the tension draining from his body. "Scarlet, sweetheart, I didn't know you were missing from my life. And now that you're here—both you and Daisy—I don't want to let you go. Ever."

"You don't have to let us go. Ever," she whispered, eyes shimmering with unshed tears. She glanced at the clock and smiled. "We still have some time before I need to officially be up. Will you let me make love to you?"

Every cell in his body shot to attention, and his blood surged south. But he shook his head. "Baby, you don't need—"

She pressed a finger to his lips. "You made me feel amazing and cared for and loved last night. I want to do the same for you. Let me?"

God, this woman slayed him. Unable to resist, he pulled her in for another kiss. "I'm all yours, sweetheart. All yours."

CHAPTER TWENTY-FOUR

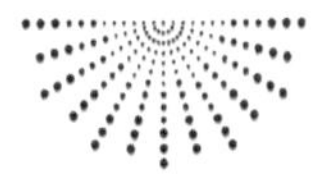

"Well, aren't you a chipper one this morning?" Martha teased as Scarlet grabbed a fresh pot of coffee from the beverage station.

"Why wouldn't I be?" she replied in a singsong voice. Martha followed hot on her heels as she refilled mugs at the gossip train table. "It's a bright, sunny Friday and the start of a holiday weekend."

And last night had been the most amazing of her life. As for this morning . . . having Matt share with her what he had? Yes, it hurt her heart to know that he'd suffered such betrayal. However, it also made her heart so damn full that he'd gifted her with his story, that she'd been able to comfort him with her words and her body—just like he'd done for her.

Their budding relationship meant the world to her. *He* meant the world to her.

"Thank you, hon," Mrs. Abbot said once her coffee was topped off. "How are you and Daisy getting along at Matt's place?"

Mrs. Green gestured to Scarlet with her mug. "I'd say they're getting along swimmingly by that hickey on her neck."

Scarlet's mouth dropped open as she gasped and slapped a hand over her neck.

"Bonnie," Mrs. Yoshida admonished, though she was chuckling. "Don't embarrass the girl." She winked at Scarlet. "It's on the other side, dear."

Scarlet could only gape like a fish at the women, who stared at her with twinkling eyes.

Then they all burst into laughter.

"Oh, honey," Martha said, wiping a tear away. "If only you could see your sweet little face."

Ohmygod, these ladies . . .

Scarlet set the pot of coffee down and covered her heated cheeks with her hands. "Guilty as charged."

"Oh no, dear." Mrs. Yoshida shook her head. "There's nothing to be guilty about with that one. All those muscles and manly goodness? It's more like yay for you!"

"Absolutely," Mrs. Green agreed. Then she pursed her lips. "He's quite a bit older than you, though, isn't he?"

Scarlet sucked in a breath and nodded. She hoped they weren't going to judge.

"Is he good with Daisy?" Mrs. Green asked.

She couldn't help her smile. "Matt's wonderful with her."

"Don't you mean *Matty*," Martha teased, and the ladies laughed.

"My point is"—Mrs. Green waited until the table's attention came back to her—"so what if there's a big age difference between you two? You're both adults. The man obviously knows you're a package deal and loves your little girl. And Daisy loves her Matty, too. Besides, if I could bottle up the way that man looks at you . . ." She shimmied her shoulders while her compatriots hooted.

Scarlet didn't want to ask, but curiosity got the better of her. "Um . . . how exactly does Matt look at me?"

Mrs. Abbot threw her a wink. "Like he wants to gobble you right up, hon. Yay you, indeed!"

Grabbing the coffee pot, Scarlet grinned at her favorite women. "Not gonna lie, ladies. You won't be hearing any complaints from me." Waving goodbye, she left Martha with her friends and continued to the next tables, chuckling the entire time.

Scarlet scanned the tables as she finished putting on a new pot of coffee. Paula was covering the far side, and everyone looked to be good, so she snagged a fresh rag and headed to the front to wipe down menus. The glamor of her job never ended.

Glancing out the front door, she frowned. The parking spots in front of the diner were angled, but a car had pulled in perpendicular to the curb. She debated whether she should say something as the driver's side door opened. A man emerged. He was hunched over and wearing a heavy jacket. She winced. It was supposed to reach nearly eighty degrees today, but whatever. To each their own, right?

Menus now clean and dry, she placed them into their bin. The front door opened. She glanced up to greet the new customers. And froze.

The man in the heavy jacket staggered toward her. With each labored step, his jacket parted. She gasped at the bright-crimson stain covering his stomach.

Scarlet was moving before she could think. Reaching for the man, she called out, "Martha! Ray! Call 9-1-1!" She slung his arm over her shoulder, then grabbed him around his waist and tried to take some of his weight. "Sir, you need to sit."

A customer rushed toward them with a chair. Scarlet

took a step, and the man fell on top of her, bringing them both to the ground.

Somehow, she managed to scramble out from under him and get to her knees. With the help of another customer, she rolled the groaning man onto his back. His hands were pressed to his abdomen, but the amount of blood seeping past his fingers was staggering.

Shockingly blue eyes captured Scarlet's gaze. Something tickled the back of her mind, but it vanished when the man coughed and moaned in pain. His face was ashen.

"Hang on, sir," she said, untying her apron. She trembled as she shook out the extra pens and notepads she kept stashed in it. Pushing his hands away, she applied pressure to his wound with the balled-up apron. "I'm so sorry," she whispered when his lips parted with another sound of anguish.

"The ambulance is on its way," Martha said from behind her.

"All right, everyone," Ray called out, one arm around his wife's shoulders. "Let's not be looky-loos. If you want to be useful, you best send some prayers up to whoever your god is."

"I have more towels, Scar," Paula said, passing her a fresh one.

Taking the new towel, she tossed her blood-soaked apron to the side and reapplied pressure to his wound. She met the man's eyes and tried to give him a reassuring smile. "Did you hear that, sir? The ambulance is on its way."

He shook his head. "Too late."

Her gut clenched. The man's voice was barely above a whisper, and the resigned look on his face threatened to break her heart. "Please hang on. Don't give up. I can hear the sirens. They're close. I promise."

"You don't understand . . ."

She could barely hear him, so she leaned closer. "What don't I understand?"

He shuddered. "They're coming for you, Sienna."

Ice raced down Scarlet's spine.

She reared back as if the man had struck her. She could only stare at him in shock.

He groaned again, and she realized she'd let up on the pressure. Correcting her mistake, she found her voice. "What did you call me?"

"Don't matter. They want her." His body seized, and his eyes nearly rolled into the back of his skull. When the shaking stopped, he whispered, "They blame you, and they're coming. Not long now. They know. One for one—"

The front door to the diner burst open, and two EMTs—Nora and Colton—rushed in.

"We've got it from here, Scarlet," Nora said, gently pushing her aside.

Someone gripped her by the elbows and eased her to standing. She didn't know who. Didn't care. Her mind was in chaos.

She glanced back at the man. They'd put an oxygen mask on his face, and his eyes were shut. All the blood rushed from her head. She reached out and grabbed the nearest person.

"I got ya, darling," Ray said, wrapping his arm around her waist.

Ray and Martha continued to speak to her, but Scarlet didn't hear. The only noise in her ears was the erratic thumping of her panicking pulse. Because she'd realized something. The man being attended to, the one Nora and Colton were loading onto a backboard?

He was the mystery man who'd been looking for her.

"Honey, are you okay?" Martha's voice sounded far away, like she was at the end of a long, dark tunnel.

Scarlet shook her head.

Sienna.

The man had called her Sienna.

Vomit surged up her throat, and she slapped her hands over her mouth.

"Matt," she croaked, battling the nausea. "I need Matt."

CHAPTER TWENTY-FIVE

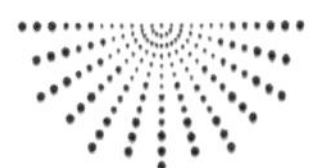

"Pause it," Matt instructed Bean. The figures on her left monitor froze. "There." He pointed at the woman carrying a black duffle bag. Turning to Bean's center right monitor, he pointed again. The same woman, but eight minutes earlier. "Look at the duffle bag. Look how in the later video, the handles are strained."

"Holy shit," Bean said with a sigh. "She took the kid out of the house in a damn duffle bag?"

Matt frowned. It never failed to amaze him how sick and fucked up some people were. "It's looking like it."

"That's absolutely fu—"

A sharp knock interrupted Bean, and the door to her office swung open.

Matt's heart stopped.

Gavin stood in the doorway with Scarlet tucked against his side. She was wearing her pink waitress uniform, but the entire front was soaked in blood.

Matt was in front of her on his next breath.

"Scarlet, baby," he murmured as she threw herself into his arms. "Sweetheart, are you hurt?"

"The blood's not hers," Gavin said.

He met his friend's gaze over Scarlet's head, silently imploring Gavin to continue.

"A man was stabbed multiple times in the abdomen. Witnesses confirmed he stumbled into the diner, presumably for assistance." Gavin nodded to Scarlet. "She was the first to help. Ray called 9-1-1 while she applied pressure to his wound. The blood is the guy's."

Matt held Scarlet tight, and his stomach twisted at the way her slight frame quaked. "How'd she get here?"

"She came with me. I was meeting with Quinn when the emergency call came in. We went to the diner and . . . She's in a bit of shock, but she was asking for you." Gavin's expression became sympathetic as he looked at Scar. "She asked for Xander to look after Daisy."

The hairs on Matt's arms rose. *The fuck?* he mouthed to his friend.

"It's the only thing she's said since we left the diner." Gavin shrugged. "Xander checked in about ten minutes ago. All is well over there. He'll stay until you pick up Daisy."

Matt lifted his chin in thanks, then bent his knees and scooped Scarlet up in his arms. Walking back to Bean's enormous desk, he murmured his thanks when Bean spun his chair toward him. She held it steady while he sat with Scarlet draped over his lap.

"Scarlet, sweetheart, are you hurt?"

She shook her head against his neck.

"Thanks, man," he said, accepting a freshly cracked bottle of water from Gavin. "Here, sit up and take a sip of this."

Gaze locked on her lap, she took the bottle of water and drank.

Matt ran his hand up and down her back and laid a kiss to her temple. "I've got you." He glanced at the concerned faces of his friends and colleagues. "We've all got you."

Scarlet looked up, and his blood chilled at the stricken expression on her face. Aside from a man being stabbed, something else was horribly wrong. "What aren't you telling me, baby?"

His chest clenched when a tear spilled down her cheek.

"He called me Sienna," she said, voice shaking. More tears slipped down her face. "I think he was the guy asking about me, showing that picture of me." Biting back a sob, she buried her face in his neck again.

"Sienna May Robinson," Bean murmured.

Scarlet flinched in his arms and let out a small whimper.

"I'm sorry, Scarlet," Bean said. "You said I could dig, so I did."

With a sniff, Scarlet sat up, though she continued to lean against him. "It's fine. I promise." She met his gaze. "That was my old name."

"Quinn, it's Gavin."

Matt glanced over at the sound of his friend's voice. Gavin had his phone to his ear.

"I need you to send me whatever you've got on the stabbing victim. There may be a connection with Scarlet."

Matt cupped Scarlet's face in his hands, bringing her attention back to him as he brushed away her tears with his thumbs. "Talk to me, Scar. Did he say anything to you?"

She let out a shaky breath and nodded. Her eyes darted to Bean, then to Gavin. She waited until Gavin hung up before speaking. Pride surged through him. Scared or not, she was so damn strong.

"He said that they blamed me and were coming. That they knew. And he said . . ." She swallowed hard, and new tears flooded her eyes. "He said, 'They want her.' That's why I asked Gavin to call Xander. Do you think he meant Daisy?"

Matt hugged her tighter. "Breathe, sweetheart."

"Did he give any indication who 'they' were?" Gavin asked.

She sniffed. "No. He said something about how it's not long now and 'one for one,' but I didn't understand. I was in shock that he'd called me Sienna in the first place."

"Once I get the guy's info from Quinn, I'll find everything there is to know about him," Bean said, tapping the tablet in her hand.

Matt frowned, and he scrubbed one hand over his jaw.

Scarlet linked her fingers with his. "What are you thinking?"

They want her. The fact that this guy had most likely been referring to Daisy made his blood boil. One for one . . .

Fuck.

"Do you think someone found out you were pregnant? You said you were pregnant at the trial, right?"

Scarlet paled. "But I wasn't showing too much, and I purposely wore loose clothes."

"But it's possible someone could have figured it out?"

She squeezed her eyes closed. "I never said anything during my testimony, but my lawyers and handler knew, so it's possible."

"If this guy was able to find you," Gavin said, "then it's plausible that whoever 'they' are did, too. They could have seen you with Daisy and done a rough estimation of her age."

Matt pushed past his simmering anger. "Bean, can you find out who the family members and close relations of Steele MacBride are? The same for the three club members he killed."

"On it," Bean said.

Scarlet looked at him in question.

"'One for one,'" Matt murmured, squeezing her hands. "What if whoever this is wants to hurt Daisy as . . . payback . . . for one of theirs being taken away? The guy said they blame you. If we assume it's for someone's death—either Steele or one of the three—then that possibility makes sense."

She sucked in a breath and shuddered. "Ohmygod, that's terrifying."

Matt lifted her chin with his fingers and waited until she met his gaze. "No one is getting near Daisy. *No one.*"

"Agreed," Gavin said, tone curt. "Consider Xander Daisy's personal security officer from here on out."

"Thank you," Scarlet whispered in a shaky voice.

"Nothing to thank me for. We take care of our own." Gavin nodded at Matt. "You and Daisy are his. That makes you ours as well."

The surprise on Scarlet's face had Matt pressing a kiss to the top of her head. Because Gavin had told the truth. She and Daisy *were* his. And he'd do everything in his power to protect them.

CHAPTER TWENTY-SIX

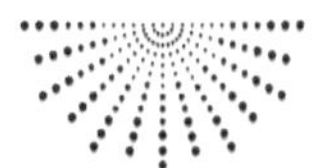

S carlet was a freaking wreck. There was no other way to describe it. Sleeping in Matt's embrace, enveloped in his strength, had helped. Until she'd woken up. Then reality had crashed down all around her.

It was Saturday, and she'd never been more grateful to not work the weekend shift. The last place she wanted to be was the diner where that man had—

Nope. Not going there.

She was home with Daisy and Matt, and she was focusing on that.

Her daughter's high-pitched giggles filled the air, along with several deep rumbles of laughter. It wasn't just Daisy and Matt, she reminded herself. Xander was here, too. As were a couple of techs from Hudson Security, who were upgrading Matt's already extensive security system. Apparently, there were "blind spots," but additional cameras would fix that problem.

Following the voices, Scarlet came to a halt as she turned the corner to the great room. All the furniture had been pushed to the edges. In the center were various cushions, chairs, books . . . All sorts of things that made zero sense to her. Matt and Xander were in the middle of the mix, arranging pillows and placing more items among the cushions.

"Mama!" Daisy exclaimed, bouncing up and down at the far edge of the room. "Matty and Xandy are making an ossticycle course for me and Mr. Slothy and Baby Unicorn and my new Squishys!"

"And your other stuffies," Matt chimed in. "You want to make sure they all get a turn, too."

Daisy's answering nod was sage, her blue eyes big. "I don't want any stuffy to be sad."

"That's right," Xander said. "I'll help you and the stuffies. That way, they get to know me better and aren't scared of me. Because, you know, I'm kind of a scary guy."

"You're not scary, Xandy," Daisy said, giggling. "You have a bun on top of your head like Mama!"

Xander chuckled and shot Scarlet a wink. "That I do, kiddo. That I do."

Scarlet's heart squeezed at what the men were doing. She knew Daisy recognized Xander from Rebecca's, but the man was still quite intimidating. He stood just as tall as Matt's six-four, was stacked with muscles, and gave off a serious alpha vibe. But evidently, building an obstacle course and sporting a man-bun negated all that in the eyes of her four-year-old daughter. The tough personal security officer had even been dubbed *Xandy*.

"All right, Otter Pop," Matt said, standing to survey their work. "You and Xander walk Mr. Slothy through the obstacle course while I talk to your mom, okay?"

Daisy squealed in delight as she grabbed Mr. Slothy and rushed to the starting point. Matt gave Xander a chin lift, then claimed Scarlet's hand and led her out of the room. Trepidation stirred in her gut when he closed the door to his office behind them. Something in his expression told her this wasn't him sneaking her away for a good time.

"Bean has new info," he said, pulling an additional chair behind his desk.

The trepidation transformed into full-fledged worry, and it sat like a rock in her gut. Yup. No good times here.

She took the seat next to Matt as he opened a couple of tabs on his computer. Bean's grim face filled the monitor. Seconds later, the screen split. On the left were three boxes: Bean, Gavin, and her and Matt together. The other side looked like Bean's laptop screen.

"Hey, guys. I'll get right to it," Bean said. "Unfortunately, the mystery man remains a mystery."

"Morning," Gavin said with an equally somber expression. "Quinn called this morning and let me know the guy didn't make it. Lost too much blood. He was stabbed in the gut fourteen times."

Bean sighed. "The man's prints aren't in the system, so we still have no ID. The car he drove onto Hudson was reported stolen five days ago. However . . ." Bean chewed her lip. "I do have footage from the ferry that shows the actual attack."

A video began playing on the right side of the monitor, and Scarlet held her breath. There was no audio, but the security feed showed the mystery man walking to his car, which was parked on the ferry's upper deck along the exterior row. He opened the driver's door and settled inside.

Scarlet's eyes widened as another figure quickly approached. The stocky man—at least, she assumed it was a man, considering his size—wore dark pants, a bulky jacket, and a dark ball cap pulled down low to shield his face. Before the guy in the car could close his door, the newcomer leaned into the driver's side. His right arm was a blur of motion.

Her stomach lurched. The guy in the car was getting

stabbed. Over and over and over again. He had been given no chance to defend himself, no time to even struggle.

The attacker straightened, tucked something in his jacket, closed the car door, and walked off. With his back to the camera.

Thirty seconds. That's all it had taken to end a man's life and get away scot-free.

Thirty. Damn. Seconds.

The video stopped, and Scarlet blinked. Matt's hand squeezed her shoulder, and she glanced at him. But she had no words.

Bean cleared her throat. "In matching up the times, it looks like the mystery man—the one in the car—drove right off the ferry and went straight to the diner."

Where he had tried to tell Scarlet something she still didn't understand.

With shaking hands, she rubbed her face. "Now what?"

"Now I'm tracking that car's plates, finding out where it's been since it was stolen. Hopefully, that'll give us some insight into what the mystery guy's motives were. Also, Quinn sent me a photo of his face, so I set it up with my facial rec program. I'm running it against the different DMV databases. It may take some time to ID him, though." Bean shrugged. "I'm sorry I don't have better information for you."

"The person who stabbed the guy. Any additional footage?" Matt asked.

"Negative," Gavin said. "Quinn's checking with the ferry and their waste management crew to see if any clothes or other evidence were dumped, but so far, nothing."

Matt leaned back in his chair and crossed his arms. "He could be on the island."

"Yeah," Bean said. "But even if he left, he could be working with a larger group."

"Ohmygod," Scarlet whispered, closing her eyes. There were so many unanswered questions. So many unknowns.

"Next steps?" Matt asked, covering her clenched hands with his.

She held on tight.

"I'm still running the next of kin and known associates of the four deceased club members," Bean said. "The preliminary reports show that the relatives that aren't in jail or prison are still in the South Dakota area. After Steele was put away, there were nearly two dozen more trials involving the remaining club members and known associates over that next year. Almost all were found guilty and sent away."

"Did they all end up in the same prison?" Gavin asked.

Bean pursed her lips. "Not all. Looks like five or six ended up in the same prison as Steele, but the majority did shorter sentences in jail. A number of them have been in and out of jail since."

"For the ones that are out or about to be sprung, pull their mug shots and send them to Quinn," Gavin said.

"Already done, boss. Also, with the facial rec, we'll get notified if any of them hop on a ferry coming this way."

"Good work, B. Scarlet?"

Her gaze shot to Gavin's. "Yes?"

"We'll keep Xander on Daisy. Have you met Natasha Silver?"

She shook her head.

"Well, you're about to. I'm assigning Tash to you for the next couple weeks." Scarlet's eyebrows rose in surprise, but Gavin kept talking. "I'll have her swing by your house today so you can meet her."

"Okay, um, but do you think that's necess—"

"Yes," Matt said. "Until we know who the players are and whether it's you or Daisy or both of you being targeted, it's better to play it safe."

Gavin nodded. "Agreed. We'll give it a week, then reevaluate. I'll check in with you two lat—"

A loud ding drew their attention.

"Hang on," Bean murmured. Her brow furrowed in concentration, and Scarlet heard the furious clicks of the woman typing. "Got him."

The right side of the screen changed to a video of the mystery man entering a gas station. The camera provided a full, clear, color view of his face.

"That's Michael Wilson," Bean said. "Thirty-nine. Resides in Beulah, Wyoming, which is right across the border from South Dakota. No arrests. No warrants. Not even a parking ticket."

Another image appeared. A Wyoming driver's license. Bean enlarged it, and Scarlet gasped. She knew her eyes were bugging out of her head, but ohmygod . . .

Seconds of silence ticked by before Matt muttered a curse. "Pull up Steele's photo, B. Side by side."

"Oh wow," Bean said at the same time Gavin asked, "Are they brothers?"

Looking at the photos of the men next to each other had Scarlet's heart hammering in her chest. Her palms grew damp. This was not good. Not good at all.

"Maybe, but it's more than that," Matt said, tapping on his phone. He held it up and showed Gavin and Bean his screen.

Scarlet didn't need to see. She knew what he was showing them.

"Holy shit," Bean said on an exhale.

Gavin made a noise in the back of his throat. It sounded a lot like a growl. "Okay, then. Scarlet?"

She looked up, but before meeting Gavin's gaze, she examined the photo on Matt's phone screen. It was of Daisy. Close up. Her mouth and chin were stained blue and red from popsicles, and her face was lit up with joy. Her bright-blue eyes twinkled with laughter. Bright-blue eyes that were the exact same shade as Steele's. The exact same shade as Michael Wilson's.

"Scarlet?" Gavin repeated.

When she finally met his gaze, the intensity in his expression should have scared her. Or at least made her nervous. But it didn't. Instead, it soothed her. Gavin was on her side. On *their* side.

"We *will* protect Daisy. I swear it."

She nodded. "Thank you."

"I found their connection," Bean said.

Another mug shot appeared on the screen. This time, of an older woman with the same bright-blue eyes.

"Tracy Ruth Wilson. Bio mom to both Steele MacBride and Michael Wilson." Bean's eyes narrowed as she read something offscreen. "She had four kids. Three boys and a girl, but Steele looks to be the only one she didn't have custody of. He was raised by his dad, Rory MacBride, aka the president of the Reaper's Assassins Motorcycle Club. Five months after Steele died in prison, MacBride was arrested for killing two cops. He got two consecutive life sentences and will be at Jameson Annex, South Dakota's Level V facility, until he dies."

"Are they affiliated with any of the larger MCs?" Gavin asked.

"It looks like they're allied with Hells Angels." Bean sipped a fluorescent-green drink. "Which makes sense if they're running guns and drugs in South Dakota."

"What about the other siblings and the mom?" Matt asked.

Bean circled her cursor over Tracy's mug shot. "This is from the mom's most recent DUI arrest two and a half weeks ago. She's still in jail. She couldn't post bond, so she'll probably be there another month or so. Nothing yet on the other siblings—not even driver's licenses—but I'm on it."

Matt stared at the photos onscreen. "I'm wondering if Wilson was possibly trying to protect you. Or at the very least, trying to warn you."

Scarlet folded her arms over her chest. "Yeah, but from who?"

Matt shook his head and scowled. Seeing the frustration in his eyes, she took his hand in hers.

"That's the question," Gavin said. "All right, we'll keep digging over here."

"If we pull enough strings, something's bound to unravel," Bean added.

"In the meantime, Tash will be swinging by. We'll update her beforehand. Stay vigilant. And, Scarlet? We've got eyes on you and Daisy."

"Thank you again. Both of you."

Matt disconnected the video call, and Scarlet released a long sigh. They didn't have much, but at least they had something. Granted, she didn't know how it was going to help. Still, it was more than they knew this morning. That had to be positive.

CHAPTER TWENTY-SEVEN

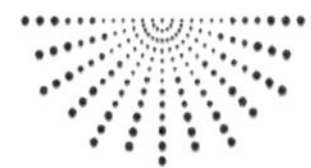

The Fourth of July weekend had come and gone. They'd taken Daisy to watch the fireworks, and the following days had been ridiculously uneventful. Which was good. No one had broken any bones. Or broken into their home in the middle of the night. Or stumbled into the diner all bloody.

In fact, the highlight had been taking Daisy to get her cast removed. Her arm was healing well, and for the next two weeks, she would wear a forearm splint with, of course, a pink-and-purple unicorn cover.

So . . . things were good. Well, except for the lack of progress on her case with Hudson Security. Which was making her a little bit crazy. No level of uneventfulness could ease Scarlet's roller coaster of emotions over the potential danger to Daisy.

Tash had come by the house last Saturday to introduce herself. One glance at the woman, and Scarlet had been beyond intimidated. Dressed in black slacks, a light-blue blouse, and a blazer, Tash had looked like she belonged on the cover of some power-CEO magazine. Not to mention she was a legit Gal Gadot doppelganger. Even Daisy had gasped and excitedly talked about how Matty and Xandy were friends with Wonder Woman. And if all that wasn't intimidating enough, Tash had a slight accent that Scarlet couldn't quite peg. Because of course she did.

However, when Tash had met her at the diner early on Monday morning, Scarlet had done a double take. Gone were the sleek, fancy clothes. Instead, the other woman had worn jeans and a sleeveless white top with a wide brown belt and white sneakers. Which had only downgraded her from a power-CEO magazine to Hudson Island's tourism brochure. The woman was drop-dead gorgeous no matter what clothing she selected.

Mercifully, after five days of Tash's presence, the PSO had dropped a few notches on Scarlet's scary-intimidating scale. No one would ever describe Tash as warm and snuggly, but Scarlet had discovered the woman *was* nice and friendly, though a bit serious. However, she supposed that was the nature of Tash's job. She wasn't getting paid to be Scarlet's BFF; she was getting paid to protect her.

At first, Scarlet hadn't believed she needed someone to follow her around during her boring day-to-day life. But now she would happily admit she'd been wrong. Knowing someone was watching out for her helped immensely. Yes, she was still a fidgeting wreck, but she could be a much bigger fidgeting wreck.

As for today's steadily growing nerves? They had nothing to do with the unknown threat. They were for tomorrow. Matt's brother and sister-in-law were coming to the house for dinner.

Speaking of . . . Scarlet glanced at her watch, then scanned the playground. No sign of Xander or Tash, but she knew they were there . . . somewhere. They always hung around until she and Daisy were locked down with Matt for the evening.

Paula had wanted to pick up an extra shift, so Scarlet had taken the afternoon off and used the opportunity to spend some one-on-one time with Daisy. They'd had milkshakes at the diner, and now she was letting Daisy burn off some of the sugar on the playground. But they still needed to swing by the store to pick up groceries for tonight's and tomorrow's dinners.

"Come on, Daisy. It's time to go!" Scarlet called out.

Her daughter ran up with Mr. Slothy tucked in the crook of her splinted arm. "Can I go down the slide one more time?"

"No, baby, we have to go to the store. We're going to meet Matt's brother and sister-in-law tomorrow, remember?"

"What's a sister-in-law?" Daisy asked, taking Scarlet's hand.

"Well, Matt's brother is Jake, and Jake is married to Carmen," she explained as they crossed the street to the small grocery store. "So that makes Carmen Matt's sister-in-law. It's like she's Matt's honorary sister because she's married to his brother. Make sense?"

Daisy went silent for a moment. "Mama, can I have a sister?"

Scarlet coughed, choking on air. "Uhhh . . . I don't really think . . ."

Her mind went blank. Usually, she was good at coming up with some sort of BS explanation. But right now? Nope.

She spied a familiar face at the far end of the block. *Oh thank god.*

"Look, Daisy. It's Matt," she said, pointing down the sidewalk. Her steps faltered when a woman walked out of the store—and straight into Matt's arms.

Scarlet froze.

Matt bent down and kissed the woman on the lips, then

tugged her against his side. With his arm all snuggly around her, they headed Scarlet and Daisy's way.

Scarlet gripped her daughter's hand tighter. Holy shit, she was going to be sick.

"Mama? Why is Matty kissing and hugging that lady?"

She glanced down, and the confusion on Daisy's sweet face was like a punch to the gut. She picked up her daughter, set her on her hip, and hugged her close.

"Um . . ." Tears welled in her eyes, and a few slipped down her face. Holy crap, she couldn't breathe. "I don't know, baby," she whispered, swiping away the tears.

She needed to move. She needed to be anywhere other than rooted to this spot. Because Matt and his . . . whatever . . . were a half block away.

A deep, throbbing pain radiated from Scarlet's chest. She felt like she was going to die.

"Mama, look!" Daisy cried with glee. "It's two Mattys!"

Scarlet's gaze swung back to the couple and—

She blinked. She wasn't sure what she was seeing. It was the lovebirds . . . and Matt. Again.

"Matty!" Daisy screamed, madly waving her splinted arm while clutching Mr. Slothy in her hand.

The Matt who wasn't holding the other woman turned. His face lit up as he waved at Daisy. But when his eyes shifted to Scarlet, his smile faded. He muttered something to the lovebirds, and before Scarlet could blink, he was in front of her, dropping a kiss to the top of Daisy's head with a "Hey, Otter Pop." Then his hands were framing Scarlet's face and he was pressing a quick kiss to her lips. "My brother and his wife came a day early."

"Your brother?" Scarlet's feet remained rooted in place. Things were *not* clicking in her brain.

He nodded, and she glanced behind him. The couple was approaching, and the concern in their eyes was evident.

"Sweetheart, what's wrong?"

Adjusting Daisy's weight on her hip, she let out a breath. "I thought . . ." *That my heart was getting ripped from my chest.* "You failed to mention your brother was your *identical twin.*"

It should have been comical how Matt's and Jake's eyes widened in unison. But it was too soon for her to find humor in the situation.

Matt grimaced. "Oh shi—oot. I'm so sorry, Scar." He pulled her and Daisy into his embrace.

"Holy crap, Matt," the other woman chided, shaking her head. "You seriously didn't mention you had a *twin?*" She turned to Scarlet with her hand outstretched. "I'm Carmen. Jake's wife. I'm sorry if our earlier PDA gave you a heart attack."

Carmen was stunning. She and Scarlet were roughly the same height and body type, but that's where any similarities ended. Carmen was Asian with long, sleek black hair. Hell, everything about the woman was sleek. Her clothes, her makeup, her jewelry . . . Not showy at all, but definitely fancy.

"Nice to meet you," she said, shaking Carmen's hand. "I'm Scarlet. This is Daisy."

Carmen smiled at Daisy, then raised an eyebrow at Matt. "He's usually smarter than this."

"Not really," Jake said with a smirk. He held his hand out. "I'm Jake. Matt's younger and more handsome brother."

Matt slapped him on the shoulder. "Eight minutes, dude. And we look exactly the same."

After shaking Jake's hand, Scarlet watched the brothers playfully bicker. They really did look identical . . . but they also didn't. Not only was Matt a bit leaner, but he also held himself differently. She couldn't quite explain it, but seeing the two of them standing together, she wasn't sure how she'd mistaken Jake for Matt.

"Matty," Daisy called out, reaching for him.

He took Daisy in his arms and popped her on his hip. "Otter Pop, what do you think? Am I taller than my brother, Jake?" He nodded at her, mouthing, *Yes.*

Daisy shrugged her shoulders. "Mr. Jake has bigger arms than you."

Jake hooted with laughter. "Daisy, my girl, I *knew* I was going to like you!"

Her smile was shy as she snuggled into Matt.

"I really am sorry we gave you a scare back there," Carmen said from beside Scarlet.

"It's okay. You know, I was just thinking—now that I'm looking at the two of them—I'm not sure how I thought Jake was Matt."

"Well, still. I say you blame Matt for not telling you about the whole twin thing."

"Yeah." She chuckled, pressing a hand to her heart. "That would have been a useful nugget of info."

"I know we just met, but here's the thing, Scarlet. That man?" Carmen glanced at Matt. "You don't ever have to worry about him straying from you. Especially since he's so . . ." Carmen sighed, and Scarlet was taken aback by the tears swimming in the other woman's eyes. "I haven't seen him this relaxed, this happy, in years."

Scarlet began to shake her head, but Carmen gently nudged her shoulder. "Trust me. I've known these two for decades, long before Jake and I got together. You're good for Matt. And with everything he's been through . . ."

"He's good for me and Daisy, too."

"Good," Carmen said. After a delicate sniff, she shook her head and squared her shoulders. "Now, since we gave you a heart attack, let us treat you guys to dinner. Deal?"

Scarlet smiled. "Deal."

CHAPTER TWENTY-EIGHT

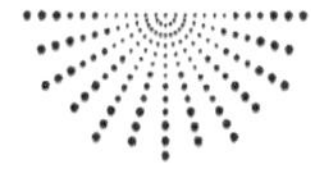

Five days later, Scarlet scanned the crowded bar area of Monty's Tavern and smiled. Her stress levels were decidedly lower. After having dinner with Jake and Carmen on Friday night, they'd ended up spending the entire weekend with the couple, and it had been . . . surprisingly wonderful.

Jake and Carmen were awesome. She loved the way they looked out for Matt, and they were fun to be around. Plus, their interests sparked a million stories. Her jaw had dropped when she'd found out Jake was the creator of her favorite game on her phone, and she'd been inspired when Carmen had talked about the nonprofit she ran that provided clean drinking water to towns and villages in developing countries. Then, when Gavin had joined them for dinner on Saturday night and the guys had talked about these crazy superspy cameras Jake had developed, her mind had officially been blown.

In any other situation, Scarlet would have been ridiculously intimidated by the couple. After all, there was successful . . . and then there was *them*. But she wasn't. Because it was Jake and Carmen. Matt's family. And they'd immediately put both her and Daisy at ease with their warmth, humor, and obvious love for Matt.

Now, taking a sip of ice water, she glanced around the crowded room. Four had roped off the entire bar area for a "private party," and Daisy, Rocco, and two other little kids had commandeered one corner. Xander and another one of Hudson Security's PSOs stood nearby, watching. Not that anyone would be stupid enough to try anything tonight.

They were gathered for a mid-week surprise party to celebrate Cade and Poppy. The event's theme was a combination of "Welcome Home" and "Congratulations," and their friends from town, De La Rosa Gym, Hudson Security, and Hudson Tactical filled the space. Meaning the sheer number of straight-up badasses in the restaurant was a little ridiculous. Not to mention the amount of testosterone.

A sharp whistle cut through the din, and the crowd turned toward the entrance. Seconds later, everyone shouted "Surprise!" as the happy couple entered the bar.

Scarlet grinned at her dear friend. Glowing—Poppy was absolutely glowing with joy.

She patiently waited her turn as the couple hugged their way through the crowd. Then she pounced.

"Congratulations," she said, hugging Poppy tight. "I'm so happy for you!"

"Thank you!" Poppy stepped back and wiped away a tear. "It was so fabulous."

"You'll have to tell us all about it. The trip, the food . . . All of it! But come on, girlfriend, how did he pop the question?"

Poppy's grin widened, and fresh tears filled her eyes as she looked across the room at Cade. With a giant sigh, she said, "You guys."

Scarlet was all smiles, as were the surrounding women.

"The morning after the big fights, we were obviously still

in London. Cade ordered room service for the two of us. I was still in bed when he brought the tray in. And . . . there it was. The ring was right next to the strawberry crepes."

Clasping her hands to her chest, Scarlet let out a squeal. Then a strong arm draped across her chest, and Matt drew her against him, his lips pressed to the top of her head.

Poppy's jaw fell open before she flashed them a grin. "You know, Matt, Cade said he took your advice on the whole proposal thing."

"Is that so?"

Poppy nodded, eyes ping-ponging between them, and Scarlet couldn't help but laugh.

"But if you'll excuse me." Poppy snagged Scarlet's hand and tugged. "I'm stealing this one from you."

"As long as you bring her back," Matt called as they hurried away from him.

Poppy mock-glared at her. "Uh, when did *that* happen?"

She smirked at her friend and lifted her shoulders in a bored, casual shrug. "What do you mean?"

Poppy's eyebrow arched.

"Okay, okay," she said, unable to contain her laughter. "It's crazy, right?"

"It looks cozy to me."

Scarlet scanned the room and smiled when Matt caught her eye. "It is, Pop. It really is."

Poppy pulled her into a hug. "I want details, girlfriend! All. The. Details!"

***

"Did you have a fun night?" Matt asked, following Scarlet into the house. With Daisy comatose in his arms, he closed the door to the garage behind him.

Scarlet disarmed the alarm, then returned to him to

remove Daisy's shoes. "I did," she said with a grin, resting her hand on Daisy's back. "If you put her in bed, I can get her all changed."

With a nod, he carried the little girl to her room and gently laid her down. While Scarlet gathered Daisy's pajamas, he ran his hand over the sleeping child's hair. His heart seemed to sigh at the contact.

"Thank you for this, Scar."

"For what?" she asked, appearing next to him. She expertly changed Daisy into a sleep dress.

"For letting me be part of your life—Daisy's life. It means everything to me."

Scarlet's hands stilled in the middle of pulling off one of Daisy's socks, and she peered up at him.

Worry slithered down his spine. He couldn't read her expression.

She let out a breath and returned to her task, getting Daisy changed. In a matter of minutes, the little girl was curled under her blanket with her stuffies.

Scarlet snagged his hand and pulled him out into the hallway.

His worry grew; she had yet to say anything.

Once they were in their room, she closed the door and locked it. Then leaned back against the door.

"Scar?"

"There's nothing to thank me for, Matt," she said softly. "You being part of our lives is everything. Not the other way around."

He pressed his lips together. "Sorry, baby. We're just going to have to agree to disagree on this one."

"Do you know what one of the best things about tonight was?"

He shook his head.

A small smile tipped her lips. "Seeing how happy Poppy is with Cade and knowing that I'm just as happy."

His heart filled. God, he loved her. So fucking much. "Come here, baby."

Her smile widened as she pushed off the door and closed the distance between them. When she was a step away, he wrapped his arms around her and lifted. Her legs locked around his waist. With one hand under her delectable ass, he snaked the other into her hair and kissed her. Devoured her until they were both breathless.

He pulled back and met her gaze. "You make me so damn happy, Scar. You have to know how much I love you."

"I love you, too," she whispered, eyes shining with hope and desire. "I never dreamed that I could meet someone like you."

"You're everything to me. You and Daisy have become my world. To cherish. To protect. To love. Let me show you how much."

"Yes, please." Scarlet unhooked her legs from around his waist and dropped her feet to the floor. She gave him a gentle shove, and he took a step back. Her grin was sweet and sexy and wicked all at once. "But me first."

Before his brain could make sense of her words, she lowered to her knees. He sucked in a breath as her hands made quick work of his jeans, shoving them to his ankles along with his boxers.

His heart raced, and every muscle in his body tensed when she took his rock-hard cock in her hand, stroking him with a firm grip. Her dark-brown gaze captured his and the sexiest smile he'd ever seen lifted her lips. Then her tongue darted out and licked him from his balls to the tip of his dick.

"Holy fuck," he groaned, winding a hand through her hair.

"Like that?" she teased, her tongue flickering the sensitive underside.

He growled and tightened his hold on her hair.

Smiling, she pressed wet kisses along his shaft. "I take that as a yes."

"Holy shit." His hips jerked forward. He was desperate for more. "Suck me, baby. Fucking swallow my cock."

And she did.

Her mouth was fucking heaven. He wanted to throw his head back and lose himself in the sensation, in the feel of her sucking him off. But there was no way in hell he was taking his eyes off her. Watching Scarlet take his cock, watching her take him deep down her throat, watching her head bob up and down on his dick was almost too much. He desperately wanted to fuck her mouth and come down her throat.

His spine tingled in warning.

No, not yet.

If he was coming, it was going to be in her tight, wet pussy. With one last thrust, he pulled out of her mouth. She groaned a complaint, and he grinned. *Goddam, she is so fucking hot.*

Matt picked her up off the floor and tossed her over his shoulder fireman-style. Her laugh turned into a moan when he slapped her ass and squeezed her cheeks. Stepping out of his pants, he placed her on the bed with a growled, "Clothes off, baby. On your hands and knees."

Removing his shirt and socks, he grabbed a condom from the nightstand and rolled it on. Turning back to the bed, his cock hardened further at the sight before him.

Scarlet. Naked. On her hands and knees. Legs apart so he could see the glistening lips of her pussy.

Holy. Fuck. He'd never seen a more gorgeous fucking sight.

In an instant, he was positioned behind her. He rubbed the head of his cock over Scarlet's folds, teasing her, and she moaned, "Yes, Matt. More."

"You want me?" He pressed into her heat a couple of inches, then withdrew.

Her hips lurched backward, following him. "Please, Matt."

Hands on her ass, he squeezed her cheeks, spreading and molding them as he watched his cock slowly disappear into her core. "You want me to fuck you soft or hard, baby?" He pulled out slowly and was transfixed by her juices coating his cock.

"Hard," she moaned, rocking against him.

He thrust into her. "Like that, sweetheart?"

"Yes, yes, yes," she whimpered.

When her hand reached between them and she began strumming her clit, something inside him broke open. *Mine. This woman is fucking* mine.

He slammed back into her. Hard. Over and over again. Their groans filled the air, and the sound of their bodies slapping together was obscenely loud. He knew they needed to be quiet, but he just couldn't. She was too fucking amazing.

He was close, and he needed her to be, too.

"Get yourself there, baby," he murmured.

He pressed a hand to her back, and she lowered her chest to the mattress, moaning at the new angle. Her inner muscles clenched around his cock. He gripped her hips tight and pumped faster. With a cry, her body tensed and trembled.

"Holy fuck, yes." His heart hammered in his chest as he slammed into her one final time, clutching her tight against him. Stars filled his vision as he came.

For a moment, they were both still, their loud breaths the only sound.

"Ohmygod, that was amazing," Scarlet murmured with her face buried into a pillow.

"Agreed." Chuckling, he pulled out and pressed a kiss to her shoulder blade. "I'll be right back."

After taking care of the condom, Matt grabbed a wash-cloth and wet it. He returned to the bedroom and smiled. Scarlet hadn't moved. She was still on her knees, face buried in a pillow. Crawling onto the bed behind her, he kissed her left ass cheek, then her right, and wiped the washcloth gently between her legs. Her eyes remained closed as he eased her onto her back.

Lying on his side, he traced his fingers from the base of her neck to her breasts, then down around her belly button to the top of her mound. Goosebumps rose on her skin, and a possessive satisfaction filled him.

He needed to have her again. No question.

"You still awake, sweetheart?"

Scarlet's answering grin was satisfied and sleepy. "I can be. With the right motivation."

"Good," he said, nudging her thighs open. Her grin grew as he settled between her legs and moved down her body. "Because I need more of you."

After worshiping every inch of Scarlet, they lay together, limbs tangled in the center of their bed. Matt couldn't get enough of this woman. He really couldn't. He'd taken her twice, and already his cock was stirring, begging for more.

Trailing the tips of his fingers down her spine, she shivered. And he smiled. There was no denying it. *This* was what he wanted.

"Will you stay?" he asked.

"Oh, I don't think I can actually move." Rolling onto her back, she let out a blissful sigh.

"Mission accomplished, then." He kissed her lips. "But I meant, will you stay *here*? Move in with me?"

Surprise flashed over her face.

He hurried on, "I know your place is supposed to be

ready to move back into sometime next week, but I don't want you to go."

"Matt . . . are you sure?"

"More than anything, I want *this*." He squeezed her tight. "Going to sleep with you. Waking up with you. Having dinner and movie nights with you and Daisy. All of it. Before you and Daisy, this was just my house. A place where I lived. But now? It's my home. Because of you and Daisy."

Her mouth fell open. Shock and hope and love flickered across her face. Then those beautiful brown eyes filled, and two tears spilled over. He brushed them away with his thumbs.

"I love you, Scarlet. So much." He shifted to settle between her spread thighs. "Stay with me?"

She nodded, and he dropped a kiss to her forehead.

"Live with me?"

Again, she nodded, and he kissed the tip of her nose.

"Marry me?"

She gasped, and Matt held his breath. Then her lips stretched into the most beautiful smile he'd ever seen. With tears sliding down the sides of her face, she nodded again.

"Yes," she whispered.

His mouth claimed hers, and his heart soared.

CHAPTER TWENTY-NINE

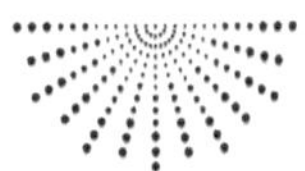

The Friday lunch rush was winding down, and for that, Scarlet was thankful. She was leaving work early again today so she could run over to her apartment to pick up a dress. Her dinner date with Matt had obviously been postponed with all the craziness—the man being stabbed, the amped-up security, Jake and Carmen's visit, and Poppy and Cade returning home—but Matt had insisted that tonight was the night. It would be their first official date.

She'd been fine with staying in. Not because she didn't want to go out with her wonderful man—and yes, he was *her* man—but because no matter how great things had been lately, no matter how much joy and love and laughter she'd experienced over the last week, she couldn't shake the paranoia. Everything was going too well, and she had a feeling that the proverbial other shoe was about to drop.

They were still keeping security tight—Xander was currently with Daisy, Tash was sitting in the diner's waiting area, and Bean had all her program things running—but Matt thought going out, just the two of them, was low risk and would take her mind off things.

It helped to know that Daisy would not only be with Rebecca, Dante, and their family tonight, but that Cade and Poppy were planning on joining their get-together as well. Matt had even said Xander was happy to join the crew if it would put her mind at ease.

The thought made Scarlet rush to the beverage station and place the coffee pot back into its stand. Pulling her phone from her apron pocket, she sent a text to Xander.

SCARLET

If you're really sure you don't mind, can I take you up on your offer to watch Daisy at Rebecca & Dante's tonight?

Xander's response was immediate.

XANDER

Of course I don't mind. I'll touch base with Alvarez on what time you're dropping Daisy off. You just have fun tonight.

After sending a thank-you text, Scarlet let out a breath and tucked her phone away in her apron. She could do this, dammit. She had no reason to be nervous about going out on an official *date* date with the man she was completely stinking head over heels for.

Love, Scarlet. You're in love *with him.*

A smile lifted her lips. She was. She absolutely was one thousand percent head over heels in love with Mateo Alvarez. And the best, most unbelievable part? The wonderful man felt the same way about her. In fact, he wanted to *marry* her.

Warmth bloomed in her chest. How was this her life?

A ding pulled Scarlet from her dreamy, swoony thoughts.

Heading to the service window, she checked the orders against the ticket, loaded her tray, and headed to the two-top.

She recognized the couple and greeted them as she placed their appetizers in the center of their table. If she recalled correctly, they were from the Portland area and had been in at some point each day this week. "How are you two enjoying your stay on Hudson Island?" she asked, setting small appetizer plates in front of them.

"Good. There's a lot to see on the island. It's been quite informative," the man replied.

Even though the man's word choice seemed odd, Scarlet's smile never wavered. "I'm glad. Is there anything else I can get you two?"

"Actually, yes," the woman said before coughing. "Sorry, my throat is just so scratchy." She sounded like she'd swallowed a frog, and she waved Scarlet closer. "See the guy eating by himself near the door?"

Frowning, Scarlet looked at the table closest to the hostess stand. The man appeared to be in his early thirties and possibly recovering from a bit of a rough night, but since he was in Paula's section, she hadn't paid him much mind. "Yes?"

"See how Martha's standing right by his table?"

Her gaze shot back to the woman, and she froze. The cold, dead stare aimed at her had all the fine hairs on her arms rising.

"That's Cutter. He loves knives. He did a number on ole Mikey, didn't he? Isn't that the spot where the dumbass bled out?"

Scarlet glanced at Cutter, and her stomach twisted when the man shot her a sinister grin. He lifted the corner of his T-shirt, revealing the handle of a knife.

"Now, if you don't do exactly as I say, you're gonna see how many times Cutter can stab her. He's fast, you know." The woman eyed her dining companion. "He got Mikey what, ten, fifteen times?"

Scarlet's mind flashed to the security footage of Cutter stabbing Michael Wilson while he'd sat helpless in his car. Bile surged up her throat.

"Sounds about right," the man said with an ominous chuckle. "Trust me, he can get at least eight or nine good ones in before even the best can react. The lady's a bit thick in the middle, but she'd be done for before she even hit the ground. She's old. I'm sure she lived a good life and all that shit. It'll be a twofer if her old man, Ray, tries to rush in."

Scarlet's ears began ringing. "What do you want?"

"You're gonna ditch Wonder Woman," the woman said.

Scarlet stole a peek at Tash, who still sat in the waiting area, scanning the people strolling past the diner. She willed Tash to turn and recognize her distress.

"Uh-uh-uh," the woman said. Her tone was melodic and so at odds with the words tumbling from her mouth. "Cutter will happily kill your precious Martha. You make one wrong move, and he'll do it."

Scarlet fisted her shaking hands and crossed her arms over her chest. Fuck this woman. Fuck all of them. If she was going down, she was taking every one of these assholes with her. But she had to be smart if she wanted to avoid casualties. "What do you want?"

The woman grinned. "Now, nice and calm, you're going to go down the hallway to the bathrooms and walk right out that exit. A couple of our friends will be there with a mini-van, and you'll get in."

A swell of anger heated Scarlet's blood. She glared at the woman, who simply laughed. Bitch.

"Oh, aren't you a feisty one? But save your spunk. Believe me, you're going to need it later." The woman nodded to the man across from her, and he rose.

"Follow me," he muttered, heading toward the hallway leading to the restrooms.

The woman grabbed a mozzarella stick and took a bite. "Hop to it, Sienna."

Gritting her teeth, Scarlet promised herself she'd make this evil woman pay. She memorized every inch of the bitch's features, then turned and followed her piece-of-shit friend.

Be smart, Scarlet!

In the hallway, she hunched over and fake-coughed. As she heaved, one hand swept into her apron and found her phone. She pulled up her messages and texted 9-1-1 to Bean.

"Hurry the fuck up," the man hissed from the exit.

Coughing louder, Scarlet locked her phone and switched it to silent. The last thing she wanted was for it to ring and get taken away from her. She pressed her hand to her chest and fake-wheezed, then straightened. Infusing desperation into her voice—which didn't take much effort—she begged, "Please, I need to get my inhaler."

The man took three menacing steps toward Scarlet, grabbed her by the upper arm, and yanked her out the door. "Fucking bitch," he muttered, effortlessly picking her up and tossing her into the waiting minivan.

She landed on her face. Her teeth clacked together and caught the inside of her cheek. Blood filled her mouth, and she couldn't hold back a moan. The sliding door slammed shut with a bang, and she summoned her strength to roll over, but a sudden weight on her back had her breath leaving in a whoosh. Something heavy—some*one* heavy—was on top of her.

Unable to move, she turned her head, ready to scream, and—

A wadded-up piece of cloth was shoved into her mouth. She tried to spit it out, but it was in too deep.

"Scream all you want, bitch," said the man on top of her. Snickering, he pinched her nose shut.

She stilled.

Holy shit. She could *not* die like this. *Don't panic! Think, dammit!*

"Nice, you're already learning, Si-Si." His familiar voice and that god-awful nickname sent goosebumps tearing across her skin. "If you don't fight, I'll let you breathe. If you do fight, I'll find something else to shove down your throat."

A whimper escaped her gagged mouth as he ran his hands roughly over her ass.

Knuckles. That was his name. One of the younger assholes she had known at the club. He'd been good friends with Zip and Jester, had idolized Steele. He'd also liked to hit while he fucked.

"Damn, Sienna. You sure have filled out."

No! Not Sienna. My name is Scarlet! Taking a deep breath through her nose, she focused on her anger and not her fear. *You've dealt with Knuckles before. You can do it again. Now think!*

Keeping still, she scanned her surroundings. She was on the floor in the back of a minivan. One of the middle seats was still in, but the other middle seat, along with the entire back bench seat, had been removed. The windows were heavily tinted.

Shit! What else?

A familiar horn sounded.

"Just one," the driver said.

Her eyes widened. They were at the ferry ticket window!

Taking another deep breath, she screamed with everything she had. But the second the sound left her lungs, blinding pain exploded at the base of her skull.

Everything went dark.

CHAPTER THIRTY

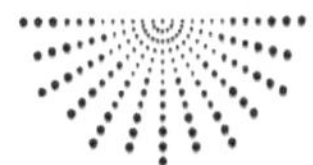

The door to the conference room crashed open, and Matt jumped to his feet.

"Bean, what the fuck?" Gavin shouted.

Ignoring them both, she parked herself at the end of the conference table and whipped open the lid of her laptop. Her fingers were already flying. "Tash apprehended a guy at the diner, but not before they took Scarlet."

Matt's blood turned to ice. "What the fuck did you just say?"

"Listen," Bean barked, eyes focused solely on the screen in front of her. "Fifteen minutes ago, Scarlet sent me a 9-1-1 text. I called Tash immediately. She went to find her, but Scarlet was gone. And then there was this fucker with a wicked knife at the diner, and he grabbed Martha. Thankfully, Tash is a badass and was able to get Martha away from the guy unharmed. They fought, but she subdued him and—hang on." Bean tapped her earpiece.

For the longest five seconds of Matt's life, she remained silent.

"Copy," she said at last, meeting his gaze. "Quinn's crew

arrived at the diner, and Tash reconfirmed that Scarlet's gone."

Gone.

Matt saw red. "What the fuck, Bean? She texted you fifteen minutes ago, and you're—"

"You're wasting my fucking time, Alvarez, and every damn second counts. I run this fucking show, so sit down, shut the fuck up, and listen."

Despite how angry and desperate he was, the look Bean sent him had his balls shriveling.

"Breathe, dude," Gavin said, slapping Matt's chest. "Trust Bean. This is her thing. She's got this. She'll get your girl."

Still glaring at him, Bean tapped her earpiece. "Esme, you copy?" As she listened to whatever Esme was saying, she slid a small box across the table to them.

Gavin snatched it up.

Earpieces.

"Comms." Gavin handed Matt one while he placed the other in his ear. "Once B switches us on, we'll be able to hear everyone. But she controls access."

"Boss, Esme says the chopper will be ready in five. Owen's flying." She glanced at Matt before returning her attention to her computer. "I'm tracking Scarlet's phone. The last location was right outside the diner. Then it drops. Either it was turned off, or the vehicle she's in is interfering with the signal, or she's down by the ferry terminal. It's shit coverage over there no matter what carrier you have. While we're waiting for her phone to ping again, I have a number of surveillance programs set up and running."

He opened his mouth but slammed it shut when Bean leaned back in her chair and held up a hand.

"If it makes you feel any better, your girl's got skills. She's smart." She nodded to the Smartboard as a video popped up. "I tapped into the footage from the main dining area. It has the guy who took Scarlet and the guy Tash apprehended hiding their faces from the cameras."

"Which means they've been scoping out the place," Gavin said.

"Exactly. But aside from Tash and Scarlet, no one—not even Ray and Martha—knew that we installed a new camera in the hallway to the bathrooms." Bean crossed her arms over her chest and smiled. "Your girl got him to turn around and face the camera."

She played the video, pausing when the guy began stalking toward Scarlet. Two mug shots appeared onscreen, one belonging to the man and one belonging to a woman. "Randy Klien and Melissa Aber. Both from South Dakota."

A second video appeared onscreen. It began playing, and Matt watched a man and woman—presumably, the people from the mug shots—sit at a table in the diner and talk with Scarlet.

"You can see when they point out the guy with the knife." Bean's cursor hovered over the guy Martha was serving. "Look at Scarlet's expression here. Clearly, she's worried."

Matt's stomach dropped.

"I assume those two threatened Martha," Gavin said.

"Agreed. Because in a minute"—Bean fast-forwarded the video—"Scarlet follows Klien down the hallway. Unfortunately, we can't see anything once she's out the door."

"She left with him willingly to protect Martha." Matt scrubbed his hands over his face. Of course she would sacrifice herself for the other woman. "I'm gonna wring her neck when I see her," he muttered.

Gavin chuckled. "Riiight, tough guy."

"And that's why you love her, Alvarez," Bean chimed in.

"Yeah," he said, dropping his hands to his sides. He leaned back in his chair. "One of the many reasons why I love her."

"While we wait for Scarlet's phone to ping, we'll follow

Klien and Aber," Bean said, then waved at her laptop. "Facial rec has them on the ferry to Whidbey. They're on a single motorcycle, and I'll track them with the traffic cams. The ferry took off before the knife guy was apprehended, so I think they're still sticking to whatever their original plan was. And hopefully, that plan will lead us to Scarlet."

"This is Esme. Do you copy?"

Bean tapped her earpiece. "Go ahead, Esme. You're on comms with the boss and Alvarez."

"Owen's ready. Wilson, Carmichael, Riviera, and Bonson are all ready to go. Tash is less than five minutes out. There are extra supplies on standby. Who do you want, Gavin?"

His friend looked at him, then said, "Me and Alvarez. Wilson, Tash, Riviera, and Carmichael. I want Bonson to retrieve Xander and Daisy. She comes directly here, and we lock down."

"Can someone pick up Poppy and bring her here, too?" Matt asked. "I want to make sure Daisy has someone she knows aside from Xander."

"Of course, Matt," Esme said. "Gavin, Tash is pulling in through the gates now. Everyone's ready. I'll be on standby. Out."

"Ready?" Gavin asked as he rose.

Matt nodded and stood.

"Wilson and Tash will take lead. Then Carmichael and Riviera. You're with me."

While Matt wanted to be the first person to break through whatever door Scarlet was behind, he knew that wasn't wise. He gave Gavin a chin lift.

"I'll open comms for everyone once you're airborne," Bean said. "As usual, I'll let you know what I know when I know it."

Gavin squeezed her shoulder when he walked by. "Thanks, B."

"You got this, boss."

"Thanks, Bean," Matt said, pausing beside her chair. "I'm sorry about earlier. About yelling and losing my shit."

"No worries, Matt. I get it. And rest assured, I have a shit-ton of programs running on this. We'll find your girl."

Ten minutes later, Matt had changed into black tactical gear and strapped himself into his helo seat with a headset covering his ears. He examined the cabin as they took off, and his eyebrows rose.

He knew Hudson Security had a number of helicopters in their fleet, but this one was the largest. The H160 seated twelve passengers in three rows of four seats, but currently, the middle row was removed. In its place was a stretcher, and a couple of duffels holding weapons and equipment rested on top.

Matt hoped to hell they wouldn't need the stretcher.

Gavin's voice came through his headset. "Alvarez, you obviously know Tash, Wilson, Carmichael, and Riviera, but have you met Owen?"

The pilot waved a hand. "Nice to meet you, Alvarez. Welcome to the team."

Matt knew he shouldn't be surprised that Owen was a woman, but he was. He hadn't heard of many female combat pilots.

"Well, I'm gonna say it since Owen won't," Tash said.

A groan came through his headset, and when the guys around him chuckled, he assumed the disgruntled person was Owen.

Tash continued, "You should count yourself lucky, Alvarez. It's not every day you get your ass flown by a decorated Night Stalker."

"No shit?" The Night Stalkers were the best of the best. The specifics of what they did were classified, but it was safe to say that the country's elite special ops groups worked hand in hand with them. "I appreciate this, Owen."

"New guy or not, we take care of our own, Alvarez."

"We have clearance to land at Naval Air Station Whidbey Island," Gavin said. "Unless we hear from Bean in the next few minutes, we'll wait there. Once we get the intel, we'll move."

Everyone confirmed, and Matt settled in for the short flight. The terror he'd felt when he'd first learned Scarlet was missing lingered in the back of his mind. But his years as a detective had taught him that he needed to lock that shit down. If not for himself, then for his teammates.

He glanced at the men and women around him—all dressed in matching black tactical gear and armed with both lethal and non-lethal weapons—and a sense of calm settled over him. This team, no doubt, was also the best of the best. He trusted them to do their jobs and not let their emotions get in the way. Just like they trusted him to do the same.

They would rescue Scarlet. And then he was never letting her out of his damn sight.

CHAPTER THIRTY-ONE

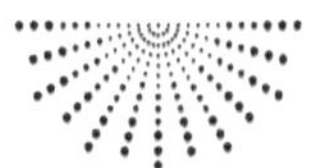

Blinking her eyes open, Scarlet winced. Her head pounded with each beat of her racing heart. Miniscule movements made her realize that her legs were strapped to a chair and her arms were tied behind her back. With what? No clue.

Leaving her head bent to the side, she tried to appear unconscious. Her mouth was dry as a desert, and every muscle in her body throbbed. She had no idea how long she'd been out.

Voices—too many to count—came from the other side of the room. Hopefully, no one was paying attention to her.

Peeking down at her lap, a tiny seed of hope bloomed. She was still wearing her apron. And it looked as though it still held the extra notepads she always kept tucked in there. If so, maybe her phone had stayed inside, too. God, she hoped so.

"Where's the fucking kid?" a deep voice boomed.

She flinched, then scolded herself for the mistake.

"Kid's under lock and key, Psycho. If she's not with the

fucking bodyguard, she's with the fucking boyfriend. There's no way to get to her."

"Bullshit!"

A loud crash startled Scarlet, and in her peripheral vision, she saw a pair of scuffed black motorcycle boots stomping her way.

"What the fuck, dumbass? You know chloroform doesn't work like it does in the fucking movies! You need to keep that shit *constantly* over her fucking face!"

The boots rushed out of her vision, and the sound of a fist hitting flesh had her heart tripping. Then the boots were back. Right beside her.

"I know you're fucking awake, Sienna."

The jig was up. She raised her head and met the bright-blue gaze of a very angry man. She didn't recognize him, but judging from the familiar color of his eyes, he was related to Steele. And to Daisy.

The only other person she recognized was Knuckles. And wasn't that all sorts of fucked up. But she took some satisfaction in seeing his lip was split and bleeding. There were two younger guys who looked close to her age, and then the "couple" from the diner. She scanned the younger guys' faces again and confirmed that neither was the scary-ass Cutter guy. She hoped that was a good thing.

"You need to get the kid here."

She glared at the blue-eyed man. "No."

He tsked and shook his head. "Daisy is *my* blood, Sienna."

Scarlet hated him. She had no clue who he was, but she hated him. "She's *my* daughter. She's *Steele's* daughter. Not yours."

Actually, Daisy was *Matt's* daughter, but Scarlet would play along with these assholes. She'd do anything she needed to stay alive and return to her family.

"I'm not going to hurt her, Sienna. She's my niece. Hell,

she's going to be the fucking princess of the new Reaper's. *I'm* her next of kin, and Daisy needs to be with her people. Where she fucking belongs."

Over my dead body. "Fuck you."

He tilted his head to the side, then smashed his fist into her face. Fire consumed her cheek; blood pooled in her mouth. But she didn't recoil or cry out. She refused to give him the satisfaction.

He extended his phone to her. "You're calling the day care, and you're gonna tell those fuckers that your brother is going to pick up the kid for a surprise trip. Then Cutter will bring Daisy to us." He showed her his phone's display with the number of Rebecca's day care queued up. "Do it. Now."

She turned her head and spit blood on the floor. "Fuck. You."

The man's face flushed bright red before his fist smashed into her face again. And again. And again. Until she crashed sideways to the ground.

Someone yanked her upright, setting her chair back on its feet. Her head spun. But as her eyes refocused, she steeled her mind.

She would do this for as long as she needed. She wasn't saying a damn thing.

"Jesus Christ, Psycho!" the guy from the diner shouted. "Let's fucking storm that day care and just take the fucking kid already!"

Psycho glared at his associate. "What? We shoot our way in, take the kid, and then what, fucker? Wait in line to get on the fucking ferry while the police swarm us? It's a fucking island!" He shook his head. "Dumbass."

"This is bullshit. What the fuck do we even need the fucking kid for? The bitch is right—the kid is *Steele's*, not yours, so why the fuck do you even care—"

Scarlet yelped at the gunshot, and she watched in horror

as the guy's head exploded. The woman from the diner screamed as she rushed to him.

"Family," Psycho said, his voice calm and lethal. "Family is the most important thing."

The woman stopped screaming. The men quieted their cursing. Even Scarlet's heart skipped a beat. Holy shit. No wonder they called him Psycho.

He extended his phone to her again. "You're going to call them. And you're going to have them give Daisy to Cutter."

"Or what, Psycho?" she sneered. Maybe not the wisest decision on her part, but what was he going to do? Shoot her? Then how would he get Daisy?

He stared at her for a moment. A menacing smile crept over his face, and she fought a shiver. "Or I'm going to call Cutter. First, he'll gut Martha and Ray. Then, he'll go after the rest of the diner people. Then—"

Explosions rocked the room. Blinding light had Scarlet slamming her eyes shut. More explosions sounded and her ears rang.

Then, just like that, the barrage was over.

Scarlet cracked her eyes open, and the smoke swirling in the air made them water and burn. Six black-clad figures stormed the room. Shouts to get down mixed with curses and wails. A gun fired, and someone groaned.

Silence descended. The only things she could hear were her racing pulse and that damn ringing in her ears. Tears streamed down her face. Partially from her irritated eyes, and partially from the pain of where Psycho had pummeled her face. It hurt to blink. Hell, it hurt to breathe. But she'd take these black-clad strangers over the crazy motorcycle club members any day of the week.

One of the black-clad people approached her. Their gun was pointed at the ground, so that was a good sign, right?

When they called out, "Alvarez! Over here!" her heart stopped.

Another black-clad figure rushed toward her. Dropping to their knees at her feet, they ripped off their face mask.

She stared at him for a second before a violent sob tore through her. The intensity of it made her moan in pain.

"I've got you, sweetheart," Matt murmured, running his hands gently over her shoulders.

Two more figures in black appeared behind him. They raised their face masks. Gavin and Tash.

Tash moved to kneel behind her, and Scarlet heard the click of a camera. Then the PSO murmured, "Hold still while I cut these ties off you."

The second her hands were free, Scarlet hissed out a breath. Agonizing tingles shot from her wrists to her shoulders and then back down.

"Hang on, sweetheart," Matt murmured, grabbing her arms and gently massaging them. "Getting the blood flow back is a bitch."

"You're telling me," she croaked. But she was so damn thankful he was here.

"You did good, Scar," Tash said, moving to crouch beside her. "Hold still again, and I'll get the zip ties off your ankles."

She nodded, and a wave of exhaustion washed over her. "Daisy?"

"She's totally fine," Matt said. Once Tash cut the ties holding her to the chair, he scooped her up in his arms. "She's at Hudson Security. Poppy and the twins are with her. She's good. I promise."

Nodding, she closed her eyes and rested her head on his shoulder. "I don't know why I'm so tired all of a sudden."

"Most likely an adrenaline crash, sweetheart. Just rest for a little bit. I've got you." She felt his lips press against her forehead. The one spot on her face that didn't hurt. "Just rest."

Sweat and dust and gunpowder scented the air. But as she nuzzled closer to Matt's neck, she drifted off with his woodsy, soapy scent filling her nose.

CHAPTER THIRTY-TWO

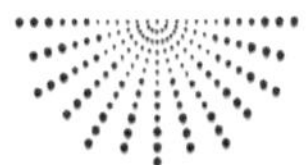

It was nearly three in the morning, and every part of Scarlet ached. She had been checked out by EMTs on Whidbey Island, and much to Matt's frustration, she'd refused to be admitted into the hospital. She was a mess of bruises and had a slight concussion, but nothing had been broken. It was nothing time and rest wouldn't heal.

She'd wanted to go home. To be alone with Matt and Daisy.

The hours after she'd been rescued were a complete blur in her mind. Highs and lows and everything in between. They had stayed on Whidbey for a while, talking with the local police before eventually taking the helicopter to Hudson. By the time they'd made it back, Daisy had been sound asleep.

Poppy and Cade had brought Daisy home from Hudson Security and waited up all night. Scarlet didn't know what she'd have done without her friends. Not only had they spent the last countless hours with Daisy, but they'd reassured her and kept her calm, tucked her in and told her that Scarlet and Matt would be there when she woke in the morning.

Now Scarlet was showered and wearing a tank top and her baggiest joggers. The cut along her lip from Psycho's fist had stung something fierce when she'd entered the shower, but decompressing under the hot water was exactly what she'd needed, had left her feeling a little less raw.

She let out a weary sigh and looked around the dining table. Matt sat beside her, Gavin and Bean across from her. One final debrief, and then she could go lie down.

"Obviously, the investigation is still ongoing," Gavin said, rubbing a hand over his tired face, "but we do know that five individuals were arrested and—" He cut himself off, glancing down the hallway to where Daisy's room was.

"You're fine," Scarlet said. "A bomb could go off in here and Daisy would still be asleep. She's *that* heavy of a sleeper. But thank you."

Gavin nodded. "Five arrested and one, as you know, deceased. His name was Randy Klien. It looks like he and Melissa Aber, the lone woman in the group, were on Hudson for about a week, scoping out the place. The leader of the group is Brady Wilson."

"Everyone called him Psycho." She shivered, and Matt took her hand in his.

"Fitting," Bean said with a roll of her eyes.

"What we've gathered," Gavin continued, "is Psycho led them to believe that you'd purposely hid Daisy from Steele. That you'd stolen her. He rallied them to come and take her back."

Bean rested her elbows on the table and stifled a yawn. "Brady Wilson—Psycho, for clarity—was the half brother of both Steele and Michael Wilson, the guy who was stabbed. They shared the same mom, but they all had different fathers. It appears that Michael Wilson either knew the truth about Daisy or didn't agree with Psycho's plan or some combination of the two, and so he tried to warn you."

Scarlet frowned. "How did they even find me?"

Bean sighed. "We don't know yet. Quinn, in his official capacity as sheriff, made a pretty heated call to your former handler with the US Marshals. Hopefully, he'll get some answers."

Scarlet wasn't sure she wanted to know, but she asked, "And what was Psycho's plan?"

"He wanted to take over the Reaper's," Gavin said. "Almost all the original members are either dead or in prison. Psycho was a little fish for the most part, but he wanted to take control. Take over as president. However, it was never going to happen because there was no tie."

"What do you mean?" Matt asked.

Gavin shrugged. "This is just my theory, but I think that Psycho being half brothers with Steele wasn't good enough. They had different dads. Steele's dad—Rory MacBride—is still alive, and even though the guy's in prison, he's still the president of the Reaper's Assassins. MacBride doesn't give a shit about the mom. He took his kid and cut all ties with the woman. If he doesn't care about her, he especially doesn't give a shit about any kids she had with a bunch of other guys. So there's no way MacBride would okay Psycho taking over his MC."

"But MacBride would care about his grandchild," Matt said as he scratched the stubble on his jaw. "Biologically, Daisy is Steele's."

Gavin nodded. "Exactly. How Psycho was going to make that work for him, I'm still not sure."

"He said something about him being Daisy's next of kin." A chill swept over her, and she rubbed her arms to fend it off. "He wanted me to give her to him. Can I assume he was planning on killing me after?"

"Motherfucker," Matt growled.

"Agreed," Gavin said. "On both counts. But it doesn't

matter anymore. The second he shot Klien, they all turned on him."

Scarlet let out a breath. At least there was that. Her mind flashed to all those people who had just stood there and watched while she'd been tied to the chair. They'd done noth—

She gasped. "What about Cutter? The guy who was still in the diner?"

"Tash got him," Bean said. "Dumbass tried to take Martha, so Tash beat the shit out of him. He was arrested and transferred into federal custody late last night."

"Good." Exhausted, she leaned back in her seat. "And everyone on your team's okay? Nobody was hurt?"

Gavin stared at her for a moment, then smiled. "We're all good, honey. And just so you know, I'm sure it will get back to MacBride at some point that he has a granddaughter. I want you both"—he glanced between her and Matt—"to trust that we'll monitor him. For as long as we need, for as long as it takes."

Scarlet's brow furrowed. "But how are you planning on doing—"

"Magic, remember?" Bean winked. "We've got you."

"We protect our own," Gavin said before tapping the table. "On that note, Bean and I will get out of your hair. Get some rest. I'll check back in with you guys tomorrow." He grimaced as he glanced at his watch. "Make that later today."

Scarlet and Matt walked them out, then made their way hand in hand to their room.

"Daisy should be up in a few hours," she said. "If you catch her before I do, can you wake me?"

Matt pressed a gentle kiss to her forehead. "Let's get you to bed, sweetheart. You must be wiped."

Her limbs grew heavier with each step. "I am," she mumbled, climbing into bed.

As Matt tucked the covers around her, she promised herself she'd only sleep for a few hours. She hadn't seen Daisy—not awake, anyway—since yesterday, and she didn't want to miss another minute with her daughter.

"Mama?"

Scarlet peeked her eyes open and came face-to-face with a pair of bright-blue eyes. Bright-blue eyes that shimmered with tears. She took in her daughter's worried expression, her trembling lips, and forced her sore body to sit up. "Hi, baby."

Calling on all her remaining strength, she pulled Daisy across her lap and hugged her tight. She knew she looked like absolute hell; the last thing she wanted was to scare her daughter.

"Careful, Otter Pop," Matt said, coming into the room and joining them on the massive bed. He positioned himself behind Scarlet and wrapped his arms around both of them.

"Matty," Daisy sniffed. "Mama has a big owie on her face."

"I know, sweet girl. Your mom got hurt yesterday, but she was really brave."

More like scared out of her mind. And so damn pissed. She wasn't so sure on the brave part.

Her face throbbed where that asshole had punched her, and there was a giant goose egg on the back of her head from when she'd been knocked out in the minivan. She had cuts, scrapes, and bruises all over her from being tied to that stupid chair with her hands behind her back, unable to protect herself from . . . anything. But having her sweet girl in her arms and being held by the man she loved?

Her life was pretty damn perfect.

"Don't be scared, baby girl," she whispered, pressing a kiss to the top of Daisy's head. "I'm going to be fine. I just got banged up a little."

Daisy sat up, and Scarlet tried not to wince as her daughter's sharp elbow dug into her side. "Did you falled down, Mama?"

She caressed Daisy's cheek. "I did. It hurt a lot, but I didn't break any bones, so that's good. I just got a puffy face and a black eye instead."

"You look like Poppy's friends from TV. Remember the FUC show we watched with Matty and Four and Gavin and Xandy and we saw Poppy on TV?"

"I do remember, baby, and yeah, I'm sure I look just like they did after their UFC fights. All banged up."

"Hey, sweet girl," Matt said, voice rumbling through Scarlet's chest. "Why don't you go pick out a movie or a show to watch, okay? Your mom needs to sleep for a little bit longer so her bruises can heal. Maybe *Kung Fu Panda?*"

Daisy shook her head but grinned. "I can't watch *Kung Fu Panda* without you, Matty. It's your favorite!"

"You're right, Otter Pop. Why don't you watch some *Bluey*, then?"

Daisy gasped, and her eyes went wide. "You don't like *Bluey?*"

Matt tensed behind her. She could practically feel his panic, and she had to bite back a chuckle.

"I'm sorry, sweet girl, but I don't." Daisy's jaw dropped, and he rushed on, "But you know, we can't like everything the same, right? I mean, I love baseball, but I'm sure you don't like watching it."

"I love baseball, Matty!"

Scarlet snorted, then flinched, both at the pain and the offended look on her daughter's face. "You *love* baseball, miss? Really?"

"Yes," Daisy huffed. Her little face scrunched.

Scarlet shook her head. "Daisy, baby, do you know what baseball *is*?"

Daisy's bottom lip popped out and began to wobble. "No. But Matty loves it, so I love it, too!"

Scarlet's heart squeezed tight. Oh, her sweet child. She glanced back at Matt, and the emotion on his face was everything.

"Otter Pop, you don't need to love baseball just because I love baseball. And I don't need to love *Bluey* just because you love *Bluey*. I love you and your mom the best, and that's what matters." He kissed her daughter's forehead, and Scarlet melted.

Daisy sighed like she had the weight of the world on her four-year-old shoulders. "I don't know what baseball is, Matty."

He chuckled. "I kinda figured that, sweet girl."

Daisy looked at her. "I love you, Mama." She puckered her lips, and Scarlet kissed her.

"I love you, too, baby."

Daisy turned to Matt. "I love you, Matty." She puckered her lips, and that look of awe flashed over his face again before he kissed her.

"I love you, Otter Pop."

"Matty, can I have popcorn and M&M's while I watch *Bluey*?"

He grinned. "It's nine in the morning. No."

Daisy frowned for a moment, then perked up and gave him her best smile. "Strawberries? Cut up in little baby triangles?"

"I think I can work that out." He bopped her on the nose. "Now go pick out your show while I tuck in your mom."

Daisy scrambled off the bed and ran out of the room.

Scarlet snuggled deeper into Matt's arms. "I love you, Matt," she whispered. "Thank you for finding me."

"I love you, Scar." His lips pressed against her hair. "Thank you for loving me. And for sharing Daisy with me."

She closed her eyes and soaked it all in. This man. Their daughter. Their future.

Her heart was so full.

EPILOGUE

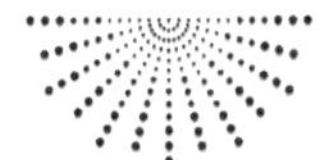

ONE MONTH LATER

I t was a cool mid-August evening. Matt smiled. He'd been doing that a lot over the last month. Scarlet and Daisy had officially moved in and having them there—knowing they all called the same place home—had exceeded his expectations. Which was saying something, since his expectations had been pretty damn high.

A week after the kidnapping shitstorm, he and Scarlet had gone out on their first official date. He'd wanted to wait, wanted to give Scarlet more time to heal, but she'd insisted, saying they had waited long enough. They'd stayed close to home and dined at Monty's Tavern while Daisy had hung out with the entire De la Rosa crew. It had been a wonderful and relaxing evening, and hands down the best first date of his life. The weekend after, they'd taken the ferry to Whidbey, gone on a small hike, and explored the little town of Coupeville. The perfect family date.

His heart squeezed. That's right. *Family* date. Because that's what they were.

Enjoying the festive atmosphere around him, Matt marveled at the transformation of Cade and Poppy's back-yard. Twinkling lights and paper lanterns were strung from the trees. Tables and chairs filled one side of the massive yard, and a dance floor sprawled across the other.

Cade and Poppy had just said their vows in a picturesque sunset wedding ceremony, and Matt was so damn happy for his friends. They'd wanted to keep the celebration small, but considering they were friends with nearly everyone on Hudson Island, their backyard was packed.

Poppy had stunned in her white gown as she'd walked the short aisle on her sons' arms. When they'd reached Cade at the front, the twins had split up, one standing up with Poppy and the other with Cade. There hadn't been a damn dry eye to be found.

The same could be said about this exact moment. Poppy and her twins had opted for a mother-son dance in lieu of a father-daughter dance since she didn't have a relationship with her parents. Carter and Dylan were swaying and swinging their mom between them, and the trio's smiles and laughter were bringing happy tears to everyone watching.

Matt scanned the crowd and spotted Quinn, with his nine-month-old daughter, Annie, in his arms and his wife, Alex, beside him. Standing with them were Joe and his wife, Roxie. While Alex and Roxie were in some sort of animated discussion with Roxie pointing to her obvious baby bump, Quinn and Joe were sneaking Annie some bits of cake frosting. By the way the little girl's arms pumped up and down, it was safe to say she was a fan. He caught his friends' gazes and shook his head, grinning. Joe brought a finger to his lips and tilted his head to the women. Matt laughed and gave them a chin lift of acknowledgement.

"How's it going, big brother?" Jake asked as he approached, then nudged an elbow into his ribs.

Matt nudged his brother back. "Good."

"Really?"

And just like that, nerves took flight in Matt's stomach. Shooting a sideways glance at his brother, he lowered his voice and asked, "You think it's still a good idea?"

Jake chuckled. "You said she'd love it."

"Right." She would. God knew he'd seen Scarlet aww-ing countless times over similar videos online. Still, worry twisted his gut. *Shit.* "Right."

Cade approached and slapped him on the shoulder. "Are you doing the overanalyzing shit again?"

"Bro, come on, you look like you're gonna puke." Jake turned to Cade with laughing eyes. "And yeah, he totally is."

Bastards. Both of them.

Cade slung his arm over Matt's shoulders and chuckled. "What was it that you said to me? Oh yes. Take a fucking breath and stop overthinking it."

Matt's gaze ping-ponged between his two best friends, and he let out an unsteady breath. "Holy shit, *I* said that?"

Cade threw his head back and laughed. "Who'd have thought, right? You also said I was making it too complicated. Which I was."

"Yeah, but it's too late for you on that one, bro," Jake said with a shit-eating grin. He nodded at the dance floor. "You're almost up."

Matt gulped. Hands patted him on the back, but he didn't feel them. He was too focused on the woman standing off to the side, having an animated conversation with one of Poppy's friends.

Scarlet looked like a damn dream. Her long dark hair was down in loose waves that highlighted its pinks, blues, and purples. She wore a simple navy-blue dress that hit her mid-thigh. Two thin straps held it up, and it hugged her gorgeous body to perfection. A body he was happily memorizing inch by delectable inch. Truth be told, he wanted to sneak her away right now. But no, he could do that later. There'd be plenty of time for that after.

Scarlet's face lit up as she laughed at something the other woman had said. And just like that, Matt's nerves settled. Because that's what this woman did. She settled him like no one else. She'd become his home, his purpose, the reason he wanted to be a better man. There was no one he'd rather spend the rest of his life with than her—and Daisy. His little girl.

Dressed in a sparkly pink-and-navy-blue dress, Daisy hopped from foot to foot with a giant smile on her Otter Pop–stained face. The twins were in charge of handing out popsicles to the kids tonight, and it was safe to say that all the children were currently on a sugar high.

"All right, ladies," TJ said into the microphone. He was not only one of Cade's closest friends and a coach at De La Rosa Gym, but also the emcee for the wedding. "Can we get all the single ladies to the dance floor, please? Poppy is going to toss her bouquet!"

Matt kept his gaze on Scarlet as she was pulled onto the dance floor by one of Poppy's co-workers. For a second, she searched the crowd. When their eyes met, she flashed him a sheepish smile, shrugged, and blew him a kiss.

His heart expanded. God, he loved her.

"Okay, ladies. Get ready," TJ said. "On the count of three, Poppy. One, two, three!"

A blur of pink and blue sparkles shot across the dance floor toward Poppy, and Matt moved closer. With each step he took, the feeling of rightness strengthened in his gut, his heart, his soul.

Laughter erupted in the crowd as Poppy turned with her bouquet still in hand. Daisy was bouncing in front of the bride, waving her arms. Poppy bent down and whispered something to the little girl. Matt smiled when Daisy clapped her hands and took the bouquet. Spinning, she darted to her mom.

"These are for you, Mama!"

"Oh no, baby. Oh, sweetie," Scarlet stammered. Her face flushed pink as she took the flowers from her daughter. Glancing at Poppy, who'd followed behind Daisy, she held the bouquet out, saying, "I'm so sorry, Pop. Here."

An excited murmur raced through the crowd.

Matt smiled. And waited.

Poppy's eyes shimmered as Cade wrapped an arm around his bride's shoulders. She shook her head. "Nope. They're for you, Scar."

Though Matt couldn't see Scarlet's expression, he felt her confusion. Still, he waited.

"Mama, look!" Daisy pointed his way. "Matty has a gift for you!"

It was as if everything was suddenly in slow motion. He stood a few feet behind Scarlet. And as she turned, he dropped to one knee.

The surprise that colored her face was breathtaking. The tears that gleamed in her eyes stole his heart. And the awe and wonder in her expression filled his soul.

"Matty!" Daisy exclaimed, slamming her little body into his.

With a laugh, he tore his gaze from Scarlet and kissed Daisy's forehead. "Want to help me?"

She nodded emphatically, so he sat her atop his knee and handed her the ring box. "Hold this for me, Otter Pop. But don't open it until I say, okay?"

"Okay!"

Matt looked back up at Scarlet. She stood with her hands clasped tightly together and pressed to her lips.

He held out his hand. Without hesitation, she linked her

shaking fingers with his. A jolt of electricity surged through him.

Everything felt right, and for a moment, he simply held her gaze. "Sweetheart, you left me speechless for nearly a year, but I promise to tell you every day, for the rest of our lives, how much I love you."

She was nodding before he'd finished speaking, and his heart soared. Grinning like a loon, he whispered to Daisy, "Now, sweet girl." As Daisy opened the ring box, he asked, "Will you marry me?"

Scarlet beamed, absolutely radiant as tears spilled down her cheeks. "Yes!"

Cheers erupted from the crowd. Matt rose, Daisy on his hip, and wrapped Scarlet in his arms. Leaning down, he captured her mouth with his.

"Mama, look!"

Turning to Daisy, Scarlet laughed. Then she gasped as she caught sight of the ring. "Matt . . ."

"Hang on, Otter Pop," he murmured, setting Daisy down. Taking the ring from the box, he placed the simple two-carat solitaire on her finger. "I hope you like it."

She stared at him with wide eyes. "Are you kidding? It's gorgeous."

He pressed a kiss to her lips. "*You're* gorgeous."

Scarlet chuckled, and he shot her a wink before dropping to one knee again.

"Otter Pop," he said, waving the little girl closer. "Did you see what else is in the box?"

Shaking her head, she nuzzled into him.

"What's that?" he asked, angling the box so it faced her.

She went still for a moment, then began bouncing. "A unicorn with rainbows!"

"That's right, sweet girl." Removing the necklace from the

box, he held it up to her. "Your mom can't be the only one getting a gift, right?"

"Mama! Matty gots me a necklace with a unicorn and rainbows!"

"Wow!" Scarlet said, lowering herself to their level.

After clasping the thin chain around Daisy's neck, he kissed her forehead. "Love you, sweet girl."

"Love you, Matty!" she exclaimed, running off.

Holding Scarlet's hands in his, Matt stood, bringing her up with him. He drew her into his embrace and kissed her once more. How could he not?

"I love you, Scarlet Miller," he murmured against her lips.

She pulled away and grinned at him. "I love you, too, Mateo Alvarez."

ENJOY THIS BOOK?

Reviews & ratings encourage other readers to try out a book & I would love your help spreading the word! If you could take a quick moment to rate and/or leave a review on your favorite book site—Amazon, Goodreads, and/or Bookbub—I would be forever grateful! Thank you!

ALSO BY CHRISTINA SOL

Want more of Scarlet & Matt?

Sign up for Christina Sol's Newsletter for a free bonus scene.

www.christinasol.com

***

The Spotted Dog Series

Redemption

Reclaiming

Returning

The Hudson Island Series

Shattered Vows

Shattered Illusions

Shattered Dreams

Shattered Secrets

The Hudson Security Series

Out of the Shadows

ABOUT THE AUTHOR

Christina Sol is an award-winning author who writes what she loves to read—romance books filled with heart, heat, and suspense.

An avid reader from the get-go, Christina was obsessed with The Babysitters Club, Sweet Valley Twins, Sweet Valley High, Christopher Pike, and all things V. C. Andrews. Her love for romance started with the Sunfire books, a YA historical romance series. Caroline by Willo Davis Roberts was her favorite of the series, and a copy of the 1984 novel is one of her most treasured possessions. Then she discovered Danielle Steele and Nora Roberts. And never looked back. She's still a voracious reader and enjoys all genres of romance but leans toward romantic suspense and dark romance.

She lives in the inland Pacific Northwest with her husband and two kids. When she's not writing, reading, or knitting, she's watching football or fueling her planner, sticker, and washi-tape obsession.

To find out more, visit: www.christinasol.com

ACKNOWLEDGMENTS

It's always bittersweet coming to the end of a series, but to my wonderful readers—thank you so much for taking the time to read Matt & Scarlet's story! I know you have a million options, and I appreciate you choosing to spend your valuable time with them. Whether their love story was the first of mine you've read, or if you've been there from the beginning of The Spotted Dog series, I appreciate you all SO much!

Shattered Secrets—from the nitty gritty details to the dreaded blurb—wouldn't have been possible without the help of Heather, Shelli, Jen, Danielle, and Megan. The feedback, honesty, and support you ladies provided is so, so, SO appreciated and invaluable!

A huge, heartfelt thank you goes out to my family, friends, and fellow writers who have provided so much encouragement. You all mean so much!

To the content creators who make gorgeous edits, and to the folks who take the time to leave a review—your enthusiasm & support truly means the world to me!

I hope you'll join me in 2025 as we spin-off & get to know the crew at Hudson Security.